I0457358

Love DRUNK

A SECOND CHANCES *Novel*

LIBBY RICE

Copyright © 2015 Libby Rice

www.libbyrice.com

All rights reserved, including the right to reproduce, distribute, or transmit in any form or by any means.

ISBN: 0-9903536-5-6
ISBN-13: 978-0-9903536-5-2

This is a work of fiction. Names, characters, places, and incidents are the product of the author's imagination or are used fictitiously. Any resemblance to actual events, locales, or persons, living or dead, is coincidental.

Gateway Publishing Ltd.
P.O. Box 1414
Golden, Colorado 80402

Cover design by Viola Estrella
Edited by Kathie Middlemiss

DEDICATION

Every word, always for Tom.

ACKNOWLEDGMENTS

Many people helped me dig into the plot of *Love Drunk*. From hacking, to wine importing, to alcohol counterfeiting, to addiction issues, this book required a great deal of research. My deepest thanks to those who assisted in getting the facts straight. I certainly took some artistic license for the sake of the story, and, of course, all mistakes are my own.

London presented a challenge for me because of her vulnerability. Trevor proved equally challenging in his steadfast decency. Thanks to so many of my writer colleagues who helped me stay true to the characters. Because of people like Viola Estrella, Jen Maitlen, and Larie Brannick, these two fell in love *their* way.

Deceiving others. That is what the world calls a romance.
Oscar Wilde

CHAPTER 1

July—Denver, Colorado

Two weeks ago, London Rose Whitley had started a date with a living man and ended with a dead one. If she'd *ever* needed to arrive on time, today was that day. Latching the door behind her with an audible click, she spied a gleaming casket sitting too still down a center aisle. Stainless steel edges peeked from beneath at least a hundred wilting roses, the metal shiny enough to catch stray rays of dusty summer light and hurl rainbows across a silent, mourning crowd.

A dead Dillon Farro still managed to rule the room.

"Always late," her mother whispered as London squeezed herself into the end of an oak pew. Dr. Victoria Whitley subjected London to a round of slow scrutiny, no doubt taking in the wrinkles in her black skirt and the way the buttons on her shirt pulled ever-so-slightly around the middle.

"Late, and not looking your best. You realize," her mom said casually, now fighting a droning organ for supremacy, "we're *five minutes* from downtown Denver, *five minutes* from your apartment. Your disrespect is unconsciously deliberate."

Same criticism, different day.

Up top, London shrugged the shoulder her mother would easily see from the corner of an eye. Below, she wound a discrete arm around her waist, pressing hard against the ache that spiked at the woman's complaint. Some psychiatrists—at least the ones who'd raised London—automatically sought reasons for behavior. A late client, they would deduce, exhibited signs of suppressed hostility. Ten extra pounds cried depression. A person who balled out the checker at the grocery store felt resentful about having his power usurped by an hourly wage earner.

According to Dr. and Dr. Whitley, actions manifested themselves like the jerking reflex after a good tap to the knee. Every last move reflected deeply seeded roots in the psyche. Lateness never sprang from a traffic jam. Weight gain didn't come from a craving for jelly donuts. Acting like a jerk could never be attributed to a bad day.

"Yes, Mom"—*what to say?*—"my being late and frumpy is an expression of power. I want to stick it to a dead man, show him he'll have to stand in line for something not particularly worthwhile."

Her mother stiffened against the unforgiving pew. "You make light of this?"

London balled her good hand. For once her mother's outrage sounded genuine, not the product of a test to see how her daughter might react. Perhaps London ought to appreciate the show of support on this baddest of bad days.

Support nearly withheld.

Her mother had insisted that London's presence at Dillon's funeral was, "a rash choice, reminiscent of the one that put Dillon in a casket in the first place." Instead of looking angry over London's audacity, her mom had grabbed her chin and peered into her face with concern, with a strained grief that implied the woman's daughter had finally tipped over the precipice between compulsive and crazy, between rash and dangerous.

They're wrong. Two psychiatrist parents didn't always know best. Their labels would *not* rise to the level of self-fulfilling prophesies, no matter how many times words like *impulsive* and *compulsive* fluttered her way.

Even Freud had acknowledged that sometimes a cigar is just a cigar.

"I don't make light of today," London insisted quietly. They could do only so much sparring from the back pew before attracting unwanted attention. "*You* do by insinuating I would ever *want*, consciously or otherwise, to show Dillon disrespect."

She'd loved him, after all.

But after two years of dating, that love had gone silent, the relationship stale, and on the day she'd tried to break things off, Dillon had ended up dead.

Before her mother could bombard her with the usual, "*Why*, then, were you late?" or "*What*, then, do you mean to say with your shabby clothing and extra pounds?" a more sinister problem fell in London's lap. A shadow crawled across her exposed knees, silencing the battle of wills raging between mother and daughter. Then came a pained scrape of a voice that nearly choked on swallowed anguish before words made their debut. "How can you sit there? Only a few feet from my murdered son?"

London looked up into a hollow, pinched face. All her determination to do the right thing vanished. Defiance crumbled to dust as deep as the kneeler crowding the tops of her tapping toes. Her mother had been right.

Nothing but insanity tinged London's decision to mourn Dillon openly.

Maybe her late arrival and ugly outfit *did* amount to a tacit admission of something deeper, like guilt and lack of belonging.

Instead of offering grudging support, Doc Victoria ought to have met her daughter on the church steps with a white jacket and a promise of padded walls.

London swallowed and stood. Gaze averted, she slunk around the man blocking her path to freedom. When her arm brushed his in passing, he emitted a low howl, as though her limbs were coated in battery acid. Jerking away, London realized pain had a *sound*, one that would ring in her ears long after she fled the echoing church.

Pain sounded like a father confronting his son's killer.

Pain sounded like Mr. Farro confronting *her*.

CHAPTER 2

Trevor gazed up at his buddy around a shiny bar bisecting his view. "Add twenty-five to each side." A cumulative three-fifty would max him out, yet he hesitated to go for gold. The trainer nearby with the do-rag, patterned track pants, and a set of eighteen-inch tatted biceps would take note. Then Trevor's numbers would end up on a white board behind the gym's front desk.

He shouldn't be anybody's goal.

Metal clanked above his head, foreshadowing the extra weight joining the bar. Not even the sound of an oncoming challenge dented Trevor's vague sense of disinterest. Once he'd been proud of the number three-fifty, or at least felt a sense of accomplishment. A guy who could bench three-fifty was strong. Strength meant speed, distance, endurance.

Strength meant power.

Hoisting hundreds of pounds in the air had built him up, helping him do all the things that mattered, like *winning*. Now it provided an easy distraction—*up, down, up, down*—which helped him forget that none of his former priorities mattered at all.

Plus a beer only weighed around a pound, give or take the bottle.

Still, his routines had become more than habit. They'd become *him*. If Trevor stopped pushing, if he quit training and never completed another Ironman or triathlon or ski race, he might as well hand his murderous ex-wife a weapon and let her pick him off, too.

Not happening.

With movements honed by two decades of repetition, Trevor curled his calloused hands around the bar. He squeezed and felt a welcome tension grow in his torso. With a deep breath, he drove his feet into the floor, locked his hips, and unracked the weight.

His friend Kevin spotted Trevor's movements with a low oath. "I won't be coming by later with an ice pack for your crying, whining pecs."

Ignoring the taunt, Trevor gulped another breath and rowed the weight downward until it touched his old T-shirt. Then he drove the bar back to lockout with a burst of coordinated power.

Resetting his lungs, he managed a quick, "Fuck off," before his second rep. Then another before his third. On the forth, Kev no longer looked on with that smarmy, self-satisfied grin.

"What have you been eating, man?"

Mostly anger strapped to the back of grilled chicken breasts. Lots and lots of chicken breasts.

Before Trevor could share about protein overload, Kevin's chin lifted and came to a slow stop. The attention once focused on keeping Trevor from wrapping the bar around his own neck homed in on something across the gym.

No doubt a woman.

Kevin's reasons for prompting a change of gym scenery in the last month had become painfully obvious. Where their old gym had been about function over form, this one had yoga classes and soaking tubs and expensive shampoo in the showers. While those things meant fuck all to Trevor, they did result in one very important distinguishing characteristic—the presence of chicks.

As Trevor stared up at a textbook case of distraction, Kev's face changed. A patient interest, able to bide its time, morphed into surprise, then panic. Without a word, Kevin wrestled the bar back to the rack and disappeared from Trevor's line of sight. So much for number five. Trevor rocked upward and let his focus follow his friend.

A developing emergency about thirty feet out hooked Trevor's cloak of apathy and jerked. *Hard.* After six months of *fuck everything* but the basics—exercise, work, sex—he saw something worth effort.

She was… indescribably gorgeous, with black curls swept away from her face, exposing a delicate profile.

She also had about twenty seconds left on her feet. Her ponytail swished less and less with each step, legs swaying heavily on the moving treadmill. A small hand groped for the machine's front rail.

Instead of looking flushed from her workout, the woman appeared to have lost every drop of blood in her soft, plush body. At the same time, she seemed unaware of her plight, almost confused about what was happening. That hand missed the rail and fluttered to her face, graceful despite her obvious disorientation, and she rubbed at her eyes like she might shake the dizziness.

Trevor lunged off the bench, the urge to protect fueling his flight across the gym. He chased Kev around equipment and people, all as oblivious to the woman's plight as the woman herself.

"Kevin, *wait*," he gritted. Trevor would handle the saving. If Kev did the honor, things would end up all wrong. Kev had a simple way with women: He crooked his finger, and they sucked his dick.

Not today.

Instinctively, he muscled his friend into the crevice between two elliptical machines. Kevin flailed for purchase, barely staving off the unexpected jostling.

"Not sorry," Trevor said as he slid past, reaching the woman's side the moment her time ran out.

Sweet, sweet skin slid beneath his hands. Her shoulders sagged as he gripped their sloping curves. When the weight of her slumped, he plucked her off the machine and lowered her ever-so-gently to the floor through buckling knees. Once flat on her back with him crouched overhead, he took a good, long look, ignoring Kev, who buzzed in the background about "dickheads" and "disrespect" and how Trevor might have "hurt her worse."

Never. A fall would have meant a concussion and broken teeth. Landing against his chest had meant a slow, careful trip to the ground.

Now her chest waved through a thin shirt with every breath. Recent months had revealed how much he liked soft, forgiving breasts that could fill huge hands. Before her defection to one of Colorado's finest correctional facilities, his wife had defined feminine fitness—tall, statuesque, *tough*. In everything but brute strength, his stunning ex had held her own. His ten-mile run had become her eleven. His forty push-ups had become her forty-five.

Rhea's stamina had won his respect. The one-upmanship—with his *wife*, of all people—had crippled his desire. Sinew and bone had a place on a woman. They belonged under a layer of softness he could sink into.

Some women had bodies built for clothes, for the drape and the crease. Others for sports, for speed and power. This one, in her pink leggings and loose tank, had a body built *for him*.

Heat forgotten long before his divorce poured into his body, renewing his appreciation for the baggy gym shorts that hid a growing problem. His roving scrutiny lingered on her limp left hand. No ring, at least not the important kind. Relief should have been out of the question after knowing her for all of thirty seconds, especially since she'd spent the duration unconscious.

Or maybe not.

Her slender fingers started to curl. Suddenly wary, Trevor let his gaze wash over the rest of her, onward and up until he collided with a pair of shy eyes. Leaf green and not quite owlish, those eyes took him in with… *alarm*, rapidly escalating to terror.

Oh, shit.

"Calm down," he soothed. "Breathe deep. That's right… One more."

Color seeped back into her cheeks and neck, probably from a fight-or-flight reflex rather than relief. For all her initial paleness, she was steeped in rich color. That high ponytail of glossy black hair pooled around her shoulders, the strands so dark they gleamed like ebony piano keys against the honeyed tone of her skin.

Nope, not pale at all. Pink lips, bright eyes… This one could be an adult coloring book.

Rather than gather her against him, Trevor ignored his instinct and inched away with little hops on the balls of his feet. He stayed in the crouch, hoping the position made him look, if not small, at least smaller.

Her lips pursed with each sucking breath. "What happen—?"

"Shh," he said quietly. "You'll be all right."

She swallowed in between pants and glanced up at the ceiling. "No, what happened?"

"You tried to take an impromptu nap on a moving conveyor."

Confusion worked its way across her features, and she stayed quiet long enough for Kev to set a paper cup of water next to her head and fade away. She didn't move to retrieve it. Finally, she muttered, "There's a first."

Before he could comment on her renewed spirit, a wince rippled across her throat and jaw. Trevor had to stop himself from reaching out and smoothing the skin in its wake. He knew a revelation when he saw one, and clarity of the unwanted variety was rapidly consuming her confusion. This beautiful woman with the cinnamon-dusted cheeks knew exactly why her body had decided on a time out, and she'd didn't welcome the memories.

Slowly, palms in the air, Trevor scuttled closer. "Can you sit up? Here, let me." He made a move to shift her, one hand slipping behind her neck, the other holding her hand. A burst of vanilla assaulted his already reeling senses. "My guess is you're dehydrated and hungry. When was the last time you slept?"

She let him pull her upright and turn her to rest against the side of the treadmill. Once sitting, her breasts bubbled up against the neckline of her tank. Her torso tapered inward and then out again at the hips.

Just a waist. Just a set of hips.

But the waist looked soft and welcoming, like he could rest his head there. The hips flared enough to lend her profile the kind of s-curve that incited fever dreams. And with both of her hands newly exposed, he saw that a short cast covered her right wrist, previously hidden behind her hip.

This one needed him. Trevor could feel it.

"You're hurt." He stoked the plaster. Maybe she'd downed one-too-many Vicodin. "Are you on pain killers, honey? Is that why you blanked?"

"Not anymore," she said softly, shrinking from the touch. "It's been a couple weeks. Four more to go."

Her voice slid into his ears and scooped out a place for her and her alone. Sweet and hesitant, she spoke as though she wanted him to listen but didn't believe he would.

"Why so woozy?" When she clammed up, he coaxed, "Tell me about your day. Nothing difficult. Nothing scary."

Tell me why you fell down? Promise you won't do it again.

"A funeral," she said, so low the admission barely cleared the buzz of machines and people. "A funeral for a friend."

Mourning. That explained the weakness. She'd gone from emotional to physical overload in the space of an afternoon. A sympathetic sound slid from the back of his throat, a sound he'd heard before but never made. "I'm sorry. Do you miss her?"

"Him," she corrected. Her lashes fluttered downward on a long sigh, leaving shadows against smooth, golden cheeks.

"*Him,*" she repeated. "My lover. My *ex*-lover. And I would give *anything* to miss him."

******

London blinked conspicuously at the figure crouched in front of her. Big and brawny. Light hair and even lighter eyes. A slash of a mouth cut into an unforgiving face.

Honesty had value. She knew that. *Of course* she did. Still, only pain and panic had made her tell the truth. Even now her throat quivered on each exhale, and she fought the urge to curl up on the rubberized floor.

Recognition pinched at the back of her skull. She longed to dismiss the sickening sense of repetition, to call it déjà vu, but waking to find an enormous man looming overhead had triggered more than a vague sense of familiarity. Shadows of her actual past danced in stark relief against the man now lurking just beyond striking distance. She saw Dillon's advance and her retreat, her struggle and then his very real death.

Shouldn't have come. Not fit for public consumption.

Murderer.

Occasionally, when she first opened her eyes, she couldn't pinpoint the reasons she'd sought to close them in the first place. In those fleeting seconds, the memories felt like a dream, until the dream disintegrated and reality rushed in like water on a sinking ship. This time, the renewed shock of it had boiled her arsenal of explanations, pulling the truth about Dillon's funeral straight to the top. When she refused further detail, he'd likely get curious about her situation—the funeral, the fainting, the cast—and try to find answers on his own.

Surprise and fear made people do things they normally wouldn't, even the sane ones. Two weeks ago those emotions had conjured up a brutality she hadn't guessed she possessed. Today they'd opened her mouth to a stranger. Her truth-telling had handed this man a weapon, and arming a guy whose left shoulder sat three feet from his right *had* to be a bad idea.

Still, the man knew she'd spent the day mourning her boyfriend, or at least trying to, and his blue eyes observed her with unnerving intent. Not disappointment. Not distrust.

This hero didn't suspect she was the villain.

The guy had no idea she'd *put* Dillon in that shining coffin already haunting the wavering undercurrents of her psyche. Self-defense or not, a slap on the wrist or not, she'd taken a life.

A trickle of blood, a broken bone, her own wheezing screams… London only wished she could block the memories, perhaps claim shock-induced amnesia like so many other victims—and perpetrators—of violence. Unfortunately, every second of the struggle played on a loop that scratched the back of her retinas.

The nagging voices scoffed at escape. *You're a wild card. Think, for once, before you act.*

Reason. Strategize.

Lie.

"What's your name?" the stranger asked.

Such an ordinary question. A wary kind of warmth flooded her system. Here they sat on the gym floor, and he sought her name like she hadn't acted the fool. Weeks had passed since her last normal conversation.

"London," she answered simply.

After a single heartbeat, the blond smiled. The shift changed everything. His initial look had most certainly been one of concern, but he'd still looked cruel. Long limbs layered with roped muscle and sharp features seemingly chipped from the face of a cliff didn't scream *nice guy*. Yet his slow smile revealed matching dimples low on lean cheeks, even laugh lines that said he knew how to have fun. Or at least he had at one point.

The smile brought out differences between this lurker and her last. This one overwhelmed with his nearness even though he held himself in check. The crew cut. The icy blue eyes. A sharp nose bisecting the angles of his cheeks.

He asked for my name.

This one looked mean and talked nice. Dillon, with his light curls and full lips, had looked nice and talked mean.

"Beautiful." The stranger reached out as though gentling a high-strung animal, half awe and half unease. Before long he twirled the ends of her upswept hair. "Tell me the rest."

"Whitley," she murmured, staring down at his busy fingers. "London Rose Whitley. My parents have never even been to England."

Silly. Twenty-six years old and still she spouted nonsense to gorgeous men. And bank tellers. And waitresses. And bartenders. To the cops who'd taken her in for questioning.

When the going grew unfamiliar, London got nervous. When London got nervous, she got awkward. Days passed without food. Nights passed without sleep. It wasn't surprising that this time, her body gave out during the power walk she needed to melt away the stomach pooch her mother saw as a sure sign of mental illness.

Possibly the same illness that leads me to kill people.

Tears threatened at the reminder, stinging and unwelcome in the back of her throat. The chaos of the last two weeks, even the last two hours, had proven one fact—if London didn't suppress Dillon's death, it would consume her. Whatever sanity she still possessed would slip away with him, another tragic consequence of that awful night.

So she'd lie. By omission or outright. With her body or her mouth.

London summoned a sparkle to her eye. She tried to join the man in his smile, but her lips wouldn't cooperate. Each stretch wilted and then faded away, until she gave up and said her lines without the comfort of an impish grin to diffuse the tension, to provide a diversion.

"Thank you," she began. The words sounded off, like high fructose corn syrup instead of sugar, and not at all like they did when she practiced common platitudes in front of the mirror at home.

Gratitude never came easy. Dr. and Dr. Whitley saw an overabundance of thanks as an attempt at ingratiation. But this man had broken her fall. Then he'd wound his big body into a pretzel so he could crouch on the floor and treat her like a normal person in an unfortunate circumstance, not an unfortunate person pretending to be normal.

He asked for my name. Called it beautiful.

Trying to ignore his touch through the sifting strands at her collarbone, London rolled to her knees. "You didn't have to help me."

"True."

"You could have let me stumble," she went on. "People trip on the equipment all the time." Except him. The man was a stranger, but not an unknown. The treadmills bordered the free weights. From her vantage point on their elevated platforms, London enjoyed an unobstructed view of the weights and the people lifting them.

For weeks now she'd watched him. Weighted pull-ups? Definitely her favorite. There was something about watching six-plus feet of defined musculature dangle metal plates from the waist and heave itself to a suspended bar, over and over again. Even those loose T-shirts he favored gave up a show. The fabric stretched over the dancing muscles of his shoulders, deferring to the perfection beneath.

No matter the exercise, the machine, or the amount of weight, he never faltered. Not like her.

He let go of her hair and began to trace the shoulder strap of her tank. "Angel, I could never let you fall."

Breath hitched at the back of her throat. Was he interested in her or in the tawdry fact she'd let slip? Despite the earnest way he looked and touched, he could be an accident watcher, a man attracted to her train wreck for the gory details sure to follow.

He wouldn't be getting them. Dillon's death might not be a *general* secret, but it sure was *hers*.

The urge to flee built with each kindness the giant dealt. If real, she didn't deserve the care. If not, she couldn't afford the trust. Time had come for a playful farewell that left him feeling like he'd done a good deed for a good girl.

Easy. Simple. Not worth another thought.

"I'll be more careful," she promised.

His warm knuckles made their way to her neck. "Like you were with your wrist?"

The question sounded light and teasing, but London knew better. Iron threaded each syllable. How often did this man hear the word *no*?

Never.

The smile she'd been striving for finally made an appearance, but she had a hunch it looked confused, lonely, probably bereft. Anything but happy. "Caution doesn't always work."

Caution had failed her when Dillon had come calling with all his strength. Not nearly as imposing as this man, yet no amount of care could have reinforced her bones within Dillon's crushing grip. A wrench, a shove, and she'd gone down. The moment her hand had connected with the ground in an effort to break her fall, she'd heard an audible crunch. She'd sacrificed her wrist for her skull.

Before, she'd had a few quirks to lament in private—Oreos with expensive red wine if the mood struck, a tendency to clean her bathroom corners with alcohol-soaked Q-tips, and a fidgety left foot, among others. *Since*, peopled watched. They *saw* the faults that had once been confined to Whitley territory.

Like now. Other gym-goers subtly observed her pow-wow on the floor—a pause in the next curl, a trip in the next step, a stretch that didn't go deep enough to skew the view.

Another spectacle to be cleaned up.

The auburn-haired guy who'd left the glass of water lingered nearby. At first he'd hovered in the vicinity, making no effort to conceal his eavesdropping. Now he climbed aboard another treadmill, a clear pretense of continuing his workout.

London had come to the gym to be anonymous, to quiet the buzzing in her head and the blame in her heart with sweat and exhaustion. If only she'd stayed standing long enough to achieve the objective.

Determined to outrun the pressure building in her chest, she planted her hands and began to push off the floor. "I'll be the definition—"

A hiss whistled through her teeth. *Pain*, sharp and stunning, spiraled from her fingers to her right elbow. Pressure on her right hand, no matter how light, worked the damaged bones of her wrist. In her haste to escape the blond's dubious scrutiny, she'd ignored the very injury on her mind.

Panting, she jerked back and prepared to topple forward, concentrating on the way the pain siphoned out of her arm with the break in contact. Before her balance had the chance to flounder, veined forearms snaked beneath her biceps. He lifted her to her feet.

Even gentler than before, he asked, "Were you about to call yourself 'the definition of careful?' I know what careful looks like, angel. *You* are not it."

London dug deep for a glimmer of righteous indignation and came up empty. Twice in the span of minutes, he'd rescued her from her number-one enemy—herself. "What's *your* name?"

He stopped laughing. "Trevor Rathlen, apparently at your service."

The frank offering cut the tripwires in her head, diffusing him as a threat. She let his unruffled presence beside what *would* have been her crumpled form on the floor bring a cleansing balm of common sense. He towered a good foot above her head, hands spanning her waist. She felt tiny and precious. Protected.

London gave up the fight.

"How?" he asked near her ear. "How did you hurt your wrist?" Her eyeballs nearly rolled in their sockets. The deep baritone slipped past her lowered defenses, a massage for the ear canal. Trevor's brand of coaxing made her want to answer.

"I fell." As far as lies went, it wasn't bad. She *had* fallen. She'd simply done so after being pushed and before doing some pushing of her own.

His grip slipped to her cast, and he lifted the souvenir between them. One hand moved to her elbow. The other outlined her half-covered fingers, never bending or hurting, just playing lightly.

"You like falling?"

Was that a joke? "No—"

"Because judging from this"—he stroked her pinky—"and what I saw today, you need to kick the habit."

London didn't consider herself overly sexualized. In fact, Dillon had insinuated the opposite on too many occasions. "*Give me more.*" "*So contained.*" He hadn't insulted their intimacy, not exactly, but he'd felt compelled to question it. When she hadn't let go quite like he'd wanted, the sex had gotten rough. Hard hands. Pinching fingers. Bruises, tiny and faint, where no one could see.

They'd been colleagues and lovers for over two years, and yet she'd always had to psych herself up for sex. If consistent, she'd been able to get away with once a week. Longer, and the nagging had started. *"Please, baby."* *"I can make it good."*

He hadn't.

So she'd taken the initiative on a regular basis, telling herself Dillon deserved a good time and that, as his girlfriend, she should provide it. Family and friends had remained in the dark, while she'd blamed the rocky waters of her relationship on past voices of authority, letting them morph into present voices of reason.

Maybe her skittishness really did arise from an *"inability to connect"* and a *"desire to be set apart from others."*

Except Trevor smelled so good she might stand in line for a piece of him, to bathe in the scent of soap and laundry detergent and man. His deep voice raised the fine hairs on the back of her neck and sent prickles to every spot he touched. If fingers could get goosebumps...

"I'll help," Trevor said, interrupting her mental summersaults. "No more dizziness. No more falling."

Sometimes promises were nice, even if they couldn't be kept. Against her better judgment, London melted farther into his chest. His throat undulated just above her hair. What if she tipped her head back and licked his Adam's apple?

"Wanna know how?"

She bit her wandering tongue.

"First, I can feed you." He scooped her into his arms and started out of the gym. "Then I can make you sleep."

She stiffened. *Nothing* could give her rest. Blood stained her waiting dreams.

"Relax." A slow squeeze compressed her hip, right at the juncture of her thigh. "I can *touch* you until your limbs go heavy and your eyes drift shut, until sleep becomes the only option."

"Do you mean—?"

"*Yes.*"

Sensuality she hadn't seen through her fear fairly oozed out of him. Somehow through the gentleness, his manner conveyed he'd be happy to eat her alive, possibly in both good ways *and* bad.

Trevor stopped in the lobby. Without putting her down, he asked the woman manning the desk to take London's locker number and combo and fetch her things. When London insisted she could get her own purse and towel, he hushed her and gripped tight.

"You're trembling in my arms. You'll fall and smack your head on the dressing room bench."

Then, without further explanation, he turned and treated the bristling receptionist to a patient stare that said, *"I'm waiting."* The woman resisted for a heartbeat, then shot both of them a scathing glance before leaving to do Trevor's bidding, her tight yoga pants highlighting her perfect—*holy mother of perfect*—backside as she sashayed toward the locker room.

That ass was all apples, no applesauce.

Trevor didn't acknowledge the tension *or* the view. He stood perfectly still with London suspended five feet from the floor, pretending the woman's reaction had been about gym protocol.

If only. Realization hit, and London's mouth dropped open. He'd spread that sensuality around.

"You two have dated," London finally croaked, knowing she shouldn't care.

Silence stretched as they waited. "Nope."

"Friends with benefits, then."

His head bent to meet hers. *"No."*

"Ah," London said knowingly, "benefits only."

He didn't bother to deny the obvious. Instead he pressed a kiss to the soft skin of her jaw. "Let's call it 'practice only.'"

"For what?"

He straightened and said two words.

"For you."

CHAPTER 3

A knock on Trevor's door split the night in two. The single staccato crack told him every detail about the ordeal waiting in the hall.

The who? Kevin.

The what? A pissing match over the incident in the gym.

The when? Oh, probably starting the second Trevor had departed said gym with one London Rose Whitley cuddled against his chest.

The why? Simple. Kevin didn't like to lose.

Trevor threw the door wide. "I did you a favor."

"See"—Kevin strolled across the threshold as though invited—"that's not entirely true. A truer statement would point out that you *owe* me a favor, but have yet to come through." Kevin splayed his hands to indicate the echoing loft Trevor called home. Slick concrete floors and exposed brick walls framed windows that yawned above the train tracks and a mesh of modern and historic architecture. Outside, Denver's lower downtown, or LoDo for short, elevated a hodgepodge to a classic. Breweries of aging red brick anchored offices of glass and steel. Clothing retailers sold five-hundred-dollar shoes from the bowels of gutted warehouses, while their sales reps grabbed their morning coffees and midday sandwiches from food trucks prowling the one-way streets.

Trevor could take or leave all the trendy, except for one simple fact—LoDo laughed in the face of his former life. Denver felt a world away from his Boulder bungalow and the choices he'd made there. At the same time, he could visit that world, and the people still living in it, whenever he could handle a reminder.

Of married life. Of the time he'd wasted. Of his own stupidity.

For a talker, Kevin didn't seem to mind silence. He let Trevor contemplate the dig and, in the meantime, meandered across the loft to the fridge. Once he had a beer in hand, he dug through Trevor's island drawers, muttering about bottle openers until, finally, he popped the top and landed on Trevor's couch.

"She's gone already?"

Trevor shrugged, focusing on the first winks of city light beyond the windows. "She never arrived."

A choking snort bubbled out through Kevin's nose, along with his inaugural gulp of Trevor's favorite beer. "I nearly ate an elliptical machine for dinner, and you wasted the opportunity? I *hate* you."

"She lives in that huge building across from the Federal Reserve, only a couple blocks from the gym. I left her with my number, resting on a chair in her lobby since she didn't want me physically escorting her upstairs."

"*Hate* you."

Kevin's inability to detect nuances gave him at least one positive trait. The man saw the world in black and white, so he had a helluva time lying— an overpaid, oversexed, insensitive pig, but a smart one. An *honest* one.

Who happened to own the building in which Trevor now lived. So, yeah, Kevin had done Trevor a favor. At the request of a friend of a friend, Kevin had made space open up in the right building in the right area. In that, he'd aided Trevor's escape from a cloistering world forever tainted by a lying wife.

Ex-wife. The "e" and the "x" were key.

Kevin took another swig. "So your plan is to what?"

"Do nothing." *For now.*

"Then my plan is to stake out the gym until she—"

"Your plan—your *only* option—is to leave her be." With each word, Trevor approached the couch, until he stood directly above his friend. "You don't go out of your way to find her. You don't approach her. If the stars align, and you somehow collide in the gym hallway out of pure coincidence, you say 'Hello, London,' maybe even, 'Hello, Ms. Whitley.' You say it like a gentleman. And then you get the fuck out of her face."

Other than government-sanctioned violence, Trevor hadn't hurt a soul since a misguided, and very drunken, bar fight in his early twenties. Yet one didn't go through life with the looks of a contract killer without experiencing other people's fear.

London had been scared of him. Whether she believed he would hurt her physically or mentally, he couldn't say. But even after she'd calmed down and trusted him to set her on sturdy ground, she'd held herself at a distance. She didn't need Kevin running after her trying to hump her leg.

In an ordinary woman, Trevor might attribute her skittishness to grief or sadness over the dead boyfriend. But London probably couldn't pronounce the word *ordinary*.

Some days his size and his hatcheted features caught the blame. He might agree today if he hadn't felt her twitch at his casual strokes along her arm and fingers, or if she hadn't licked her lips the second before he'd thrown sanity out the window and hauled her into his arms.

Kevin sank into the cushions, each vertebra curling with controlled purpose. "Good thing you're not threatening me."

"I'm *not.*"

"That's what I said." An empty beer bottle thudded to Trevor's aluminum coffee table. A pair of size elevens landed next to it. "I'm gonna let you get away with this, but that's two favors from me and zero from you. In fact, today's stunt put you at minus one. I consider myself *owed.*"

Any response would infer agreement, so Trevor simply pilfered more beers from the fridge before setting a second next to Kevin's empty. "She's not okay, you know."

His friend shrugged, but his eyes narrowed to suspicious slits. They hadn't known each other for long, and Trevor was quickly learning that Kevin didn't struggle with a white-knight complex.

"And?" Kevin drawled.

"I'm not going to investigate, so nix the silent suggestions."

"What?" Kevin sat forward, elbows braced on knees, gaze toward a bank of computers in the corner. "If I could do computer voodoo like you, I'd already know what she ate for breakfast and whether she likes Crest or Colgate."

Trevor glanced at the equipment, all neat and tidy and out in the open, not a trace of the maniacal hacker's lair shown in movies and on TV. Still, as soon as he constructed a client's computer security walls or built a new network, he set out to exploit its weaknesses.

Iteration by iteration, he broke his systems to make them unbreakable.

Inside *every* computer ever connected to a network lie the seductive and murky waters of discovery, a way to touch the world through digital tentacles. Needless to say, Trevor's day job had tempting side effects. White-hat hacking came with the territory.

Sometimes he chose to ditch the white hat.

Stretching out on the opposite end of the sofa, Trevor considered all the reasons Kevin could take his ideas, pour the remainder of his beer over the top of them, and light them on fire. "She'll come around." Meaning London deserved his trust. *She* hadn't wronged him, and he refused to react to Rhea's betrayal by preemptively betraying others in retaliation.

London's privacy would remain intact.

Kevin shook his head. "I never thought I'd see such arrogance on a"— air quotes—"*nice guy.* That woman isn't going to contact you. She'll probably switch gyms to avoid ever seeing your blunt-cut profile again. You're a diamond in the rough, *minus* the finesse of the diamond. I bet she loved your caveman routine all the way to the front desk where she requested a refund on the remainder of her membership fee—"

"She wanted to lick me." Of that, Trevor was certain.

"Ever had a fear boner?"

What? Trevor's head spun. He'd been married too long. Suddenly he couldn't even manage a speedy bout of bro talk. "*Start* making sense." Leaving London injured and alone in her lobby had left him twitchy, and he wouldn't mind working the stress out on Kevin's hawkish features and irreverent grin.

"A fear boner. You know, when a chick gets pissed off and she's in your face, maybe jabbing you in the chest with a red-tipped finger. You've done wrong, and you're in deep shit. There's fear—not the scared-scared kind, but the hot-scared kind. She wants to kill you, and all you want is to fuck."

Trevor's jaw slackened. He banged his head against the back of the couch. How could Kevin get that so right? "Yes."

"What?"

"I've had one."

"So you know what I'm saying when I tell you London had a feminine version of a fear boner today. She was terrified, yet she wanted to lick you. Big deal. It's a natural response but not one known for its longevity or depth of feeling."

Kev's ensuing pause felt like a windup to a grand finale.

"She won't call," Kevin finished. "Chicks don't have dicks, my friend. They don't think like we do, which means you fucked up my plan."

Some opinions weren't worth the breath they took to counter. Trevor thought of the women he'd had over the six months following his separation and then his divorce. Maybe he hadn't connected, but he sure had *connected*.

Women called him.

London would, too.

Wait. He met Kevin's challenging stare over the bottle approaching his lips. "What *plan*?"

******

Kevin contemplated a response. Trevor's little switch from Rambo to Casanova in the gym had destroyed his strategy so thoroughly he now required assistance. Preferably, that help would come from Trevor and his electronics ranchette in the corner.

Starting simple, Kevin asked, "What do you know about London Whitley?" He enunciated her name, all slow and careful-like.

Trevor's whole body went rigid against the cushions. The man made his money with a quick mind and nimble fingers that flew across the keys, but he spent his spare time honing himself into a lethal weapon. From what Kevin understood through their mutual acquaintances, Trevor's past layered like a jumbled, scorched lasagna—years of some kind of murky military service, then a second life of computer "security," a hellish marriage, and a divorce made for reality TV. With Trevor's background, skills, and predisposition toward distrust, Kevin could almost feel thankful for the guy's intervention in the gym.

And downright gleeful about Trevor being indebted to him.

Tension poured off Trevor in waves that might seem menacing if Kevin didn't find them so damn funny. A betting man, Kevin guessed Trevor didn't like the implication that Kevin walked a step ahead, especially when that step ambled in the general direction of black hair and green eyes too vulnerable to be real.

"I think," Trevor said, "maybe you should start. Let's begin with how you know who she is."

"This is bordering on *drama*." Rolling his eyes, Kevin came clean. "It's not what you'd guess. She's another favor. Generally when my brother does a good deed, he asks for one in return."

Six months ago Brian had called from New York out of the blue, requesting that a loft be held for Trevor. He'd explained that his friend Lissa Blanc would soon marry Trevor's younger brother, and that the whole family had been cluster-fucked by Trevor's then wife but soon-to-be ex. In sum, Trevor had needed a change of scenery *stat*, and Kevin had been in a position to help. Brian had played intermediary.

Even though Kevin had been the one to pony up the apartment, Brian saw the whole thing as an opportunity. In his brother's mind, *Brian* had found Trevor a place, and neither Trevor nor Kevin would be remiss in thanking him.

Brian Wentworth only made sense to himself, and he tended to like non-verbal thank-yous.

Circular, meet logic.

Confusion pinched brackets between Trevor's eyes. "What exactly did Brian do? My brother's fiancée asked for a favor. From what I can tell, he turned around and called one in from you. You owe *him* for doing *him* a favor?"

Kind of. "I might have made him invite me to his firm's summer party and introduce me to every single female associate beneath the age of thirty-five. He found my request a bit extravagant, but he granted it anyway—we Wentworths are a giving bunch—so now I'm back to owing him."

A Wentworth credo, really. Kevin and Brian had been trading escalating favors since they'd learned to talk. Being *owed* made the world go round. It was better than money, way better than love, and took second place only to extremely good sex. Brian would say collecting favors had bought him a big corner office in a Manhattan high-rise. Every action had an equal and opposite reaction, so no finger lifted without the leverage of one lifting in return.

Trevor didn't blink. "You're not even a rogue asshole. You actually come from a family of *born and bred* assholes."

"Precisely. My methods are ingrained. You might as well surrender."

Kevin stood with a fake yawn, weary only of the small talk. He approached Trevor's workstation, ready to come clean. "London Whitley is a wine importer and distributor. She started as a small, part-timer in college and built up the business. At this point, she runs a respectable shop for someone her age." Kevin used the word *respectable* to draw Trevor in, but he didn't mean it. London Whitley was a jade if he'd ever seen one. And he'd seen many. "WW Imports, which I'm guessing stands for Whitley Wine Imports, supplies wines to a decent number of restaurants and retailers around town."

Trevor peeled away the edge of his beer label, saying nothing.

"Lately, wines have been being returned with some regularity. If the returns were across the board, she could blame storage or maybe shipping conditions. At least she could point the finger to an inadvertent and likely fixable problem. But *all* of the bad wines originated with the same producer in central Hungary."

"You know this, how?" Trevor asked, his tone wary.

"You can't guess?" Kevin sank into an office chair abutting the desk and powered up a laptop the size of a picture window. He probably had about three seconds before Trevor removed him bodily from the seat. "That Hungarian wine producer is my brother Brian's client. While I imagine WW has been getting an earful on poor quality, the client has heard directly from several dissatisfied buyers. It turns out high-end restaurants don't appreciate bottle returns. When there's a trend, they pipe up. The thing is, after all this dissatisfaction, the client hasn't heard a peep out of London Whitley or anyone else at WW Imports."

Eerily quiet, Kevin could almost hear Trevor's teeth grinding across the room. Then, "You've been trailing her."

"Not *trailing* her." Kevin made his reply sound injured. "More like showing an active interest in the wine business and WW's tricky owner. The worst thing I've done is follow London home from work and have a lucky break when she stopped off for a little cardio."

And *Boom.* He'd conned Trevor into switching gyms within the week, no mean task since they used to work out right downstairs where it was easy for Trevor to keep up the hermit act—work at home, workout at home… Since moving in, Trevor had made contact with only a few sentient beings, including Trevor's brother and his fiancée—Cole and Lissa—the brothers' Uncle Kent, Kevin, and a few random women Kevin had witnessed slinking from Trevor's apartment in the classic walk of shame.

When Kevin had asked Trevor how a veritable shut-in managed to meet women, Trevor had solemnly said, "The grocery store."

That comment alone proved Trevor was perfect for what Kevin had in mind. Women went after Trevor in the damn produce section. London had fainted prettily and fallen from the treadmill for God's sake. She'd played the needy woman card, and Trevor had carried her out of the building. From what Kevin could tell, London had the shy, timid act down pat. All she needed was a strong, silent type like Trevor to see to her needs.

The gym move had provided double returns. Kevin had kept one eye on London Whitley and the other on all the lovelies that had been conspicuously absent downstairs. Eventually *he'd* have asked London out. Her secrets would have followed close behind.

Until Trevor had destroyed the master plan by playing prince charming.

Kevin hammered at the keyboard in front of him. "If you'd unlock this behemoth…" An unfriendly jab to the shoulder nudged him aside. "*Okay, okay, I'm moving.*"

Resting a hip on the desk, Kevin watched Trevor log on and search for London's company. In a few seconds both of them stared at a slick site, complete with wine bottles that sweated prettily amid mounds of grapes and cheese. Trevor clicked on "people," and there she was—*London Rose Whitley, owner and importer.*

Even on screen she appeared fragile, as though she sought to ward off prying eyes sight unseen.

Kevin wasn't buying. The fine features and winsome smile felt insincere. Like currency, she likely used them to purchase trust from the people she misled. "Not being a network infiltrator of the first water, I'd planned to investigate the hard way"—good food, great wine, unparalleled orgasms—"by searching her trash in the middle of night."

"Sneaky," Trevor deadpanned. "I see why your brother trusts you to carry out his dirty work."

"Luckily you intervened and fucked up my initial approach. Now this is on you, which is fitting since you're the one who actually owes the favor to me and my brother, has already boned in on the girl, and has the skills and the means to figure out what she's up to. Take advantage of that attraction, pal. Think less fear, more boner. I bet we get answers fast."

Trevor pushed away from the desk to roll across the concrete floor, hands in the air. "So I'm to whore myself out for the sake of your brother's client?"

"It's not whoring if you do it for free."

A rumble sounded deep in his friend's throat, and Kevin didn't know whether he was witnessing the coming of clenching hilarity or the apocalypse.

Finally, Trevor said, "I won't go after this woman just because a few Hungarian assholes sold her bunk pink Chablis. Who cares? The supply will run dry, and the world will keep turning."

"Not sure the assholes are Hungarian. Brian thinks there's one asshole, in particular, who happens to be an American woman with the name of a British poser."

The rollers on Trevor's chair squeaked to an abrupt halt. "I'm listening."

Kevin bit down on his cheeks. He *had* him. Clandestine hacking activities fueled Trevor's thirst to solve problems, for working through mysteries no one else could or would. An ex-wife in an orange jumpsuit fed his disdain for liars, especially the kind with lady bits below the waist.

The question had just become whether Trevor would tell lies for the sake of outing the same.

Stuffing his hands in his pockets, Kevin chose his words carefully. "The wine comes from a small vineyard in central Hungary called Tereth. With only several hectares of family-owned vines, the export numbers are small and the wines prestigious. The family has considered expansion but hasn't managed to purchase more land. For now, they work with Brian because he's based in New York, and they sell *exclusively* into the high-end market on the East Coast."

With a voice as troubled as the muscle ticking in his jaw, Trevor stopped him. "Yet Tereth wines are causing trouble here in the Wild, Wild West."

"Yes." Though they shouldn't have been. "Perhaps a New York importer might sell to a Colorado retailer, even a restaurant or a bar, but no eastern importer would sell to a western one for the purpose of reselling into the Denver market. WW got the fake wines directly from their source—maybe from Hungary, maybe from London's garage. *Never* from Tereth. Coincidentally, there hasn't been a *single* complaint about bottles sold on the East Coast. Why? Because those have traceable, documented provenance."

A tremor in Trevor's expression revealed a dawning understanding. Innocent, injured London, who couldn't hold herself up on the treadmill without a third-party rescue might not be so guileless after all.

"So, what?" Trevor asked. "These wines are like knock-off designer bags coming from China and bound for a street corner?"

Kevin nodded. "Except these kind of fakes are worse than fraudulent. They're *dangerous*."

Tension stretched Trevor's lips tight. "You assume the problem lies with London. Why don't I buy her being a criminal mastermind?"

Because London had "save me" written across her porcelain forehead. "You tend to see the bright side in the women you'd like to see on all fours."

"*Kevin.*"

The soft warning punctured Kevin's self-righteousness. Still sitting, Trevor's fists had clenched in his lap. Head bent, his friend watched them flex and curl, almost like he was imagining wrapping them around Kevin's throat and squeezing the insults away.

"Sorry," Kevin said, not meaning the apology for an instant. "That was too much." Especially since his friend was already half in lust with their person of interest. "But it doesn't change the fact that Brian initially wanted *you* to investigate, seeing how you're the one with the fancy new digs and the light computer fingers. I took over thinking she might be a pleasant *diversion*, but I don't think she'll give me a second glance after your ambulance impression this afternoon."

Kevin plucked a pen from the desk and scribbled his brother's number on a piece of scratch paper. Brian and Trevor could hash out the details of their private-investigative future all by themselves. He'd certainly done enough. Then, figuring retreat would serve him best in the face of Trevor's continually cracking knuckles, Kevin began backing toward the door.

But not without a parting shot.

"Consider the torch passed. And look at the bright side—this time you might extract your head from your ass *before* the woman you want manages to kill someone."

CHAPTER 4

The stem of a wine glass dug into London's palm. Her phone—the one Trevor had programmed with his number only two short days before—seemed to throb within the purse slung over her shoulder. Not even a crowded party could drown out the silent banter between that phone and her thrumming fingers.

She would *not* be calling him.

She snuck a sip of the wine she'd donated for the event, one of those meet-ups for young professionals seeking to network over cocktails and fried calamari. Hosted in a coworking community space housed in an old mansion, a whole lot of business casual mingled amid clusters of mismatched desks, each cluttered with the type of studied disorder that screamed *startup*—globes, circuit boards, snowboard bindings, doll heads, even a mannequin bust and a sewing machine.

So far London had talked with a biking realtor, who ferried potential buyers about town via a fleet of red cruisers, and a software salesman turned professional snuggler. That one sold non-sexual snuggling for sixty bucks an hour. He claimed to be constantly overbooked.

Maybe she should try for an appointment.

Fatigue from the failures of the past several weeks pulled at her eyelids. In another time, she'd have let Trevor take her upstairs two nights ago. When she'd halted his assistance in her lobby, he'd quietly arranged her on a leather lounger, then dug through her purse. Soon he'd had her phone in hand, tapping out a number. A responsive ring had sounded from the pocket of his gym shorts, and he'd said, "Call me when you change your mind. I'll tuck you in."

London leaned against a doorjamb leading to what looked like a reading room. People probably used the overstuffed chairs to relax, lattes and laptops balanced on laps. Add a counter, and the place could double for a

'Bucks. Perhaps *she* should consider workplace sharing. This space sure beat her ratty office, where all the money went into environmental controls for the attached wine warehouse. Wine was picky like that, and she made sure the warehouse, with its concrete flooring and towering shelves, stayed between fifty-five and sixty degrees. The warehouse even had a resident cat. Harriet watched over shipments coming and going through the loading dock with the ferocity of a tiny tiger. The animal didn't know she was on board for snuggles, not security.

In the abutting office, on the other hand, London and her handful of employees made do with ragged carpet, a collection of used computers, and a few metal desks scavenged from a 1970's cement plant. No amount of wall washing could purge the lingering scent of cigarette smoke.

Escaping that closeted room with the stale air and the stained floors had made her refuse Trevor's tantalizing offer. At least partly. Had he put all that stacked muscle to work "tucking her in," she wouldn't be here talking to alternative realtors and skilled snugglers.

She'd still be in bed with him, and that wouldn't help her understand why her business was circling the drain. *That* wouldn't move her offices from warehouse central to something more befitting of a high-end import emporium.

That wouldn't keep her lips sealed.

The sobering thought propelled her into the reading room. A blonde approached a drink table in the corner. After perusing the selections, she chose the wine London had brought.

London breathed in, then let the air escape over a carefully counted five seconds. The woman had the look of a sophisticate. She poured out the bottle's last glass, swirled the liquid gently, and took a starter sip. An immediate smile reminded London of why wine, with its temperaments and its follies, was a worthy endeavor. *A worthy life.* When the woman moved off to chat with a group circled nearby, London mentally tallied the response as favorable, if not earthshattering.

Another breath. Another five seconds.

London moved in and snatched another bottle of her problem child from the chiller she'd stashed under the table, an Olaszrizling that hailed from the Badacsony region of Hungary. The mild white tended to be a crowd pleaser, with hints of peach and apricot on the finish. While last year's shipment had been flooded with buyer complaints, this year promised a much better vintage. Within minutes of backing away, she had another taker. This gentleman read the labels on several different wines, but, like the woman before him, he opened and poured London's.

Not too surprising. Her selection offered plenty of curb appeal—noticeable, yet approachable; new, yet familiar.

The man brought the glass to his lips and turned to join an expanding group of suits. He froze.

Turning back to the table, she watched his eyes dart over the stuffed ice chest, over the cocktail napkins and fresh glasses, over the bowls of salt-encrusted nuts. Apparently he didn't find what he was looking for because without much ado, he plunked his full glass to the table and took a new one. This time he didn't pour London's Olaszrizling. He chose the exact opposite, a chewable Zinfandel out of California's Russian River Valley. New and apparently better drink in hand, he joined the conversation buzzing next to the table.

Personal preference? A bad bottle? A mistaken pour?

London nonchalantly stepped up for a taste, each exhale harder and harder to siphon slowly.

A hand covered hers, stalling her progress before pressing the bottle away. Strong fingers. Blunt nails. "Not that one."

The deep voice didn't belong to the man who'd rejected her wine. As though its low tones had been committed to muscle memory, parts of her body stretched taut. Others went liquid.

Trevor Rathlen.

Sliding her hand from beneath his larger one, she turned and let her gaze travel upward, straight into frosted blue eyes. As it turned out, Trevor of the weight bench and Trevor of the cocktail party were two different animals. At the gym, he stood out for his sheer size and command of the equipment. In a room full of men wearing adhesive-backed nametags, his charcoal and black ensemble fit in with its clean lines and understated finesse, but stood out for the very same reasons. He wasn't exactly a cheetah penned up with the bunnies—more like a healthy specimen thrown in with his mangy, dehydrated brothers.

The comparison made her rethink the snuggling appointment with a lesser specimen.

With the deliberation of a surgeon, Trevor extracted the wine from her grip. "You don't want this."

"Why?" The question popped out before the thinking that should have preceded it. Obviously with him she needed a strategy to get the answers she sought.

He shrugged and pressed close, reaching for the Zin. "Only *good* things should pass those lips."

The insult landed with the accuracy of an expert marksman shooting at a close target. London swallowed a gasp, realizing he didn't—*couldn't*—know her relationship to the wine he so casually insulted.

Which meant, London realized as her breathing raced faster and faster, that the dis reflected an unbiased opinion.

Inky liquid splashed into a fresh glass, and she wondered aloud, "You've *tried* the white?"

A shrug. "Different bottle. Over an hour ago. And saying 'a white' presumes much. I'm not sure plonk like that deserves to be called wine."

"*No.*" Heat from the crush of bodies and aging AC had left the room warm. Barely tolerable before, London suddenly felt stifled. Sweat slicked down her back, sure to bloom through her thin blouse at any moment. She'd be the token sweaty chick at the party, the one who'd brought the toxic beverages and lurked near the drink table monitoring all the action she wasn't a part of.

Trevor held out the red. "I'd hardly lie."

Ignoring him, London lurched forward and helped herself to a near overflow of the chilled Olaszrizling. Half the twelve-ouncer would beat the heat. The other half would prove Trevor wrong.

She took a healthy swig. Swallowed.

A choking cough burst from her mouth. The wine went down like a match to gasoline, literally painful to drink.

"Wrong pipe," she gasped, refusing to voice the panic overtaking her final slivers of calm. She'd imported Tereth vintages for two separate years, though the pronoun "she" applied loosely. *He*—Dillon—had been responsible for Hungary and Slovakia. After his death, London had taken Hungary and given Slovakia to Clara, another of her importers.

And her baby sister.

Complaints had plagued the first shipment from Tereth. At first London hadn't known about the angry calls and irate e-mails. Later, she'd taken Dillon's word that he was chasing the issues—hot spots in the shipping containers, over-dry corks that allowed the occasional bottle to prematurely oxidize. Dillon had been in contact with the vineyard and reported that, while frustrating, the quality issues would be handled prior to this year's shipment.

Yet the liquid sloshing in her rebelling stomach couldn't be called an improvement.

Could barely be called *wine*.

"It's…" What could she possibly say? Other bottles had been fine. This one promised to blow the lining of her esophagus. "It's…"

"Put the glass down, London."

The command should have made her angry, but instead her whole body clenched with a sick kind of attracted fear. The man had boundary issues, and London was practically *made* of boundaries. She got the feeling he relished the idea of smashing through them, one by one. The Trevor of today knew little. A careless moment at the gym had revealed Dillon's death, but after that, Trevor's knowledge hit a wall. The Trevor of tomorrow would know everything—all the personal failings that had led her to jeopardize her business, to destroy the man she'd tried to love.

Tried and failed. London hadn't truly mourned Dillon. Guilt, she realized, could never stand in for loss. Wanting to love wasn't the same as loving.

Another failing Trevor would discover if she let him.

"No," she said again, refusing to relinquish the wine with false calm. She took another blistering sip. "I like this one. Given a breather, it'll open up."

"Another drink and *you'll* open up." His tone insinuated that he meant *physically*, and not in a good way.

Maybe. The wine was *that* bad. A metallic aftertaste bruised each sip. Beyond corked or dated or tainted by heat, London tasted a failed chemistry experiment.

Trevor crowded closer. "Hand me the glass, London. I won't watch you choke on your own mistake. At least not yet."

Leaning back, she let the rim kiss her lips. Another taste. London had a *type*. She went for men with imperfections, underdogs like herself. A snaggletooth or a high forehead made a man tolerant of flaws in others. A history of second place meant a man could understand and accept the improbability of perfection.

Dillon had been attractive, but boyish; tall, but rather soft.

The man standing over her had pecs that preceded him into a room and veined forearms the width of a rolled yoga mat. He stared down at her, eyes burning with intelligence and impatience. On a breath, she prepared for another difficult swallow. "My mistake? Let's not confuse your opinion for taste."

This battle of wills would surprise them both because *she* was going to win.

But her glass was gone, slipped from her fingers during a moment of distraction. Looking around, she saw it on the table next to her hip and reached out. He caught her good wrist before she could retrieve the wine. "Turn around and walk out of this room. There's a bathroom on the left."

"I know where the bathroom is."

He didn't smile at her cheek. "Then you won't have a problem finding it."

By the time she rounded the corner, he pressed in behind her, guiding her toward a slim door that hid a tiny sink toilet combo. That press—chest to back and thigh to thigh—carried them into a room that folded inward like a closet under the stairs. A sloping ceiling indicated it had once been exactly that.

Unable to stand upright, Trevor sank to his haunches and closed the toilet lid. "Sit."

Almost against her will, she found herself lowering in front of him, meeting the irritation sparking from his gaze with weak defiance. "The wine was fine. I—"

"That wine will *ruin* you." He produced a plastic cup from nowhere and thrust it into her hands. "Swish."

Her mouth no longer burned, but the walls of her cheeks and tongue felt puckered, as though she'd sucked one too many lemons. Accepting the cup, she rinsed her mouth and leaned over to spit in the sink. "Happy?"

"I'd be happier if you didn't offer up wine that tastes like cat piss and ammonia."

Her rapid breathing stalled. "You *know* I donated that wine?"

"I know you're behind WW Imports," he answered softly. His palms grazed her knees before sliding down her calves, slow and gentle. At her ankles, he trailed away and once again delved into her purse. Pulling her phone free, he flipped the leather cover wide and held up the business card plastered to the inside. Obviously he'd seen the card when he'd entered his number the other day.

There went her future as an international woman of mystery.

"I recognized the import labels on the backs of two wines tonight," he explained. "First on the one I tried, and then on the one you *enjoyed* so thoroughly. Your tendency to stalk the 'bar' filled in the blanks. My guess is you know the wine has problems, and all these poor schmucks"—he jerked his head toward the door—"are unwitting participants in a taste test."

Exactly. But she couldn't admit as much without oversharing. "The wine is a project." A hopeless one. "If problems persist, I'll"—*do what I always do*—"find solutions."

"Admirable, since five minutes ago you were willing to risk open mouth sores to yourself and half of Denver's up-and-coming."

She flinched. He was right. She *had* set out to experiment. She *had* been willing to risk a few bad bottles in the bunch. Air that had been coming too fast stopped coming at all. What the hell was wrong with her, to think she could use unsuspecting party-goers as guinea pigs? To think she could *hurt* people?

Suddenly a face, full of shock and betrayal, floated out of reach. In her mind, the shock burst like a bubble and then faded, slowly trickling away to nothing. Accusing eyes went flat. Grasping hands fell limp. And she stood above it all. The culprit. The killer.

Impulsive. Compulsive.

Crazy after all.

Scrabbling for purchase, London tried to push up and away from Trevor's keen observations. The wine remained on the table, like a trap for the unwary. Guarding her broken wrist, she batted at the wall of Trevor's chest. Every second counted.

"Easy, easy," he murmured. "That's it." Hard hands handled her softly, pressing her quaking body back to the seat. "I'll get the wine. I'll get it for you."

A fleeting touch returned to her calves, tickling an imaginary seam lining the pair of stockings she wasn't wearing. Her legs tightened automatically, snugging the structured material of her skirt tight over her thighs.

Awareness seethed beneath her skin. Each inch that fell to those swirling fingers prickled in surrender. By the time he reached the sensitive patches behind her knees, arousal hammered at the tightness in her chest, easing the worry that had short-circuited her breathing patterns.

All the sudden the wine didn't seem so bad. Sex didn't seem so bad. *She* didn't seem so bad.

This man she hardly knew, a man who took her to task with such care, had drowned out the demons with the trace of a finger.

If only he'd keep going.

******

Trevor felt the exact moment she gave in. Wide-eyed and frantic, he'd thought she'd tear out of the bathroom and humiliate herself, snatching the bad wine and any evidence of its existence. When he stroked over the smooth skin of her legs, she jerked, then sighed. Her green eyes darkened from dry leaves to wet.

In a gesture of utter trust, she leaned forward until her head rested in the crook of his neck. "How can you touch me like that?"

Very, very easily. "How can I not?"

"I mean, how can you know where and for how long? How much pressure and when to linger? It's like your hands channel *good*."

Gripping her hair, he pulled her head back so he could gauge her reaction. "Don't you deserve it?"

Her lips parted. A single beat, then, "The wine is waiting."

Goddammit. He'd pressed too soon.

Trevor helped her to her feet, ignoring the fact that his body had decided on having her—right then, right there. No matter the size of the bathroom or the at least seventy people on the other side of the thin wooden door. No consequence to fact that he didn't trust her.

He *wanted* to. And somehow it was easy to trust wishful thinking.

London's responses felt too visceral, her fear of him and what he might think of her mistakes too real. She was selling counterfeit product, all right, but maybe she didn't know.

Brian Wentworth had been clear on the phone. Trevor had met the man only once in passing, when Brian had come to Colorado at Cole's request. Trevor's brother had needed romantic back-up with his then business partner, Lissa. Apparently Brian was practically one of the girls back in New York, and he'd been instrumental in helping Lissa graduate from Cole's artistic associate to his fiancée.

Now Trevor knew Brian had likely come so Cole would *owe* him. The Wentworth brothers doled out favors like broken genie lamps. They relished handing out aid, knowing the kindnesses were never free.

Plus "one of the girls" wasn't quite right. Fit and flamboyant and endlessly mocking, one might call Brian effeminate if they weren't looking closely. Brian watched women like a starving wolf, and Trevor guessed that playing the harmless wingman paid Brian's kind of dividends. The man knew exactly what he was doing.

The lawyer in Brian hadn't wasted a moment on their call. "London Whitley is a beautiful cheat. *You* are a beautiful genius, and you're going to build the case I need to shut her down. Much more of this and I'll lose my client. I don't like losing clients, Trevor, especially not wealthy Hungarian vintners that pick me up at the airport in a limo with a chilled bottle of rosé waiting on ice."

In the end, Trevor had agreed, but not for free, and not on Brian's terms. He'd agreed because Brian and Kevin were handing him a bundle of lies wrapped in a pretty package. Rhea had presented the same challenge, and Trevor had failed.

Not this time.

The agreement with Brian wouldn't be in writing, as the whole purpose would require Trevor to break the law. In fact, he'd already started in that department.

Explanations shuttled to the tip of Trevor's tongue. He could call his presence a coincidence. Running a computer security company dragged him to networking events all over town. Yet telling London a plausible lie would take them down a deceitful path that would only grow wider and wider.

He refused to be that guy, blurting, "I hacked your e-mail."

London froze, hand on the doorknob. "What?"

"I wanted to see you again"—he *had*, among other things—"so I hacked your account and peeked at your calendar. I attend things like this all the time to drum up business, just like you. But today I knew you'd be here."

The once-pliant body at his front straightened as though being slowly sewn upright with steel thread. She turned in place, letting herself be pressed between his chest and the door. "Why would you do that?"

Admitting the truth had been easy. Explaining why he'd decided on a course of action that could justify a restraining order called for slightly more finesse. He could be the meathead following his dick to the girl. Or he could be the computer nerd intent on flexing his skills. Maybe he was the nice guy who simply wanted to make sure she'd recovered from her woozy stint in the gym.

Which Trevor did London deserve?

He backed away, keeping his hands on her shoulders, pinning her to the door. Fuck, he'd never been able to resist her kind of argument. Blinking eyes conveyed surprise, but flushed cheeks said she found his overstep acceptable, even arousing.

"That doesn't bother you, does it?" He already knew the answer. "I invaded your world and followed you here, and you'd let me do it again."

Squirming beneath his restraint, she said, "*Why*, Trevor." No longer did she *ask*, and the demand looked good on her. Maybe this woman, who felt fear but forced strength, deserved the truth. Maybe the innocence in her voice and the courage in her eyes actually told it.

"So many reasons," he admitted. "Mostly I wanted to—wanted to see you again, to feel you again."

She nodded and let her head fall back against the wood, exposing the long, smooth column of her throat. Before he could get better acquainted with that beckoning skin, he had to come clean. She'd accepted the nice reason easily enough. What would she do with the nasty one?

"And then there's the fact I was *paid* to."

He barely caught her knee between his thighs, right before it connected with something much more sensitive.

******

One word pounded at London as she pulled her leg free and struggled with the doorknob at her back.

Paid.

Paid to follow her. *Paid* to be nice to her. *Paid* to rescue the fragile flower and ask her name.

Trevor stood aside. He didn't interfere when she barreled out of the bathroom, but when she turned toward the reading area, he spoke up. "I said I'd get the wine, London. *Go.* I'll meet you outside."

Fine. He could play fetch even though she had plenty of unsellable swill to go around, but he wouldn't be meeting her outside or anywhere else.

She didn't make it. Before she could inch out of her metered parking space a block away, Trevor plunked her wine chiller onto the hood. His sardonic, "Missing something?" translated straight through the windshield.

Paid to save her from herself.

Except she didn't know anyone who'd spring for London cleanup. Her parents seemed to enjoy her follies. Each time she screwed up, she proved them right. Otherwise, how could their story for her morph into *her* story? She paid her employees, and while she enjoyed a solid working relationship with most of them, they didn't know enough about her to be moved to intervene in her love life. Her friends existed in the abstract, more like acquaintances on an aging roster. For years she hadn't been emotionally or even physically available to turn budding relationships into actual ones. All her time had gone into WW Imports and then a man.

The *wrong* man, who hadn't lived to tell the tale. And now her business might not survive her either.

One person remained standing after the shoddy process of elimination—her little sister. Clara might just be creative enough, *impetuous* enough, to hire an escort and sic him on her wilting, risk-adverse older sibling. Lord knew Clara would cackle with glee if she saw London's latest predicament. Since childhood, Clara had insisted that London's efforts to remain calm and cautious were a waste of time. In Clara's mind, London's life had forever needed more excitement, not less.

"They're wrong," Clara had mumbled when their parents weren't listening. "I don't get it. They look at you and see the kid you aren't." Meanwhile, Clara, initially shy and quiet and well-behaved, had been free to grow daring, free to be bold, and she'd used that freedom to tantalize a stunted London into the light.

Clara's faith had been enough to make London believe that an inquisitive curiosity didn't equate to ADHD. When London had turned eleven, she'd wrecked her new bicycle attempting to jump a curb in front of the house. A neighbor boy had mocked her fall. Despite the bloody scratches oozing along her legs, London had stood and invited him to do better. In her mind, he'd most likely succeed, and she'd learn by observation. He hadn't. Johnny had fallen, too, only the fall had busted his arm against the unforgiving slope of the gutter. There in the cul-de-sac, with London bleeding and Johnny screaming, London's mother had declared her eldest a menace. By nightfall, the pills had started.

For months London had dutifully taken the medicine. But science hadn't made her better. She accidentally broke an antique stethoscope trying to hear her own heartbeat. She continued to shower twice a day, and no amount of explanation could make her use a bath towel more than once. The dinner table became a battleground, a place where London sought to assert her individuality and convince her parents that her opinions and thoughts were both real and normal. She liked peas and hated carrots and refused to believe her preferences were a sign of mental instability.

Her parents used descriptions like "acting out," "defensive," and "in denial," the same cryptic, clinical terms they applied behind closed doors when talking about their patients. When her father caught her listening outside his consulting room one afternoon after school, he accused her of violating the sanctity of his work. The dialog changed to "unconscious hostility" and "impulsive resentment" toward her parents and their valuable profession. They upped her meds that very day.

London stopped taking them the next.

Clara played equal parts accomplice, buffer, and witness. The two girls quickly developed a routine for disposing of the drugs at mealtimes. They called it the "pass and piss." Neither Victoria nor Warren Whitley watched Clara like they did their eldest, so each day Clara discreetly flushed napkins full of psychotropics into the Denver water supply.

And London learned to fake it.

She stopped fidgeting with her feet and playing with her hair. She made her bed every morning, but in a way that lacked the crisp, almost military precision of her former efforts. Her parents' home offices remained strictly off limits, and she gave up the intense and incessant questions about their work and switched to the unfocused meanderings of a child. Instead of searching for a heartbeat through her ankle, she listened to boy bands, talked about make-up, and hung posters on the wall.

All expected. All accepted.

On her twelfth birthday, she received a kit that taught her all kinds of ways to make accessories out of colored duct tape. When Johnny from next door found her making a purse in the driveway and snatched up her supplies to hold them out of reach, she didn't bother with challenges or mind games to get him to give them back. She didn't trip her tormentor or call him names. She did what was normal, what was expected: She shouted for an adult and pointed a finger.

She ate carrots.

The less aggressive, less opinionated, more demure version of herself—*Level London*—earned her parent's reluctant approval, though they remained a hairsbreadth away from calling her crazy. What drew her parents, however, repelled her sister. Clara wanted the wild, experimental London back, the one who built a fire-escape ladder out of nylon belts and insisted the two of them test it from the second floor beneath every full moon. Clara wanted the girl who rebuffed accusations of instability by challenging bullies with mental gymnastics they couldn't understand. London's sister couldn't accept that, as the years passed, London *became* the staid and careful person she'd once only pretended to be. To compensate, Clara herself grew more outgoing. It was as though the two switched places—London slowed down and Clara sped up, always wanting to drag London along for the ride.

"If 'compulsive' and 'impulsive' are so bad," Clara had complained hotly, "then be bad. Be their worst nightmare."

London had refused. "But *you'll* always know"—*maybe always be*—"the real me." And thus the duality had grown. For the world, London got good grades but not great. Her voice rarely raised beyond moderate. She minded her own business and buried her questions. She made decisions with studied care, neither compulsively fast nor indecisively slow. She researched and came to understand her parents' words and their drugs, but never told a soul about her discoveries. The Whitleys never knew she studied them every bit as much as they studied her. And when her father hypothesized over dinner that Santa Claus was really a phallic symbol entering a vaginal chimney, she had laughed in secret, with her sister, on their fire-escape ladder.

Now, taking note of the latest lapses in her carefully cultivated picture of sanity, London realized she knew exactly who'd hired Trevor. Perhaps a bit of murder had left her sister wondering whether London was finally tapping at the inside of her self-imposed shell. Clara had probably decided to push the process along. With a sledgehammer. And a man with shoulders broad enough to block out the sun.

Lowering her car window, London baited a trap. "Hacked my e-mail, did you?" *Right.* More like he'd gone where her sister had directed—*for a price*—first her gym, now her job. "How'd you manage that?"

He wouldn't have a clue.

Looking harassed, Trevor said, "Phishing software. You really shouldn't change your password every time you receive a remotely authentic-looking e-mail saying your info's been stolen. Half the time that stuff comes from the bad guys."

"Like you?"

"No." The man smiled more like a shark than a paid seducer. "I hack for the good of mankind, *usually.*"

She sat in silence. An e-mail *had* come the day before. Very official-looking, it had explained that numerous servers had been compromised and asked users to immediately change their passwords to protect sensitive information. Always the responsible citizen, London had clicked the link provided in the message and complied.

"London?" he prompted.

"Why bother? Clara could have told you where I'd be."

"Clara?"

"My sister," she said slowly, emphasizing the association, "the one paying you?"

Trever made a noise that sounded like the "wrong answer" buzzer on a game show. "Try again." Approaching the passenger side, he began tapping the window with the padded chiller. "Unlock the doors, London."

She did, grudgingly.

The chiller slid across the back seat before Trevor joined her in the front of her little sedan. The interior barely accepted his big frame, and he folded himself inside, one limb at a time. "Would you like some dinner before we discuss this wine situation?" He spoke as casually as one could when imitating origami. "You probably need food after ingesting what amounts to a toxic substance."

Three times he'd tried to take care of her in as many days. As far as paid companions went, she imagined this meant going the extra mile. Yet London wouldn't let her sister literally *buy* her a dinner conversation. Desperation needn't sink so low.

"I'm not hungry," she finally said.

"You look hungry."

"What, exactly, does hungry look like?" Because, as her mother would say, London was not it.

"You swallow more often and shift in your seat. When you think I'm distracted, you lick your lips. Inside, I saw you eyeing the nuts. You would have eaten some if you hadn't been laser-focused on the poisoned fruit."

London sat purposefully still with her arms crossed, engine idling. "You can keep the money. I'll tell Clara—and if it wasn't Clara, which I *doubt*, then I'll tell whoever signed the check—that you showed me a good time. The best."

Trevor tweaked a knee and sighed. "That's not how it works, angel." His face fell into implacable lines. "I want to believe you don't have anything to do with the counterfeits, but as this is a private investigation, you're pretty much guilty until proven innocent. You show me you're not a problem to my *satisfaction*"—he lingered on the last—"and I'll show you a good time. You can bet it *will* be the best."

Counterfeits? The physical awareness London had been fighting drowned in a rising flood of adrenaline. Trevor kept talking, a garbled mess that pressed against her ears but didn't enter. Reaching out, she gripped the wheel with shaking hands and whispered, "You're not an escort."

The indistinct roar coming from Trevor came to an immediate stop, and London couldn't help but drink in the silence. Squeezing the rubber beneath her fingers, she took a breath and counted—five, four, three… Before the air ran out, she glanced at her passenger.

Trevor's mouth had compressed into a thin line, and yet above, she saw humor simmering where she habitually spied intolerance.

"Say that again?" he asked quietly.

"My sister didn't…?" *Pay you to up my excitement quotient?* "You aren't—?"

"A gigolo?" he finished. "A gentleman of the evening? A prostitute? A card-carrying member of the Thunder from Down Under?"

A squeak whistled through her restrained exhale. "No," she said, "you're none of those things."

"Angel, the only thing I *do* for money is computers." He dug into his pants pocket and fished out a leather wallet. Soon a crisp business card sailed across the car and landed in her lap. "Things like network construction, firewalls, data storage and retrieval. You get the picture." He didn't mention anything sinister, but his earlier admission about infiltrating her e-mail told her his list of professional accomplishments extended beyond run-of-the-mill data management.

More like data theft.

"Rathlen Cyber," she read. The logo on the card featured a padlocked computer and a brain, an obvious nod to computer security. *Definitely not sex for hire.* London cringed. "Can we forget about the last few minutes?"

He folded his wallet and took his time tucking it away. "Maybe I don't want to." His voice was gently mocking. "Maybe your suggested extracurricular activities put me exactly where I'd like to be."

She swallowed against the implication, letting her hands idly stroke the steering wheel. "*If* you're a computer security guy, *and* someone is paying you to investigate me for wine counterfeiting, *and* you're willing to tell me about that someone and what they believe I've done, *then* maybe I'm hungrier than I thought."

Trevor flicked an expectant glance toward the empty, waiting road. "I know just the place."

CHAPTER 5

Fifteen minutes later, Trevor directed her into another metered space next to a converted industrial building. From street level, London could see Denver's historic Union Station. Recently renovated, the nineteenth century behemoth had been reborn into a venerable transportation queen. With a hotel, bus and light-rail stations, an entertainment complex, and a score of restaurants and shops, London assumed they'd park and walk to the crowded depot that had anchored the northwest end of LoDo for well over a hundred years.

Instead Trevor tugged London inside and onto an elevator, where he pressed the button for floor six. The main floor boasted obvious storefronts, but she'd assumed the rest housed offices or condos resurrected from the bones of the converted building.

"There's a restaurant toward the top?"

With a nod, he answered, "The best."

London couldn't afford the best. "Maybe we should grab a sandwich somewhere"—*lower?*—"else," she finished lamely.

"You don't want to miss this."

In the hall on floor six, she understood. "You've brought me home."

"For a meal," he said casually, "and an explanation—one from both of us, I think." Stopping outside a door that read sixty-six, he tapped the knob. "The night waiting on the other side won't hurt you. Promise you'll relax."

"How much wine do you have?"

"Don't you know Denver is the Napa Valley of beer?" The slide of a hidden deadbolt punctuated his question, but before she could respond, he swung the door open and gestured her inside. "Welcome to the land of hops and dreams."

She'd taken one tentative step when he added, "And dog hair."

At first glance, the loft looked pristine. Her own apartment was both down the street and a world away. Where she had compartmentalized carpet and tile, he had shining concrete floors and exposed ductwork spanning one huge room. In her home she'd framed her most beloved shots from wine-scouting trips. While the captured moments highlighted the things she valued most, her photography skills, equipment, and the money she'd dropped on framing could all use a lift. Half of her pics had been taken with a phone, more documentary than artistic.

The chalky brick of Trevor's walls popped against *real* art—prints of abstract paintings, if she wasn't mistaken, and some of the most breathtaking examples of travel photography she'd ever seen. Wine had at least given her a glimpse of the world, and now Naples and Istanbul and Buenos Aires leapt from his walls to her mind. Trevor hadn't bothered with eight-by-tens. Some works spanned a few feet, others several.

Dog hair didn't appear to be a problem.

Trevor tossed her an apron he'd fished from somewhere behind a massive kitchen island. "Put this on."

"I'm to cook?" The apron slid overhead, tied at the waist, and fell to her ankles, more hazmat suit than cooking implement. With her at the helm, Trevor had better like saltines and squirt cheese. There was cooking, and there was eating. London prided herself on the latter.

"Nope," he assured her, "more like entertain." The last word competed with a high-pitched whine that escaped from beneath what London assumed was the bathroom door.

"Entertain *him*." Trevor opened the door, and a pony-sized dog ambled out. For all the whining, he didn't appear to be in a hurry. Or, possibly, he couldn't move particularly fast given that he weighed two-hundred pounds if he was an ounce.

London instantly thought of alpine hunting lodges and kegs of brandy strapped to hulking, furry necks. This guy could probably dig to the center of the earth with those man-sized paws. Her awe fled when the dog dismissed Trevor's practiced strokes along his glossy back and turned for a go at London.

One slow-mo head butt to the thighs, and she fell in love. "You house a horse in a loft?"

"I babysit. My brother and his fiancée travel a lot for work." He motioned to the prints on the walls. "They're artistic types. My uncle and I juggle Sasha when they're on a gig."

"Is he even allowed in here?"

A low chuckle. "Not at all. But we know the owner, and Cole—my brother—pays for the privilege of ignoring the weight limit." Trevor stooped and spoke to Sasha in a smooth, affectionate tone that probably worked on animals and women alike. "Huh, baby, you're only forty pounds on paper, aren't you? Practically a wiener dog."

Straightening, Trevor reverted to human speak. "He's house trained and has the bladder of a camel. Plus he's so lethargic it's like living with a sloth. Mainly he likes long naps in the bathtub, bacon, and chicks. The order of those priorities shifts on a daily basis. I have a feeling," Trevor said speculatively, eyeing the way Sasha nuzzled her legs, "that today he's mostly into chicks. The apron should protect you from the slobber involved in his more amorous pursuits."

Hammering the point home, Sasha went in for a full-body press. He leaned into her hips and wiggled to direct her hands to all the right spots. If she stopped for even a second, he flipped his head back and stared into her eyes with a look that said, "*If you love me, you will rub me.*"

She rubbed, letting Trevor take to the fridge. Over the next several minutes she made a life-long friend, and Trevor laid the foundation for something with chicken and goat cheese and rosemary. He moved about his kitchen the same way he did the weight room—calm and methodical, a streamlined machine.

He even had fresh bread and her favorite nineteen-dollar olive oil.

Suddenly London wanted Trevor and his canine nephew to have the chick thing—a *particular* chick thing—in common.

******

Trevor laid a pile of chicken between sheets of wax paper and began to pound it flat with the smooth curve of a rolling pin. As he let the familiar process of feeding himself take over, he considered London and her reaction to the loft and Sasha the Secret Weapon.

Sasha had arrived that afternoon for a week-long stay. This time Lissa and Cole were in Puerto Rico. For once, the trip didn't involve work. The two were scouting wedding locations, planning an epic event that appealed to his soon-to-be sister-in-law's wealthy family.

London moved to the couch, where she sat and put her arms around Sasha's thick neck. The dog stayed still for a bit, doing his part to tear down the walls encasing this one quiet woman. When Sasha got tired of standing, he spun a one-eighty and sat, ass to cushion and feet on the floor, right next to London.

She smirked at the dog's human impression. "Je t'aime," she said on a sigh, letting Sasha draw her out in a way Trevor had failed. *I love you.*

Such easy affection. Most women either feared the animal as a whole or, at least, what he might do to their black clothing. His ex had steered clear, probably because Sasha had sensed the chinks in her idealized armor.

"You speak French?" Of course she spoke the most lyrical language to ever be whispered across a pillow. Trevor knew the basics of several languages and could spout serviceable German, thanks to Uncle Sam. The harsh, guttural cadence didn't compare.

"Badly," she said. "Some call French wine's second tongue."

"What's wine's first tongue?"

"I suppose the actual tongue. All those taste buds and such." She stuck hers out at Sasha and cooed, "Vous pouvez marier Harriet." *You can marry Harriet.*

A pet? As far as openings went, it was small progress, yet disclosing a pet was the first bit of information she'd offered without his needling or prodding. He could see her with a cat, one of those eye scratchers that hid behind the curtains at the first sign of company. "You've an animal?"

She nodded. "Harriet's my guard cat. She lives at the warehouse and acts kind of like a wine bouncer. It's one of her many dog-like talents."

Nice. Trevor shot Sasha an indulgent glance. "I'm not sure this one knows the difference between dogs and cats. If it's breathing, and it pays attention to him, he wants to make out with it."

Sasha emphasized Trevor's point by sniffing London's ear. She leaned in, not away, and he realized this introverted wine importer had already put him in danger of compromising his hard-won ideals. Much more of her, and he wouldn't care whether she sold fake wine, whether she knew it was dangerous, or even whether she made a fraudulent living and used her innocent looks to deflect suspicion.

Setting the chicken aside, he combined a package of soft goat cheese with generous amounts of rosemary and shallots in a skillet and began warming the mixture with a drizzle of olive oil. Digging two different beers from the fridge, he held them up with a raised brow, encouraging her to choose.

"Which one tastes more like wine?" she asked.

"We're broadening our horizons. I drank wine earlier. *Bad* wine, even. I'm giving you *good* beer." Figuring she wouldn't make a selection, he decided on an apricot ale for the lady and poured the golden liquid into a chilled glass.

He handed over the drink with a warning. "Don't let Sasha con you. He only gets beer on his birthday."

"You give him alcohol?"

"On his birthday." She was such a constrained, rule-bound little thing. "He weighs a million pounds. What's a beer gonna to do to him?"

The wheels visibly cranked in her head, and she took a small sip, more like a trial taste than actual consumption. "Not terrible."

"Delicious," he corrected. The sunny color of the beer almost matched her skin. He bet she'd be sweeter but equally appealing. Shaking his head to reset the single track of his thoughts, he retreated behind the island and forced himself to focus on chicken prep.

"So, other than beer, you like food," she observed. "And you can even cook it.”

“Food is my first love.” Too bad it hadn’t been his only. “My hobbies demand a lot of calories. Early on I decided I wanted to like consuming them.”

With each inch of beer that disappeared, London sank farther into the couch, one hand on Sasha and the other gripping her liquid gold. “I suppose energy bars and sports drinks only go so far.”

And they tasted like shit. “You speak from experience?”

The hard-won relaxation slid from her face, replaced by a wary suspicion. “Do I *look* like an athlete?”

Obviously she didn’t think so. And she was right.

London looked like a *sport*—the kind he could play for days and never tire.

Trevor busied his hands, spreading a layer of warmed goat cheese over the flattened chicken breasts. “Not particularly,” he said carefully.

At his comment, she looked down at her lap. He could see her throat working from across the room, and yet she remained quiet. The list of touchy subjects grew. She clammed up when too close to a man. She’d alternated between wanting and fearing his nearness, first on the gym floor and then in the cramped bathroom. Telling her he’d been paid to trail her had initiated first a knee to the nuts and then a conversation about moonlighting as a gigolo, and questioning her business decisions had almost gotten him run over. Now an innocuous remark about her hobbies had her curling inward to a place he couldn’t see but wanted to reach.

Who had taught her to fear and to doubt?

“You look healthy,” he continued, “all soft and welcoming and edible. You look like you’ll finish that beer and eat this chicken”—he held up the platter of meat ready for the grill—“but refuse dessert and hit the gym tomorrow so that sweet little skirt will fit just right.”

The observations that came between “healthy” and “skirt” brought her head up. Her hesitant gaze followed him out onto his suspended steel balcony.

Lighting the grill, he made a final entreaty. “Now you look like you want to believe me, and you should.” *Mostly.* Before the night ended, he’d tell her the rest, but with a minimal kind of veracity that left certain truths unsaid.

Like the fact that she was a liar and he was a trap.

******

They ate side by side, bellied up to the granite of Trevor’s kitchen island. The sun had finally faded, and despite inauspicious beginnings, Trevor had barely cranked the lights beyond dim.

Date dim, London thought.

In one sentence, he talked of wine fraud and admitted to being paid to investigate her company's alleged illegal dealings. In the next, he spoke of finding her *edible*. Drops of conversation peppered the room like buckshot, each hit falling into a bleary constellation that might be difficult to see, but if studied carefully, formed a cohesive pattern.

London's guess? Trevor spoke of attraction to gain her trust so she'd open up about her supposed lapse in business ethics. He was willing to hear her out, but he harbored suspicions and would use whatever clandestine skills he had—computers, charm, even seduction—to determine whether she'd done wrong.

She had *not*.

At least not in the way he thought.

Granted, Tereth's Olaszrizling presented a problem, but London watched her people, vetted her suppliers, and, above all, kept her finger on the pulse of the money. Bills paid. Accounts balanced. Quality fervently controlled. Tereth had been scrutinized before the first contract had ever been signed, and now some anomaly—some glitch—brought unwarranted censure to her door.

A familiar unease began to wind through London's thoughts. Obviously she hadn't been careful. Two years had evaporated in the wake of a relationship with little promise. In the meantime, WW Imports had suffered. London had done this to herself. She'd put herself in Trevor Rathlen's line of sight through carelessness and distraction.

The beginnings of panic overtook her nerves. The chicken, once moist and delicious, suddenly tasted like ground up cork. Breathing slowly through her nose, she mentally counted each chew and reached for her beer, hoping to wash away the familiar taste of anxiety. A swishing hand moved between her and the drink.

"London," Trevor said, his voice pitched low and cajoling. "Where'd you go? You were relaxed, then pensive, then calm again. Now you look like you might be sick."

Her eyes shifted to his. Mortified, she shook her head. *Not crazy. Nothing but a normal dinner between two regular people.*

Except it wasn't normal at all. "Who hired you?"

He balled his napkin and cleared both of their plates. Appearing resigned, he asked, "Another drink before we do this?"

Do this. She shook her head. The beer, not her usual choice, went down heavy and made her feel overly full.

"We'll talk first," he informed her, "about little things, even about nothing."

Standing across the island with both hands braced on the edges, Trevor looked like a rising giant. His body threw long, sinuous shadows in the low light. Yet he made kind requests even though he didn't have to ease her in.

"Why?" she wondered out loud.

"I want to know you."

I want. He said it like a man comfortable with chasing the things he wanted, regardless of the consequences.

Coincidentally, she returned the sentiment. Plus she recognized an opportunity to deflect when she saw one. "Have you always lived in Denver?"

Trevor turned to the sink, giving her his broad back. "A recent development."

Even steeped in the night, his place looked cared for. Lived in. He'd taken time with the artwork and the cushioned leather furniture. His dishes matched, and he kept beer glasses frosty in the freezer. The cords of the computer equipment consuming nearly an entire wall had been organized and labeled. The loft was a showpiece, rather like the man, and his attention to detail soothed her.

"What brought you to the mile-high city?"

He stopped washing. "Divorce."

Oh.

"Go ahead," he said. "I started this."

London fumbled for words that wouldn't sound invasive or judgmental. "No kids?"

The last dish settled into the dishwasher, and he began pressing buttons. "Just a part-time dog."

"Does your wife... er, your *ex*-wife ever take Sasha?"

"*God*, no."

London looked down at the fur ball settled between their respective bar stools. Sasha had nudged his way in as they'd sat down to eat. From there, he'd stared upward pitifully, like he'd never tried a piece of chicken on his way to a million pounds.

"I've lived here my whole life." Some days she wished she'd escaped to one of her sun-drenched wine regions, where they grew grapes in the coastal breeze. "My parents are psychiatrists who work from home. My little sister started working for me after she graduated from college. We might import alcohol simply to aggravate them, and I appreciate the irony of our efforts to kill brain cells rather than understand them."

Still staring down into Sasha's dark, adoring eyes, London *felt* Trevor turn away from the clean sink. He took her in as he repeatedly balled and snapped a dishtowel between huge hands. His gaze slid over the exposed skin of her neck, along her arms. Slowly. Always calm. Ever collected.

"My parents died—a car crash and related complications—when I was a kid. My uncle Kent took my brother and me and raised us in Boulder. He's a rock, and also part of Sasha's crew of nannies."

For some reason, she loved that the whole family pitched in to raise a communal dog. Not all were so inclusive or so accepting. "You sound close."

"We are." Back at the fridge, Trevor extracted a round, ceramic dish. "You and yours?"

Thick as frenemies. "For my sister"—the one who'd thankfully *not* hired a male prostitute to coax London onto a date—"I'd take a bullet."

He paused before nodding, withholding comment on the relatives she'd conveniently left out. The dish hit the counter next to a small plate and a matching silver fork.

So the dessert warning had been real. "That's *pie.*" Really luscious-looking pie that jolted her protesting taste buds back into action.

"Strawberry rhubarb," he explained. "You can take the man out of Boulder, but you apparently can't keep him from bribing his brother to play courier from the Boulder farmer's market."

"You made this?" And offered it to her like she could afford the treat. She didn't miss hearing the usual questions—from her parents and then Dillon—about whether she'd exercised today or the combined health quotient of her lunch and dinner.

"I did promise you the best dinner in town. Will you indulge with me?"

More like indulge *in* him.

"Who hired you, Trevor?" Incessant questions kept her from slipping into that dangerous state called *trust.*

Shoving his hands through his hair, he stalled. After a few rough passes over the scalp, he said, "Someone who helped me when I needed an escape."

A favor, then. Of course. "From your wife?"

His bitter laugh held a warning. "From myself. From my life. My wife wasn't the problem. Rhea won't be seeing the sunny side of a prison cell for decades, if ever."

London sensed that his comment foreshadowed the arrival of information she wasn't going to like, and a wave of wariness balled in the back of her throat. What had this woman, his *wife,* done to so effectively tamp Trevor's easygoing openness? She gripped a fork and cored out a bite of pie, straight from the source. Sweetness slipped between her lips, providing a respite but not a response. She chewed slowly, and settled on a comment that would allow him to dictate the parameters of what he revealed.

"Tell me."

Trevor mumbled, "This'll teach me to open the gates." Then he jabbed at the now desecrated pie sitting between them. After making short work of a mighty bite, he said the only words that could possibly move their situation from complicated to impossible.

"She killed her lover." The pronouncement was low and grating in the quiet space. "For two years, her lies prevailed. For two years, I slept next to a murderer."

He didn't say *with* a murderer, but the subtext swirled in a deep, unreachable place in his eyes.

London reared backward, nearly falling from the stool. "What?" The question was feeble and reed thin.

"I think you heard me." Trevor stepped around the edge of the island, not stopping until he stood between her knees. Her legs grazed his hard body, and she *felt* him stiffen. "My wife was a beautiful, strong, take-no-prisoners kind of woman. Rhea liked men. Rhea liked women. I knew this before we married, and her sexuality didn't, and still doesn't, matter. After all, she married *me*. I trusted her to swing solely in *my* direction. When she found a woman she couldn't live without, and also couldn't have, she took drastic action. I suppose you could call it the if-I-can't-have-you-no-one-can route."

London had known powerlessness, but this felt like being tied to a tree in the path of a team of blind, deaf lumberjacks. "I'm sorry." She wanted to sound confident, a mere bystander hearing a tragic tale and feeling understandably sympathetic. Instead, her condolences eked out in stilted, choked degrees. "So… incredibly sorry."

And she was. For his wife's mistakes. For his, too.

But mostly for her own.

He caught her injured wrist when she reached to steady her perch on the stool. Trevor seemed to gravitate toward that hand, but after that first time in the gym, he hadn't pressed her for more details about the injury. Instead, he said, "Wonder why I'm telling you this?"

One could say that. Two encounters and he'd revealed deeply personal secrets with a frightening level of detachment.

Or perhaps patience. Trevor's staged reveals could be part of a larger plan. *"Will you walk into my parlor?" said the spider to the fly.*

"The answer is simple," he explained. "Someone helped me out of an untenable situation after I'd been lied to. Now that person thinks he's being lied to—indirectly, at least—by *you*. I've promised to solve the mystery. To do that, I'll solve *you*."

Even if she consciously refused, the ever-growing lump in her throat acknowledged the unstated implications of his words. Trevor Rathlen—huge, intense, disturbingly calm and thorough—was coming for her.

"I want to believe you're telling the truth about the wine, that you know as little about that Hungarian travesty I tasted tonight as I do." He spoke with a dangerous softness as he brought her casted palm to his cheek and rubbed. "At the same time, don't think I didn't catch how easily you turned the tide of conversation from you to me."

Her broken wrist throbbed beneath his fingers. The wrist had snapped seconds before London had taken a life—her lover's life, to be exact. How cruel that she and Trevor's ex shared *that* kind of history.

Both of them killers. Both of them keen to hide the fact from the same man.

"I played this your way," he said, "and now you know my story, while I know nothing of yours. And *still* I want to believe." Brows lowered over hooded eyes, he looked disgusted with his own capacity for trust. "See that computer in the corner? That's Brutus. With the stroke of a finger, I can know everything you're withholding. Computers really are weapons, the assassins of our time. Don't make me go there."

Staring over his shoulder, London said, "As if you haven't already." He'd hacked into her e-mail, after all, and intercepted her evening. Then he'd blithely told her all about it.

"Child's play, London. I haven't so much as Googled you. *Yet.* I don't want you to be the bad guy, which makes me the stupid guy."

She licked the back sides of her teeth, searching for the words that described his strategy. "So you're dangling a carrot? Telling me all your dark secrets in hopes that I'll roll over and reveal mine?"

Not a chance.

He smiled—a wide, devastating grin that brought out his dimples and reminded her she dealt with a dangerous breed. Trevor was equally beautiful and frightening, thoughtful and diabolical, patient and ruthless.

"No," he said softly. "I told you because for a moment I forgot that you're nothing more than the kind of job I was born, trained, and always predisposed to complete. For a moment you were the first woman in months I've wanted to put my hands on and still remember your name after you're through calling out mine."

"Trevor." She breathed out his name, caught in the fantasy his admission evoked.

"Which means we'll work together." He stepped back, all business. "If you've told the truth, and you truly have no idea how you happen to be simultaneously blackening a reputable vineyard's reputation *and* endangering the public, we'll find answers with each other's help. I'll do my job. You'll do yours. I'll stay in *front* of your walls, rather than dig under them."

A reputable vineyard. The statement was telling. In some roundabout way, Tereth had recruited Trevor. She found herself nodding automatically. At least he *wanted* to believe. She could imagine a worse start, and, given the intrigue surrounding the situation and the fact that she shared Tereth's desire for answers, she could use his help. Why not take it?

A sigh built behind her lips. Perhaps Trevor would prove a lucky break, releasing her from the weight of sole responsibility. Over the swooping slope of her exhale... five, four, three... his parting words killed all sense of relief.

"If you've lied"—his touch trailed over her cast and up her arm before he leaned forward—"I'll stop helping your cause. Brutus and I will start dismantling it."

CHAPTER 6

The next morning came too soon. In the light of day, London could no longer lull herself with the false sense of security—of safety—that came with Trevor's nearness. Despite their dinner and drinks and poorly suppressed attraction, the man had been hired to prove her a fraud, and she woke with the terrible feeling that, however unwittingly, she might actually be one.

Now London found herself in a race to discover what was happening behind the scenes in her *own* business. When one accepted help from the devil, one had to know more than he did.

Starting small and practical, London stopped at her favorite bakery and splurged on bagels for the office. Her people took to hard questions better with full mouths. Later, from the vantage point of her desk and only halfway through *half* a blueberry bomb, she managed an opener between delirious visions of a betrayed Trevor tearing the building apart, board by board.

"Let's talk." She had no need to bother with an e-mail since all three of her colleagues sat within a ten-foot radius.

Grey Cordon glanced up first. The shaggy towhead seemed an unlikely candidate to work with her most discerning French suppliers in Burgundy and the Loire Valley, but something about his easy American charm brought smiles to the faces of the most discriminating of wine snobs. That and the man had been known to utter, to himself of all people, "My life *changed* with my first Domaine de la Romanée-Conti." Grey balanced his vast knowledge with a breadth of appreciation and a belief that wine was meant to be enjoyed. Give him a thirty-dollar Shiraz from Australia's Barossa Valley or a 1945 Château Mouton-Rothschild, and he'd recommend a fine pepperoni pizza for either.

Or both.

Which meant Grey would always be her favorite.

Trent Rolande swiveled his head around to face the forming group, fingers still flying across laptop keys. Trent generally got a late start before heading out for sales meetings in the afternoon. Clean-cut and dressed in his stock uniform—a blue suit that complimented his dark good looks—Trent knew wine well but customers better. A salesman first, Trent could sell grandma's fermented apples to a billionaire. He exuded a sense of urgency that made buyers feel *lucky* to purchase from WW.

Which meant London had to secure future opportunities for him to sell.

Last to tear herself away, Clara Whitley spun in her chair and steepled long, elegant fingers beneath a pixie-like face gone bright with curiosity. London's little sister straddled the importer-distributor line. She worked with a few vineyards in northern Italy, where London had previously devoted much of her time. Now that London had added Dillon's territories in Hungary and Slovakia to her own list, she suspected Clara's importing activities would grow increasingly Italy dominant.

Clara had originally believed in the romantic notion that wine importers live a jet-setting lifestyle supported by champagne wages. When the drudgery of a truly government-regulated environment set in—federal and state licensing, intricate tax provisions, foreign shipping hassles—she'd realized that selling, rather than importing, opened a host of possibilities more suited to her skills. Buyers, whether liquor-store managers, restaurant owners, or individual collectors, were drawn to Clara's fire. Wine loved her.

Which meant London would always love wine.

With London importing and scrambling after the leftovers—accounting, market analysis, and inventory—she and her motley crew did all right.

Or they *had*.

Attention captured, all three employees regarded her with a combination of sympathy and caution. The last weeks had been chipped and abraded by Dillon's death. London hadn't faced charges. She'd been questioned, obviously a person of interest, but Dillon's fall, no matter how unlikely or how bloody, had quickly been ruled an accident.

No one to punish. No one to blame. Only a gaping hole of guilt and dull remorse to fill.

In the big picture, London's life paralleled the one she'd led before, except she was one boyfriend—or, she supposed, ex-boyfriend since she'd broken things off minutes before the accident—and one wine importer short. With a mountain of possibly tainted Olaszrizling napping in her warehouse, she didn't dare contemplate hiring a replacement. If the wine couldn't be sold, WW Imports would be lucky to stay afloat.

She'd fail again, all her promises—to Grey and to Trent, to Clara, and to *herself*—broken.

Keeping her tone light and encouraging, she waded in. "We've a problem."

Trent arched a calculating brow. "Another one?"

What's one more?

"A small one," London hedged. Compared to killing an employee, Trevor Rathlen was a mere blip. "It's about the Olaszrizling." They'd each fielded an angry call or two over the previous season, but, like her, they'd counted on seeing the issues resolved in this summer's shipment. "The new shipment is likely not authentic."

Clara's face tightened, and she spun in her office chair. "Fakes?" She reached for a pile on her desk and held up a handful of invoices. "It's been selling. No deliveries yet, but it's marching off the shelves."

London eyed the stack. "Stall on delivery, and take all the Tereth out of your sales samples." Until she understood the problem, they'd sit on every bottle. "For whites, focus on the Loire Valley Sauvignon Blancs, even the sparkling."

Trent nodded, head cocked. "In the meantime, what happens to the Hungarian stuff?"

"Nothing."

The room slid into a kind of questioning silence, the crunching of toasted bread worse than the music of bored crickets. London looked to the door leading to the warehouse. Today she almost hated what was on the other side.

"From what I know"—*a whole lot of nothing*—"Tereth isn't happy. They've sent reinforcements to determine what we're up to. That Tereth wants to investigate tells me we're in deep." A vineyard that suspected internal quality issues would look inward. No vineyard would investigate an inside issue through its external supply chain. Tereth legitimately believed its wines were being faked. By sending a man like Trevor Rathlen after WW, Tereth had made it plain that a long, pointed finger extended across the Atlantic, straight at her miniscule corner of the wine world.

London took another bite. Stalled. Swallowed. "Since we're not *up* to anything, I'm sure we'll work out the misunderstanding and move on."

Grey let out a low whistle from the corner. "Our wine is inferior, and our own supplier has sicced the dogs on us."

Just one dog, but he's part bloodhound and part pit bull, with the tenacity of a border collie in a cattle pen. "We'll have company skulking around the warehouse—a computer guru I've agreed to cooperate with in determining the actual source of the Tereth wine. Do as he asks, will you? At the same time, I'd appreciate you confining your cooperation to *business*." They had to play nice. If not, London got the distinct feeling that despite his respectful, civilized veneer, Trevor would simply break into her computer system, if not her building, and take the information he wanted.

Grey, Trent, and Clara traded looks before their bemused attention refocused on London. She'd hoped to skirt the issue, but like most things lately, no such luck. With a subtle movement, she inclined her head toward Dillon's empty desk.

Clara didn't exactly do a face palm, but it was a close thing. "You want us to keep quiet about Dillon."

"*No.*" There went any hope for subtlety. "Dillon's a former employee. Anything pertaining to his role here is relevant. His current"—what to call it?—"*status* is not. Knowing that Dillon is dead won't help us find the source of some bad wine." *Nope.* That would only humiliate London and cause a guy with Trevor's history to dislike and distrust her from the outset. "What happened with Dillon was both accidental and *personal*—a wrong-place, wrong-time incident completely unrelated to Olaszrizling."

London closed her eyes. *Five, four, three...* Saying words that reduced death to an *incident* ushered in a new low. Her parents would call that kind of ability to separate true evidence of psychopathic tendencies.

"Sure, boss," Trent said, his smooth bass gearing up for the inevitable pitch and levelling the awkward that stilted the group. "From what I know, Dillon Farro worked here for three years and then moved on."

Clara, as usual, said exactly what the others danced around. "I assume your computer whiz won't unearth records that say 'termination via head wound?'"

Two, one...

London blinked at the ceiling, fighting a host of inappropriate responses—*no laughing, no crying, no screaming.* "His last check was directly deposited into his account as usual. I assume it became a part of his estate. Other than that, there's nothing."

Grey scooted close and squeezed London's shoulder. "'Moved on' it is, then."

Weren't those the words of the hour? The chair beside her sat empty, the man who belonged in it dead, and they spoke of moving on. Like any other day, the line at the bank would be long. Traffic would be slow. London wouldn't be able to reach the bowls on her top kitchen shelf. All the minutia of life would remain exactly the same even though one among them didn't have a life anymore. How could the line between alive and dead account for so little?

And yet for so much.

Clara chimed in right as London pictured Trevor piling up the heavy metal desks with his bare hands, dousing the room with alcohol from her own stores, and torching the building. "Do whatever it takes on this," her sister said solemnly. "We've got you."

Thank God.

Because pressed between dangerously bad business at her front, a taboo past at her back, and a relentless man likely to squeeze the two together until London popped like a hot grape, she would no doubt need safe ground to land on.

******

Trevor glared at Kevin, who'd sprawled across the floor with his head relaxing in the curve of Sasha's furry stomach. The man refused to acknowledge that Trevor's occasional canine visitor wasn't actually a life-size throw pillow.

Plus Sasha liked acting the part.

The three of them, Sasha included, had been on speaker phone with Brian for nearly half an hour discussing *London-gate*. So far Trevor had reached three conclusions completely unrelated to the goal of the call: Brian was a sadistic son of a bitch far too in lust with hearing himself talk. Kevin had mentally tried, convicted, and hanged London the moment Trevor had mowed him over in hot pursuit of London's treadmill. And, most of all, Trevor should have told both men to suck it when they'd demanded help.

But the thrill of the chase had felt too much like old times. Complacent to the point that his wife had committed murder under his nose, Trevor would never again let himself stray so far from his roots. Once, he'd been the guy who *knew* things—patiently, quietly, sometimes violently—yet he hadn't known about Rhea.

That ignorance was almost the worst part of his wife's betrayal.

"She doesn't have it in her to counterfeit." *Maybe*. Even *hopefully*. London might not be guilty as charged, but she hid secrets behind stiff lips. The second he'd opened up over dessert, she'd closed down. Barely five words had escaped that lush mouth before she'd practically rushed the door, promising to do "her part" despite her haste to escape.

When his wife had started hiding—first an affair and then a crime—she'd clammed up. Saying nothing naturally decreased the risk of saying the wrong thing.

What was London refusing to say?

Brian's droll voice sounded through the cell-phone speaker. "You know this because by now you've inspected her operation from the inside out? Tell me. What's with the shipping records? How about the invoices?"

Kevin snorted from the floor. "Don't ask, brother. You won't like the answer."

"Nooo?"

Before Trevor could stomp the teeth out of Kevin's big mouth, the guy opened the floodgates. "Our boy here would rather feed our suspect *pie* than actually do what he's paid for."

"Right." Trevor cracked his neck, spinning to face his friend. "As opposed to Kevin's brilliant plan, which involved going through her trash after taking her to bed and fucking her into compliance."

Kevin absently stroked Sasha's floppy ear. "Women *talk* to men they fuck. A few nights of the Kevin treatment, and she'd leave her secrets lying on the sheets."

Pompous ass. "Or smother you in your sleep." Trevor rolled to his desk and reloaded London's pic from the WW Imports website. After spending an evening with the owner of those green eyes, he saw things in the photo he'd ignored before.

"London Rose," he murmured to himself. Then louder, he said, "She's exhausted, not to mention working herself to the bone. Look at this. Even her marketing photo shows strain." He traced her face with a finger, noting the down swept gaze and subdued smile. The picture was dated the previous year, after the counterfeiting had already begun. If London had planned to get rich quick from cheating the masses, it sure didn't show.

He heard Brian typing through the speaker. Then, "I didn't ask what she looks like. I didn't ask whether either of you want to take her to bed. I asked whether she's tanking my client's American rep. Though honestly"—the man whistled, long and low—"what a mouth. Maybe I should hop a plane."

The urge to *bloody* a mouth rose sharp and hot. Both brothers clearly chewed Viagra for breakfast. Before Trevor could respond, Kevin cut in. "Calm down, big guy. Brian won't get anywhere near your prize. Even if he was serious, I wouldn't let him. Your girl has a devious streak. We'll leave you to it."

"Look," Brian said. "Get inside her computers. Check the shipping records, the invoices. Stopping fantasizing and get inside *her* for all I care."

"You don't want that," Trevor responded. "The second I have her, the deal's off."

"What, you don't kiss and tell?"

"I don't kiss and *work*." That kind of job went by a different name. And what was with all the people assuming he'd fuck for money?

Brian let out a noncommittal grunt. "So don't kiss her. Your loss, looks like. But get the secrets, because… Trevor?"

"Yeah?"

"That wine might be deadly."

CHAPTER 7

There were wine lovers who swore the finer the crystal, and thus the thinner the glass, the better the wine. London believed a wine glass acted as an accoutrement of sorts, much like a perfectly aged cheese or a morsel of smooth, dark chocolate. Accoutrements could enhance the flavor of a wine, but they could not *make* a wine.

Wine, like a grand dame presiding over a majestic estate, could speak for itself.

No explanation, then, would fully convey why London stood at the door separating her office from her warehouse, holding an empty pitcher, a wine opener, a box cutter, a notebook, and a lead-crystal glass made with an exceptional level of craftsmanship.

Tonight she failed to believe in the same way atheists caught in the throes of natural disasters had been known to pray.

The glass had become her prayer, even though she didn't think it would do any good.

No, the wine would rise or fall on its own, crystal or Dixie cup, foie gras or Spam in a can.

Fluorescent light flickered overhead, and despite the dry summer heat outdoors, she shivered against a blast of air conditioning. A pallet sat in the middle of the concrete, piled high with cases of Hungarian Olaszrizling. Her sister claimed the wine was selling all across town. That meant at least some of the bottles were more than good enough to drink, while others reminded her of the pills her parents pushed, only crushed and shaken with a liter of Kool-Aid.

Tonight she would taste methodically, without relying on the varying palettes of party goers. She would also log the results. For every. Last. Bottle. Compressing her loot between her forearms and chest to avoid her injured wrist, London lowered to the floor in a wobbly fold next to a box of waiting bottles. She slashed the seal, opened the first soldier to meet her fingertips, and poured out a taste.

The light color spoke of rolling hills and wet days along the shores of Lake Balaton. The familiar scents of lemon and a hint of almond rose from the glass. Then, finally, a taste.

Dried fruit. Fresh-cut grass. A noble beginning. The inaugural sip was good enough to sell a bottle or two. Good intentions demanded the wine end up in the empty pitcher, not her stomach if she had any hope of completing her study. Yet who was she to waste a success?

Lately they'd been so few and far between.

London swirled and savored. She leaned over the waiting spittoon and… swallowed.

On to the second bottle.

Two hours later, London was feeling smug. Two cases had undergone if not a clinical inspection, then at least a *thorough* one. Eighteen of twenty-four bottles had passed muster, which hinted at better times ahead. The presence of viable bottles lessened the probability of counterfeiting. Why would some bottles be fake and others legitimate? Perhaps this was a case of hot shipping crates and subpar corks after all.

Midnight had come and gone, and in losing sight of her spitting rule for the decent samples, London had managed to warm herself from the inside out. Hand over hand, she crawled up the side of the pallet, belatedly realizing the stack hadn't shrank nearly enough for her to declare a win. Careful to support the edges just right, she eased another box of wine from the top of the pile.

The bay door used for deliveries gave a mighty clunk. A torsion shaft overhead started to spin and, with it, her door—the only thing separating London from the waiting night—began to open. Inch by inch, light poured into the warehouse from the blackness outside. London struggled to replace the box, but it teetered on the edge of the one below it, finally falling to the floor. Glass crunched, protesting its rough treatment. Before the door stopped moving, the box wept its first signs of wine.

When the grinding came to an abrupt halt, London stared into a pair of headlights.

"Hello?" She wanted to yell, to sound like a woman not to be trifled with, but the greeting barely registered. The bright light triggered a shifting between her ears, as though her brain cells were knocking together. Instead of a pleasant buzz from the wine, London felt the first stabs of an impending headache.

Bending down, she retrieved the box cutter. Many a deadly deed had blossomed from one of those tiny knives.

London, unfortunately, had proven herself deadly when warranted.

A little louder this time. "I said, '*Hello*.'"

"Such a hostile greeting, though I suppose that's all you have to offer the world."

The voice didn't belong to anyone she expected. Not an employee. Not a relative.

Harriet, in all her calico glory, landed lightly on the wine pile, teeth bared in an unwelcoming hiss.

That disembodied voice came again, slinking around the edges of the light that let sound succeed and sight fail. "Is this the kitty I've heard so much about?"

Not a stranger, then.

Not a friend, either.

An indistinct outline, tall and imposing, began to cut across the glare. London squinted into the light, then blinked. Nothing brought the shadow into focus. "I can't see you."

"No? How inconvenient." In a wink of insight, the owner of the voice registered, just as two legs became three. A long, slender object protruded from one arm, almost scraping the floor.

A weapon. In the hand of Dillon's father, a man who believed—who would always believe—that London had murdered his son in cold blood.

"You know," came the voice, "Dillon used to insinuate you weren't all that bright. I believed him, up until the moment the police knocked on my door. Now he's dead, and you're free." He paused, and she felt the man take in the open bottles she'd set in a row. Almost as though she digested the scene through his eyes, London understood Turner Farro's disdain when he noticed the smashed box flowing with a river of wine. "You're not so stupid after all. Indeed, here you sit drinking the night away, impervious to the carnage you've wrought."

Not drinking, *per se*. "Working," she corrected. "Dillon's wine—"

"Yes, let's discuss *Dillon's* wine. He did his best to help you bring in more for less, to help you grow out of the garage operation you are and into the—"

"His *help* might put me out of business."

"Is that why you killed him?" The weapon in Turner's hand rose, then struck the concrete, sending out a menacing wave of echoes.

What? The noise sent shards of pain skittering through London's head, and she struggled for an elusive breath. "It was an accident," she insisted, "like the reports say." *And the witnesses. And the reams of video feed.*

Dillon had pushed. London had fallen. When he'd appeared overhead, imposing and aggressive, she'd wobbled on the twisted, broken wrist beneath her hip and kicked out. Balanced on a precipice with nowhere to go but down, Dillon had fallen into a twisted, bloody heap. Red Rocks amphitheater wasn't famous solely for its acoustics and the recording artists they attracted. Hundreds of steep steps led to the open-air stage, and a hundred more trailed upward through the seating stretched before it. The dangerous beauty occasionally bore witness to sights and sounds more terrible than talented.

Turner Farro stepped forward, far enough from the high beams to reveal a broken man, albeit a blurry one. At the funeral she'd retreated out of respect, giving him first her back and then her absence. Tonight she took a good, long look. His waistband sagged above dingy jeans that might have clung to those hips for days. Above, his hair had grown wild, the usually sleek strands of silver unruly, as though he'd spent too much time literally with head in hand.

Regardless of how this man had spent the last few weeks, he was no longer gripping his skull in hapless grief. Instead, he gripped a crowbar. Despair had fled, replaced with the bright-burning torch of hatred and the single-minded purpose of a man who'd been wronged. While his clothes and hair said disheveled and harmless, the look in his eyes hinted at aggressive and deadly.

Leaning on the curve of the bar like a cane, Mr. Farro came forward in clunky, dragging steps. Yet she knew in her bones he wasn't injured. Like his son before him, the man excelled at games.

Dead eyes skimmed the pallet of wine. He nudged the leaking box on the floor with a slow foot. Then he studied the row of bottles she'd opened and sampled—every one nearly full.

"I've been cleaning my dead son's home. When I found Dillon's keys and the garage code, I didn't expect you to be here," he murmured, sounding distracted.

"Yet here I am." The metal handle of the box cutter dug into her fingers, protesting her grip.

He looked up. "I couldn't be happier." The bar tapped the concrete like a countdown. "Do you think my son felt fear when you swung at him?"

On that final, unanswerable question, the crowbar lifted and came crashing down. Bottle shards flew, and London reeled away toward the back side of the pallet. The scent of wine soaked the air along with the ricocheting screech of fracturing glass. Once the noise died down, he shattered another of her test bottles.

Then another.

London moaned helplessly into the racket, ignoring a tremor that started deep in her core. She eyed the open bay door at Turner's back and considered the unlocked office at hers. About twenty feet separated her, in either direction, from whatever Dillon's father would do when the easy targets ran out. An unopened bottle rolled at her feet, and she shoved the box cutter in her back pocket and palmed the bottle neck like a club. Or a missile.

A mediocre weapon for the one functioning hand.

She'd never learned to brawl. Becoming *Level London* had meant she'd barely traded in unkind words. *Shameful.* London had spoken softly, demurred quietly, even cried silently—and alone—so others wouldn't be bothered. A shudder rippled over her shoulders and down her throwing arm. She'd *had sex* with this man's son. She'd stayed quiet when he'd gripped too hard or entered too soon, simply because she couldn't imagine others' reactions to the hidden bruises, to the secret tearing.

She'd let her lover—her *employee* for Christ's sake—make her bleed without the slightest hint of protest.

Until the night he'd gone too far.

Sweating and shaking and refusing to venture within reach of a madman, London took advantage of Turner's preoccupation with her earlier experiment. She stepped back, took aim, and hurled the bottle at his chest like a Frisbee.

The missile hit but didn't break, not until it bounced off forgiving flesh and exploded on the hard concrete below. The blow had to have hurt. Too bad it hadn't maimed. If anything, rather than slowing the violence, she'd enraged the offender.

"Dillon did feel fear, didn't he?" Turner asked conversationally.

No, London thought, *but maybe he should have.*

"Like you," Turner continued, "he was afraid he was going to die. Did he beg for mercy? I *hate* that you might have reduced my son to the pathetic desperation I see before me."

That unflappable, almost bored drawl made London wonder whether Dillon had really lost his mind when he'd attacked that night, or whether he'd been raised to be an abuser all along. Suddenly Dillon's offhanded insults and mounting judgments felt like an escalation toward the violence that had ultimately come.

"Don't question me," Dillon had said, with a perfect imitation of his father's sneer. *"You* think *you're the boss because I let you think it. You* think *you run your company because the illusion entertains me."*

Level London had been a fool in her insistence on not rocking the boat. Foolishness, as she well knew, came at a high price. Mr. Farro was proof she still had more to pay.

Nausea gurgled in her already unsteady stomach. London grabbed another bottle from an open box on a shelf to her right and did something she'd only seen in movies. Again holding the smooth, sloping neck, she struck at the edge of the metal shelving, *hard*, over and over again, until the glass cracked and the bottom fell away, leaving a jagged club she brandished at her front like a torch to a cave of wolves.

Retreat came one rearward step at a time. Only problem was Turner matched her inch for inch, all the while gripping that length of iron that could turn her bottle to sand with a few well-placed blows. Dizziness whirled behind her eyes, and London gulped a steadying breath, ready to fight a flood with more water.

"You don't look well, London. Maybe something you drank?"

The moment she isolated the strand of fear running through her body and tugged it from her spine, a low growl sounded against the barren floors of the warehouse, replacing the noise of breaking glass with the threat of broken bones.

A peek over her shoulder revealed that someone else had gotten ahold of her security codes. Trevor watched the scene steadily, his gaze stoic and utterly unreadable. Next to him, his borrowed dog bristled, teeth bared in a clear one-eighty between lover and fighter.

Shadows thrown by shoddy light and high shelves carved the arcs of Trevor's face—his brows, those cheekbones, that jaw—all of them powerfully sculpted. During the day, Trevor could look brutal, dangerous even. In the waning light, he looked barbaric and... scary.

London hit her knees. Trevor might be her second break-in of the night, but she'd never been happier to see another living thing.

******

"Friend of yours?" After finding a list of passwords tucked away in London's e-mail contacts—that one minor infraction was paying endless dividends—Trevor had come to have a look at the place. Never would he have expected to find London fighting off a crowbar-wielding attacker with nothing but a wine bottle and grit.

At that, he fell a little bit in love.

And a lotta bit suspicious.

Ignoring her noncommittal grunt of a response, Trevor strolled forward to where she'd slumped on the floor. "You, London, are full of surprises." He turned to the man who'd been so ready to hurt her a few seconds ago. "And you? Are leaving."

London's phone sat a few feet from her legs. Instead of dialing 9-1-1, she'd engaged in a dangerous game. For some unknown reason he would *very soon* know, London didn't want to involve the police.

Trevor clasped grasping hands behind his back. They twitched, wanting to punish this man who grew brave when he faced off against an untrained, terrified, and if Trevor wasn't mistaken, tipsy woman. He wouldn't. Years ago Trevor had honed his body into a weapon because it had been one. Today it merely *could* be, if he so chose.

His adventurous computer skills hadn't sprouted from a classroom and a pile of student-loan debt. Trevor had paid for them in a currency he no longer cared to use. Blood stained his hidden hands.

No more. Not for anyone or any reason.

The intruder lowered his arm, looking stumped. "Who are you?"

"The computer guy?" Trevor offered.

"You don't look like a computer guy."

Trevor drew closer with each word. The man's limp arrogance did Trevor a favor. A few beats of simple talking and slow steps, and the intruder barely gripped his makeshift club. He'd traded the braced stance of attack for the relaxed posture of disbelief.

"I get that a lot."

"Trevor," London cut in between labored breaths. "He wouldn't have touched me."

Trevor tossed the statement atop London's growing pile of lies. The faintest tremor behind her plea betrayed the fact that London had believed she would end up too familiar with the business end of a crowbar. Deflection, no matter how pretty the mouth spouting it, wouldn't work.

This man, who'd finally wised up enough to start backing away, had been ready to lay hands on her. Her father? A jilted older lover? The mysterious cause of the broken wrist? Trevor schooled his features, hiding a hurricane, a raging inferno of a death wish for whoever would cause her more harm.

He kept it hidden maybe because, or maybe *despite*, of the fact that one of those people could eventually be him.

Quelling the burn that grew in his muscles when they wanted to do something he couldn't let them do, Trevor went stock still. Not a blink. Not a finger twitch. If London wanted to trade cops for a civilized diffusion that sent this guy packing, he'd grant her wish. *Anything* in exchange for an explanation.

And explain she would.

Without so much as raising his voice, Trevor jerked the crowbar from the man's grasp. He threw the weapon aside, its landing jarring against the silence. Sasha's whine rose over the clanging that rang through the night. Earlier a hand to the scruff had calmed the dog down, but Sasha had been an inch away from dining on the guy's thighs.

Those protective instincts told Trevor much about who he was dealing with. The dog was a better judge of character than most people. A gentle giant who was almost always harmless, except for when he wasn't.

In the same methodical way he'd disposed of the weapon, Trevor lifted the man off his feet and dragged him to the open bay door. The guy kicked and squirmed, lashing out with colorful threats to Trevor's life and limb before Trevor chucked him into the darkness beyond the headlights. Two thumps said the guy had bounced off the side of his truck and landed on the concrete.

Perfect.

Once Trevor stepped back inside, the door began to grind to a close, and he saw London stood on the other side of the warehouse near a bank of switches and buttons.

One disaster averted, he stared into the swimming green eyes of another.

CHAPTER 8

"There was a time when I collected secrets." Trevor's voice rumbled across the warehouse from where he stood next to the closed bay door. Where Turner Farro's overt threats had left her shaken but bold, ready to fight and to win, Trevor's controlled calm left her damp with clammy sweat.

Taking in the broken bottles, the discarded crowbar, and the puddles of wine polluting the path between them, London knew she'd misjudged Trevor in accepting his help, but not telling him everything.

More like anything.

Trevor had happened upon a physical fight for her life and disarmed Dillon's dad with less effort than it would take to pry a toy from the mouth of his dog.

Plus, no one could digest this scene without serious questions about what she'd gotten herself into.

Trevor started forward, slow and steady. "Back then I did a lot more than work a keyboard and a mouse to learn what I needed to know. I haven't used those more *stringent* techniques for a long time. Lately I've been about as dangerous as a child with an iPad."

The way he casually remarked upon his harmlessness told London he could end that streak at any time. Who exactly was this man with his equal ease with computers and violence?

Trevor paused and toed a broken bottle out of the way. "Look where decency has landed me. Without the threat of something stronger than a computer virus, people think they can lie. My wife did." The last was low and hard, not like the Trevor of their first two meetings.

One last step brought them face-to-face. Looking up, London held off a creeping sickness and watched the strong lines of his throat undulate with each word.

"You would do the same," he said. "Wouldn't you, my sweet, innocent little London? What I just interrupted is *not* playing out in wine warehouses across the city. You're different, yet you insist otherwise. Look at you now—eyes wide, chest heaving. You'd give me anything to stem the questions, let me do anything to put my mouth to another use."

"No."

At least not to shut you up. Tension strung Trevor's body tight, and she sensed his need to wring answers from her like water from a sponge. He had ample reason to distrust, but she didn't feel the bite of his hands.

It had to be the numbness spreading from limb to limb that made her want to.

"Prove it," he said, still too quiet and too calm. "Tell me why you're here in the middle of the night. Talk of those shattered bottles we agreed to investigate *together*. Explain how they came to be the centerpiece of a table for two, you retreating and that guy"—Trevor gestured over his shoulder toward the closed door—"advancing."

"Together?" London choked, unable to help herself. "Is that why you came here well after midnight when I'm normally gone? To collaborate?"

He leaned in, pinning her at his front. Without warning, his thumb traced her lower lip. "I let you change the subject before. Not this time." He pressed and the flesh gave, opening her mouth.

Trevor's form swayed in front of her, except she didn't feel him move. He stood heavy and solid, and she blinked, trying to clear her whirling vision.

"This time," he said, "we skip the storytelling." Light fingers trailed over her eyelids, lazy and affectionate, so at odds with the accusation in his tone. "The panic here tells me you're about to evade my questions, just like you did the other night, and I'd rather move on to something better."

Lips parted, eyes shut, London jerked when the softness of his tongue stroked over her mouth. Again and again, he licked until she opened up and let him in. That first slide inside—tongue against teeth and then beyond—jolted her already stressed system. Breathing hurt.

Wanting him hurt worse.

She gave in, clutching at his massive shoulders, seeking to borrow strength so she could bring him to his knees in the same way the first taste of him threatened her on every level. This was different than ever before, a treat to seek out, not avoid.

Trevor tasted like cinnamon and smelled like soap and laundry detergent. Clean and real.

Deceptively simple.

He pulled back. "You're driving me crazy. Saying one thing. Doing another. Almost getting your head bashed in. Tasting like a promise—"

Trembling, she brought a finger to his lips to stem the admonishments. His eyes flared, and he nipped her finger, only when his teeth closed over her flesh, he didn't let go. Instead he stared across the barrier of her hand with a challenge, tongue slowly stroking her fingertip.

The blatant eroticism brought forth a sudden, clenching reaction. While her mind screamed, *Yes!* her body rejected the overload. With a groan, London tipped over a hidden precipice she'd been approaching for the last hour. Saliva flooded her mouth. The numbness retreated, replaced with a stabbing heat that pitched her surroundings into white noise.

"Let go." London cried out and lurched to the side. Pools of lava seared her eyes, and her vision winked in and out. She lurched to a nearby waste basket and lost the contents of her stomach. Agony pricked like needles along every inch of skin, and she couldn't draw sufficient air.

"Trevor," she gasped, gripping the wall for support. "Trevor."

Before her hold slipped, she felt herself lifted high against an unforgiving chest.

"*London.*" His urgency registered even as her surroundings faded. "Talk to me."

Wetness streaked her cheeks, and the pain left London praying she wept tears, not blood. "I messed up."

******

Messed up?

That kiss had been the first thing Trevor had done right in months. He knew when a woman wanted him, and London had been there, ready for him to taste a whole lot more than her mouth.

Now this. Cradling London's soft little body, Trevor spun for a closer look at the warehouse.

What had his tiny rogue been up to?

Glass bottles, many broken, littered the floor next to a pallet stacked with boxes. He'd immediately understood that the pallet contained questionable Hungarian wine, but on closer inspection, he realized the intact bottles on the floor had been opened. An empty glass and a notebook lay abandoned at the end of a row, surrounded by the shards of fallen comrades. Each tapped bottle looked almost full, but not quite. By his estimation, she'd dug into over twenty.

"You *drank* the counterfeits." Incredulity made the observation harsh, and he bit down on the insides of his cheeks.

"No," she replied weakly between labored breaths. A drop of blood eased from one nostril. "Most were okay. I—I spit the bad ones out."

Obviously not. Feeling helpless, Trevor dragged her closer, tighter, to stop the tremors radiating through her limbs. A burning heat seeped through her clothes and into his arms, yet her face was bleached bone white.

It took him thirty seconds to backtrack through her office and to buckle her into the truck he'd parked out front.

"Hang on, honey. Talk to me."

"Can't…" She bucked against the seatbelt, seeming to seize involuntarily.

"You *will*." He slammed the door. In another five seconds, he'd shut Sasha in London's office, and they were in route to the hospital. "How many samples? Can you tell me how much you had?"

"Twenty-four bottles, one taste each." Then she repeated, "I spit the bad ones out. I swear."

Mind whirling, he calculated her consumption to be around two to three glasses in all, depending on how many samples she'd managed to swallow. Had the wine not been tainted, she'd sport a buzz and a smile.

"Trevor," she said, sounding truly afraid, "I can't"—she scrubbed a hand over her face—"I can't *see*."

He reached across the seat and tucked a wayward curl behind her ear. "Close your eyes. That's it. We're almost there." Her tears tore a hole in the sandbag of guilt he'd hoisted right about the time he'd found her alone and hurt and fending off a crazy. The sparkling drops fell silently from her chin. Trevor had witnessed pain, but as London curled inward and convulsed, he recognized a body in the purest form of revolt.

And he understood that if she could bounce back, he'd do everything in his considerable power to ensure she never endured such pain again.

At the emergency room, Trevor talked when London couldn't. He told the doctors he suspected she'd ingested fifteen to twenty ounces of counterfeit white wine. They demanded the origin and then wanted to know what the substance might contain. When he could only offer a shrug, the prognoses began to fly as fast as the needles and tubes used to bombard London's dainty frame.

"Blindness…"

"…kidney failure."

"…several cases of coma—"

"She's seizing!"

Through it all, Trevor stood unnaturally still beyond the curtains that separated the frantic activity surrounding London from the rest of the room. He listened and learned. Most likely, the wine wasn't wine at all, more like fruit juice and methanol. A substitute for its safer sibling, ethanol, methanol was an industrial form of alcohol, commonly used as a solvent and in anti-freeze. London's body was converting the methanol into formic acid, and as the acid built up over time, it had begun to attack her nervous system, mixing the signals traveling to and from her brain.

She *could* go blind. After he'd egged her on, challenging her to prove her innocence. In one sentence, Trevor had spouted off about doing her the great favor of working *with* her to resolve the counterfeiting problem. In the next, he'd threatened to expose her and dismantle her life's work if their efforts revealed things he didn't like.

The realization took him down hard. A woman pretending at ignorance didn't risk life and limb for answers she already had. The risk alone proved London didn't understand who, or what, was behind the bunk wine, at least not entirely. On the other side of the curtain, London fought for her sight, maybe for her life.

The *why* of her outlandish actions suddenly became clear. Bullied for answers, London had resolved to get them.

Discreetly. Away from prying eyes and prophetic threats and the chance that she could do someone harm. He'd bet that, like him, London hadn't considered the possibility that the bottles might contain something more sinister than badly fermented grapes half turned to vinegar.

Trevor backed away from the curtain and the frenzy behind it. He'd been a bastard because he'd felt it his due, painting all women with his wife's broad brush. Except London had chosen to hurt herself before anyone else—again, his fault after he'd accused her of using the other guests at the networking event as guinea pigs. In not taking a gentler approach, he'd pushed her straight into a hospital bed.

Shit, as they say, had just gotten real.

Staring at the dull floor between his boots and the shifting curtain that hid the agony London faced because she'd fought too hard to redeem herself, Trevor landed on the conclusion that her earlier dissembling made no logical sense. If London didn't have a hand in a plot to make or sell fake wine—a fact he'd become convinced was the case—then why had she been so quick to shut him out? In her position, he'd have parted with the proverbial key to the kingdom and let him have a good, long, *un*satisfying look if for nothing other than to rub his face in a pile of wrong assumptions. Instead, she'd proclaimed her innocence while sitting on the evidence and pushing forward with her solo investigation.

London's promise to work with him had been nothing but hand waving. *Subterfuge.* Since she didn't need the ruse to hide a penchant for wine fraud, she needed it for something else.

Trevor pushed off the sterile wall that did nothing but reflect the sounds of London's distress and send them ricocheting around in his head. He needed coffee, black as tar and twice as strong, to tackle a looming wait and an infernal question: What, if not the stout body and long neck of a killer bottle of Olaszrizling, was the shape of the skeleton in London's closet?

CHAPTER 9

A steady beep in her ears. Disinfectant in her nose. A thin mattress at her back. London rolled onto her side and studied her surroundings. Out of the corner of an eye—*a functioning eye*, she silently rejoiced—she spied a shape shifting on the couch in her hospital room, which reeked of antiseptic cleanser and cafeteria peas. A closer look revealed a massive, hunched form passed out beneath a pitiful excuse for a blanket. Over Trevor, the thing looked like an undersized beach towel.

Time had blurred, and she didn't know what *night* meant, exactly. She recalled an IV and its removal, several pills, and even a supervised shower. Did the sequence mean she'd drunk the wine three hours ago? Twenty-three? More?

Trevor rolled, and suddenly his light eyes glittered like bottled fireworks in a shaft of streetlight streaming through the window shades.

London shifted her scrutiny to the floor, not pretending sleep, but also not alerting him to her watchfulness.

"You're awake," came his low voice.

Caught. "You're *here*," she replied.

A slow, curling unfurl brought Trevor to his feet. In a step, he stood by the bed, one hand stroking the railing that caged her in. The angles of his face appeared severe in the low light. Heavy brows shadowed his eyes. A straight nose intersected lean cheeks. Still lips perched above an uncompromising jaw.

So solid, and yet that hand moved along the steel rail in a ceaseless, almost yearning rhythm. If she could convince him she'd played no part in the counterfeiting scheme, maybe those fingers would move to stroke her.

"I'm sorry about—"

"Tell me why." He spoke through clenched teeth, but he also took her hand. His fingers were cool and strong, dwarfing hers in a reassuring grip.

"You accepted my help. Then you pretended otherwise. You…" He trailed off before adding what she knew would be a comment about the risk—from the wine, from the poison, from the drugs meant to counteract and dilute the poison and ease the pain.

"My risk to take," she began again. "You shouldn't have to be here. I didn't intend any of this."

The rail at her side lifted and folded out of view before she felt Trevor's weight on the mattress. Without dropping her hand, he sat down, one hip propped next to her thigh. "I *don't* have to be here. I want to. I want to know why a woman, *obviously* innocent of what I've accused her of, has so much to hide. Why doesn't she call the police when her warehouse is ransacked? Why is she in the warehouse alone in the first place? Why does she seek answers by putting herself in jeopardy?"

He leaned in and smoothed back a tendril that had fallen over her forehead. "Most of all, why does she apologize in the middle of the night when she's only hurt herself?" The questions slid her way, cool and level, but his voice had taken on an edge. He believed she hadn't masterminded the wine, but he saw her later choices as desperate and inexplicable and designed to keep him in the dark.

Meaning he saw them for exactly what they were.

London knew Trevor had been giving her the benefit of the doubt. Tonight his questions were multiplying faster than she could derive ways to maintain his ignorance. Without a doubt, the Olaszrizling in her warehouse was fake. Beyond fake, really. Her health scare proved the wine was the worst sort of counterfeit imaginable—a carelessly mixed concoction not meant to fool consumers as to its authenticity, but designed to move bottles off after-market shelves and get people wasted… if they were lucky. Some bottles tasted better than others because with volatile ingredients and a complete lack of quality control, each mix was a crapshoot. Sometimes the person doing the mixing got it right. Other times he didn't.

Worse, Dillon had to have known. In fact, Dillon had to have orchestrated the scheme right under her watchful eye. If she'd made this discovery before Trevor had shown up with his suspicion and his mysterious benefactor, she could have cleaned house, so to speak. The bad wine could have poured itself down the drain. New house rules could have required London to place all orders, ensuring every single wine came straight from its authentic source.

Now atonement meant more than quietly moving on. WW Imports had to answer—*she* had to answer—for her negligence. Whether he knew it or not, Trevor sought to trace the path of that negligence, which linked directly to Dillon and a life cut short.

Trevor wouldn't find gold at the end of the rainbow until he knew who Dillon was, where Dillon was, and *why*.

She flinched at the inevitable. Trevor meant to find where the not-so-metaphorical bodies were buried.

Once he knew, his warmth would withdraw from her side. His hands would pull out of her hair. He wouldn't put that slow, insistent mouth to hers ever again.

The realization slipped right past the drugs that made her feel light and optimistic. "It was an accident," she whispered. Trevor's wife had lied to him. So had London, even knowing his Achilles heel. Could he believe the two were different?

Sliding his roaming touch to her face, Trevor silenced her with a finger over her parted lips, looking resigned to her silence. "I know, angel, but last night I moonlighted as a paramedic. Never ask that of me again."

London tried to smile behind his finger, letting his assumption fill the night. The poisoning *had* been an accident. Unfortunately the accident she needed him to understand loomed larger than a failed taste test.

Dillon couldn't *stay* buried, figuratively speaking. If London didn't tell all, then Trevor would eventually lose patience. If he moved on with that named computer of his, he'd end up confronting her with the facts and, most likely, a number of ways to make her pay for his being used by a surplus of lady murderers.

She was beginning to understand Trevor as the type with a long, slow fuse that led to a devastating powder keg.

Secrets and strategies swirled in her head, mixing with a need that had begun to pulse between them the moment his mouth had overtaken hers in the warehouse. The two of them played with a fire that flared hot, but unstable. London should play the game of Trevor safe. She should keep her cravings buried and hand over what she knew about her flailing company, including its most problematic ex-employee.

If she did, Trevor would immediately learn about Dillon. The move would resolve his suspicion professionally—a good outcome because he'd be out of her hair with the least amount of hassle—but also push him away personally.

A not-so-good outcome.

Maybe an intolerable, unacceptable, *unspeakable* outcome.

The idea of revealing facts certain to repel the intense and complex man overhead made her stomach pitch and roll, a warning that for the first time her body had ideas, too. A prickle beneath the skin, a warmth between the thighs—both said London didn't want to be staid or level anymore.

You're on a bed. Barely dressed. His hands are on you.

Keep them there.

Because she knew she would lose him sooner or lose him later. The question had become: How much of Trevor Rathlen could London have before he became a casualty of her gravest mistake?

70

******

"Trevor."

His name sliced through the charged silence. In that way London had of saying a lot with a little, her tone struck him as subtly, *meaningfully*, different than her earlier apologies and then her desperate pleas for help in the warehouse.

This time it contained a *request*.

Her reclining position let the hospital gown fall against her skin, skimming over the bountiful curves that had blown his imagination all through her shower earlier in the night.

By then he'd known she would be all right. With the scare over, her biggest problem would be lingering headaches and dehydration, which had left plenty of bandwidth for him to be jealous of the attending nurse.

He'd cracked down on how badly he'd wanted into that sterile little bathroom because *no way* was he lusting after a woman in need of a crash course on the nobility of truth.

Unfortunately, his lofty, better-than-thou ideals hadn't tempered the urge to distract the nurse with lies about buzzers and sirens in the hall so he could sneak in and go down on London in the shower. Only sturdy locks had kept his ass squarely on the couch.

Now her eyes held a dark invitation instead of her customary uncertainty. It seemed London didn't trust him enough to tell him what she was hiding, but she did trust him enough to *touch* him.

To let him touch her.

Maybe Kevin had had the right idea about women—*sex for secrets*—all along.

London, sleepy-eyed and relieved, looked perfectly willing to be plied.

Trevor shifted away and rolled his head back. When he spoke, he did it to the ceiling. "I know that look."

The London he knew would reply with another apology, an instant and visceral retreat from her tiny step toward what she wanted.

Except she didn't. "Really?" London whispered. "What does it mean?"

Anticipation thickened their mutual stillness, and his cock. No matter how badly he wanted them to, the overhead tiles didn't get any more interesting upon increased inspection. Barren and white within a metal framework, they practically dared him to turn back to what mattered in the room.

To temptation. To madness.

When he risked another glance, London hadn't budged. Green eyes met his stare evenly, as though their battle of wills, her injuries, the counterfeiting, even the remaining mysteries they both knew she guarded, all belonged somewhere far from her bed.

Freshly scrubbed, London smelled of soap and lotion. Moonlight gleamed against a natural glow that had replaced her earlier pallor. Black curls tumbled across her pillow in artful tangles. Fresh and unkempt, she looked impossible but real, a magazine spread that wasn't.

He leaned in, caging her torso with spread arms. If she wouldn't guard herself, Trevor didn't have the strength to do it for her. "That look is a *demand.*"

"For?"

"*Me.*"

Beneath him, her chest expanded on a slow, deep inhale.

"And, London?" he said. "Unlike you, I won't renege once I decide to give you're asking for."

******

London flicked a look at the closed door. It was the middle of the night. She felt infinitely better. Surely the nurses had more important patients to worry about, at least between dusk and dawn.

"No one's coming," Trevor predicted. "They know I'm here. They know I'll buzz if we have a problem."

The natural progression of his words didn't need saying: *We* don't *have a problem.*

Corded arms flexed at her sides, and London found herself questioning her boldness for unpredicted reasons. Oh, she could handle the break from her usual safe, unassuming persona. Every muscle, every inch of her skin, craved this wicked adventure. But in the dim light and deep shadows, Trevor looked almost *too* capable of providing it.

One of his strong hands slid to her hip and began to massage in slow circles. Heat seeped through the thin cotton gown. The hospital getup took easy access to another level, and he would surely detect her lack of underwear. For long moments, he squeezed and rubbed, only moving to the other hip after her muscles had gone lax against the sheets.

While his touch skimmed her body softly, London felt the coiled power in his frame, the damage he could do if he wanted. Poised on a knife edge between anticipated pleasure and remembered pain, she floundered. In her experience, going to bed with an angry man tended to hurt.

Most of the time sex with Dillon had been average, bringing little pain or pleasure. But there had been exceptions. Early on, London hadn't understood the relationship between their days and their nights. Toward the end, she'd come to see that lashing out unexpectedly in bed had been Dillon's ultimate power trip. Pain had never sprung from angry sex or even make up sex. It had always arrived in the middle of middling sex, when she'd been trying hard to enjoy herself, to convince herself she liked him or even sex in general.

Unpredictable though it was, London had found a correlation between painful intimacy and Dillon feeling disrespected. Maybe she'd overruled a decision of his at work. Maybe she'd said no to sex in the first place, and he'd cajoled her—gentle and ever misleading—into the act. Sometimes she swore he'd wanted to punish her imperfect body—the softly rounded tummy or the thighs that would forever touch. He'd never said so, but Dillon had sometimes gotten rough hours after criticizing a chocolate bar or a slice of pizza.

Like a character study of a world-class victim, each time she'd believed he would be fine. Most times he had been. Now her memory seized on the times he hadn't.

On the times she'd paid dearly for picking the wrong man.

How could she trust herself? Trevor handled her with care—velvety and dark and oh-so-enticing—but she'd mislead him. She misled him still. A past life said such dishonesty elicited retaliation.

Dillon's rough had left marks. Trevor's might leave scars.

Light strokes trailed up her side, across, and then down, until Trevor kneaded her stomach just north of the secret skin that waited for him to arrive. Her breasts felt heavy, her thighs determined to part regardless of logic's dictate. All her imperfect places had decided they deserved a perfect lover.

All the while, her mind screamed that he, too, could be a ruse. Only a far more dangerous risk than Dillon had ever hoped to be.

From her stomach, he inched downward, until he circled her pubic bone with two fingers. Around and around. Up and down. Tickling motions that didn't tickle at all. The magic caress taunted her, at odds with the fierce determination in his face. He blinked, then looked up. "Your body, it's…" He licked his lips. "I wish I was an artist like my brother."

"Trevor," she began.

"Your mouth won't confide in me, but your body says everything I want to know. Look at this." He stroked a single finger between her thighs. "Your perfect, perfect body trusts me."

"Trev." Tussling with her thoughts, fear and need crashed against a crumbling cliff of restraint.

He surged up off the mattress. Before she knew it, he'd knelt at her bedside and replaced his hand with his mouth. Mother of God, he kissed through the gown, hot and wet. His tongue pushed the cloth against her, drawing it along her skin. Around and around. Up and down.

Divine. Trevor was a thousand-dollar Bordeaux on a starry Paris night. A gasp escaped in her indecision. Then another. The sounds were short, but they got her mouth practicing. "Nothing rough," she blurted, not making any sense when he touched her like freshly blown glass—not yet cool, not yet set.

He stopped.

"I don't like it rough," she repeated, and then babbled on. "I know that's weird and that people are all about the crazy stuff, but I don't like for it to hurt, and I'm not really up for being held down or for all the different… implements."

Chest heaving, London looked down at a stillness she wouldn't have thought possible in a man like Trevor. Hard, dangerous eyes met hers, blue gone black in the shadows. She could practically see gears grinding behind them, sifting through their encounters to make sense of her request.

"Hurt?" By the time he landed on the hard "t," understanding had dawned.

After a beat, he slid his hands to the mattress and pushed up. "Rough." The word drew out, low and raw, like he wanted to test its meaning on his tongue to see if she could possibly be saying what he thought.

Unwanted heat stole upward from beneath London's flimsy gown, until her face burned with embarrassment. She had *and* hadn't meant exactly what he thought. The plea had bubbled up, not because she saw Trevor as the type to mishandle a woman, but because she had thought Dillon equally incapable of bringing pain.

Not that asking would make a difference.

He reached for her casted wrist. Her arm might have been a butterfly wing for how softly he stroked the plaster. "Someone hasn't been careful with you."

"It's not that."

"It is *exactly* that."

"*No*… you're so big."

"Yes."

"And you're angry with me for jumping ahead with the investigation."

"Maybe."

"You're frustrated because I keep my business close to the chest."

"Definitely."

"So I thought I'd set boundaries, in case, you know, you like it that way."

Before she could further mangle the reasons he might take sex to the wrong level, he leaned in and pressed the full length of his torso to hers, hard against soft, unforgiving against pliant. London froze as he licked his lips and angled his head so a scant inch separated their would-be kiss.

"You thought you'd tell me you don't like it rough, that you don't like *implements*, just in case I'd been planning to punish you, right here in this bed, for not cooperating outside of it."

For a moment, he stared at her mouth. Then, slow and sure, he skimmed her lips with his tongue, offering everything if she would only take it. Sexual energy rocketed between her parted lips, and he became all that was warm and inviting and… necessary.

London soaked in the invitation, wanting to accept just when he pulled away. Trevor linked a hand behind her nape and, with the barest pressure, pressed her cheek to his. "My mind," he whispered, letting his breath warm her face, "might be tasked with besting you. My body only knows the opposite. I'll take you any way I can get you. I'll *like it*, too."

He moved closer, so his mouth moved against her ear. "I'm going to find the man who took your passion and gave you fear—"

"No." *Not possible.*

"And when I do, he and I will talk about *rough* and its place in the world." Trevor didn't get colorful with the threat. He spoke softly but with a conviction that said the perfect place for Dillon's rough would be in Dillon's cracking bones.

Again, impossible.

Trevor straightened and looked at her then. His expression might as well have dripped blood, and she felt herself blanch at the violence etched upon his features. Though directed outward, and on *her* behalf, seeing his transformation made her jumpy.

After a moment, the tension deliberately relaxed. His mouth quirked into a half-cocked grin.

"For now, let me show you how good gentle can be."

CHAPTER 10

"Do you like sex?"

Did he like sex? Had Einstein liked math? He could tell her that—remind her that any man who needed to be asked should find the door—except he sensed the answer, as well as the answers to the questions sure to follow, would mean everything.

This woman would kill him, and he would enjoy the dying.

"Yes," he said, all seriousness. "All kinds."

Married sex for Trevor had been hard and fast, two dominant players clashing like phoenixes fighting for a pyre. Pleasure had come in the way one might enjoy winning a wrestling match. Since the divorce, sex had been too anonymous to have character. Women saw his size and all the blunt edges and assigned him a type, much like London had done in assuming he'd mix her pleasure with pain.

Only those women had *wanted* Trevor in the role—the king who'd come to conquer. They'd wanted to be held down for a rough fuck meant to be felt the next day.

He'd obliged. No complaints.

So why did the idea of getting tender with a beautiful woman lying on a hospital bed with fear on her face nearly split his zipper?

Because it's real. Their moves regarding the wine had been choreographed. He'd stepped in; she'd backed away. He'd made demands; she'd retreated to do the exact opposite.

Wanting him didn't follow the charted routine, and fearing what she wanted had revealed her true colors. London Rose Whitley was a deep, dark purple tinged with crimson edges, all of her encased in golden shellac.

And someone had cracked her. Trevor had forgotten what it felt like to want to kill, to be willing to do it.

To *actually* do it.

He'd remembered those needs the moment London had haltingly admitted she didn't like to get freaky. And why.

Trevor shifted on the bed. Her proximity made him want to tap her outer casing on his way to the red, to the woman, inside. But London wasn't that easy. Break through her protection, and he might break the woman.

Instead he'd have to learn her code.

Satisfaction tugged his lips into a real smile. *Lucky him.*

London watched warily as he let the realization take over his face. Looking nonplussed, she asked, "How many *kinds* would you say there are?"

Of sex? "Two. Sex either makes you see stars or wastes your time."

Her plush lips formed a perfect *oh*.

"You've been *wasting time*." *So have I.*

A nod.

"Want to see stars, London?"

Her next move showed in the unconscious way she shifted to drag her nipples against the cotton of her gown, in the fluttering pulse at the base of her neck, even in the dart of her eyes to his flexing hands. He waited her out, ready to take, yes, but mostly to give.

Another nod.

The slight incline of her head lit a match to the craving smoldering in his veins. Trevor bolted upright, intent on learning her needs with his life's best game of trial and error. But when he touched her again, he felt a slight tremor.

Not good enough.

Ever so slowly, he extracted his hands. Arousal was paramount, but perhaps ease took precedence, at least this time. Setting the scene, he rose from the bed and wedged a chair beneath the doorknob. The room's outer door didn't lock, but the chair would assure at least a warning before an impending interruption.

Back at the bed he took both of her hands and employed a weapon that had never come easy.

Words.

Letting his gaze scorch the cotton hiding her body, he said, "If I ask, will you give?"

London's lids slid shut, and she shimmied against the gown again. Her slender fingers thrummed against his palms like they wanted to lift to those nipples that had swollen and grown sensitive. "What will you ask for?"

"Pleasure, mostly." *Yours.*

She exhaled sharply. Then he got what he came for—a final, languid *nod* that mimicked a new pliancy in her posture. London tried so hard to mask her thoughts, but the way her body told stories was remarkable.

He kicked off his shoes and slid to the end of the bed, facing her with his knees bent, caging her legs. Leaning back on his elbows, he began to weave a web. "Keep your eyes closed. That's right. Now picture me."

A flutter betrayed the activity behind her closed lids. London was struggling with his instructions. How like her.

"Your nipples are hard, London. They're reaching for the gown, and I can tell it feels good when you rub them back and forth against the material."

This time she reacted automatically, swaying in that way that gave each pebbled tip a subtle graze.

"They need more."

"Yes," she murmured.

"Touch them. Circle each nipple with your fingers."

Her eyes popped open.

"The gentlest touch," he said, his voice deep and approving, "is no touch at all. At least not from me. At a point, you'll snap. You'll beg to feel me. And then I'll know you've broken through the fear and that you trust me not to go too far."

Her hands rose to her breasts, not to titillate, but to cover. "You want to *watch*."

More than anything. "Will you let me? Will you give me that? I'd never hurt you. I won't even *touch* you unless you demand it."

"And if I demand it right now?"

He took in the placement of her hands—arms crossed, one palm and one cast thrust over perfect breasts. "You won't." *But you will.*

She stared him down across the length of the bed, and damned if he didn't see the push-back as progress. "Relax for me. Move your hands away. Better yet, keep them there." But for a different purpose. "Your breasts look heavy, so round and full."

Tense muscles released incrementally with each word. London didn't remove her hands, but by the time he suggested they stay, she'd begun to move them in tiny circles. Now her legs shifted in front of her, ending in pearly pink toenails at the juncture of his thighs.

She sighed, needy and sweet, and inched those shapely legs apart. The room's deep shadows didn't reveal the kind of detail Trevor craved, but he had a good idea of what awaited him beneath the fabric. He clenched his teeth, then remembered that London's ultimate reveal depended on the story he was spinning.

A story of this gorgeous woman getting exactly what she wanted.

******

Trevor stayed put, but he looked ready to drag her from the bed and eat her whole. The arousing requests were one thing, *his* obvious arousal quite another. Another inch and her toes could fondle the evidence staining against his jeans.

A test, then.

London lowered her casted wrist, then let the fingers of her good hand trace the outline of one areola. Need surged in a blast of white hot heat. Her nipple stiffened even more against the fabric. Wetness slid between her barely parted thighs.

Who was she testing?

Normally touching herself didn't bring such a charge. She knew exactly what she was dealing with and what she'd get from the effort, so where was the thrill? But now she did as instructed while taking in his broad shoulders, his harsh jaw and giving lips. Those hooded eyes and intense stare.

Before he could ask, she trailed her touch across her chest to give the other nipple equal attention.

He seemed to give himself a shake. "Like that," he said, his voice like crunching gravel but still reassuring. Still making it clear she called the shots. "Make them both ache."

Unyielding hands landed on her ankles, and a jolt sizzled up both legs. When she looked at him in question, he merely quirked a brow. *No more than this*, he silently assured her. *But this much, I need.*

Without an answer, she continued exploring… Over her ribcage, past her navel. Then lower. She couldn't see her skin through the gown, and she wanted to. She wanted *him* to see it. Her fingers gathered the excess fabric, slowly revealing her knees, then her quads, then her thighs.

Trevor's hands twitched against her feet. He squeezed. "Show me, London. How do you say it in French? *Ta chatte. Votre belle chatte.*"

God help her, she did. With a final pull, she slid the gown to her stomach. Her skin usually looked naturally tan, but in the low light streaming through the window, she appeared ghostly. The paleness of her stomach and thighs popped against her trimmed black curls.

Soft curls.

Exposed from the waist down, London had never been the object of such intimate scrutiny. She felt vulnerable, but free. *Safe.* Then she noticed his look.

Starving, riveted. Dangerous. His grip tightened. He didn't bother to hide the strain.

"Lovely," he said in a deep rumble that shot more heat to that place they'd both focused their attention.

Glistening curls.

His grip circled her ankles and spread her legs. Not a lot, but enough. "Touch," he rasped. "Make yourself sigh for me, and I'll be your slave."

A positively *wonderful* idea. "No."

No? Had she lost her mind?

With a will of its own, her mouth took over. "You, too." When he merely arched one tawny brow, she went on. "I don't want to touch myself"—*yes*, she did—"alone."

The idea of a solo show sent equal trills of excitement and fear careening down her spine. Hot, but lonely. Much of her sexual past had been entirely focused on another. Trevor focused exclusively on her.

She wanted both.

Dragging her heels inward, London let her knees fall open, revealing herself completely.

Trevor froze, and his expression melted in almost imperceptible degrees. "*London.*" He refocused on her face. "What do you need?"

To have a man ask me that question. She could have cried joyous tears. Would have, if she hadn't been poised on the edge of a physical cataclysm. Trevor *shook* with the restraint he exerted to stay on his end of her bed. His eyes glittered with the need to finish what they'd started. And yet...

What do you need?

In that moment, she knew she didn't want *all* give or *all* take. She wanted the mutual, unforgettable kind of passion that tied two people together in ways that went far beyond physical. "Show me," she said. "Show me *you*. Let me watch *you*."

With his eyes half-lidded, he grasped the bottom of his T-shirt and tugged it over his head. The move revealed an expanse of smooth skin. As she'd already known, Trevor didn't do soft. Without an ounce of fat on him, the heavy lines of his shoulders and torso tapered to trim hips and arcing muscles that arrowed their way south.

Her own hips lifted in response. Instead of feeling exposed, London craved *equity*. Staring down the length of the golden treasure trail impeded by his jeans, she moaned from the back of her throat, sounding wild and desperate to her own ears.

"Is that code for *you like*?" Trevor didn't wait for her answer. He popped the top button and pulled until his zipper splayed wide.

London blinked. Fully hard, the tip of Trevor's erection had escaped from the band of a pair of navy boxer briefs. Heavy. Gleaming. Flushed. One glimpse of the wide head made it clear she needed to see the rest of her treat.

"Touch yourself," she whispered, "in the way you asked of me."

He chuckled. "I don't think I can replicate what I want from you. Wrong parts. And, besides, you didn't do it."

I will. I'll do anything. Everything.

Looking at the outline of his cock, London let her left hand wander with a mind of its own. She began with one feather-light caress along the seam between her legs. She'd grown so wet, it was impossible not to imagine him sliding inside her, easily moving through enflamed tissues that had already issued their welcome.

London might have started all this unsure of his restraint, but like he'd said, her body knew better. The achy, quivering need said all they needed to know. She arched, shamelessly circling her clitoris, tormenting, not doing anything to take herself over the edge.

On that, she'd changed her mind. Trevor had claimed she could demand his touch. She rose off the pillows on a helpless whimper, reaching for him with both hands.

"I… Please…"

He glanced up, jaw loose, blue eyes burning. As he registered her plea, surprise crept into his expression. "Oh, angel. It's all right." In a fluid move, he swiveled his legs beneath him and rocked upward between her thighs. "I *did* say I'd be your slave."

Obeying her shameless plea, he pressed her back into the bed, kissing each eyelid with inconceivable tenderness. His fingers found her, sliding deep into her slit. He petted her with soft strokes, talking in throaty endearments.

"You're as wet as you looked," he rasped. "Soaked. I could drink you down. That makes me happy." His warm, calloused fingers teased and circled until shivers sparked all over her body. Could she possibly want it… harder?

Rougher?

She rocked against his hand, moaning, nearly incoherent.

"Trevor." She slid against the sheets in the direction of his teasing touch, trying to impale herself. *Be a good slave and—*

Two fingers slid inside. Still gentle, still easy. But also thick and very, very fulfilling. She cried out, past all sense.

"That's the way. You want my touch. You *crave* it."

True.

Her head thrashed on the pillow in a gesture that might have meant *no*, but really meant all kinds of *yes*.

"You want it harder now." He pulled out and eased back in, then began a lazy rhythm with only those two fingers. "Maybe next time."

Still moving in and out, maddeningly slow and soft, Trevor leaned forward. He licked a hardened nipple through the gown she'd bunched around her waist. The hot, wet slide of his tongue joined his fingers.

Around her peaked breast, he whispered, "And now for what you've been waiting for. The proof you need—about yourself and about me." His thumb joined in. The first stroke slithered over her swollen sex until it rubbed around the base of her clit in a wide circle.

She gasped and bucked.

He didn't falter. "Ah-ah-ah. You asked. You *get*."

Another run around the base. Then, all at once, he pressed those fingers deep, slid his thumb over her throbbing nerve center, and closed his teeth, ever so carefully, in a barely-there scrape across her nipple.

London clenched with delight, imagining more than his fingers filling her. Receiving that final thrust, she bubbled over into an orgasm that assaulted her in spasms she never wanted to end. The release brought relief, but also a greater need for Trevor to give her more.

And for her to touch him in ways she had a feeling she'd quickly learn to like.

When she grew overly sensitive, Trevor pulled back and dragged her hospital gown down her legs, covering her heated flesh. His erection strained against his underwear, but when she reached for him, he pressed her hands away and zipped up.

"Exquisite woman," he murmured. "Now you know." He leaned in to take her lips in what felt like a parting kiss.

Yes, she knew. She had withheld information and taken risks he didn't understand. She'd ignored his wishes, lied to him about her plans, and put herself in danger. He knew too many of her explanations contained half-truths. Despite their strain and her unintentional, but frankly flagrant, disregard, the man had flown her high and dropped her over a pillow of clouds into a puddle of want.

He rose with a grace that seemed unnatural for one so big. Shrugging into his T-shirt, he hopped off the side of the bed. At the couch, he knelt down for his shoes, tying the laces with single-minded focus. "I can play your way, London. If you want a gentleman between your thighs, you'll have one." He stopped tying and strode toward the hall, stopping to calmly remove the door-stopper chair. Finally, hand on the handle, he glanced back. "Out of bed, where you're not nearly as honest, I won't be nearly as accommodating."

CHAPTER 11

"My sister isn't an idiot." Clara's hot indignation pulled London from an uneasy slumber. She stayed still for the sake of learning what delights waited on the other side of her closed lids.

"Debatable," said an unfamiliar voice.

"Not even sure it's that," said another. "Or are we *not* standing at the bedside of a woman who accidentally put herself there with wines she knew were bad?"

"*Suspected* were bad," Clara cut in. "The exercise was *about* knowing. You might have done the same."

A snort.

"My daughter didn't make a stupid choice." *Thanks, Mom.* "She made a rash one, which is perhaps her greatest weakness."

Such faith.

London opened her eyes to find bright afternoon light and a noisy chain of visitors surrounding the hospital bed. Her lone sentinel from the night had multiplied. Most she recognized. Others might have wandered into the wrong room.

Victoria and Warren Whitley stood at her feet. Clara flanked her mother, who absently rolled a prescription bottle between long fingers. A hospital had never been the place to face-off against the Drs. Whitley, and with London in the bed because of her own mistake, the balance of power tipped heavily in her parents' favor.

Clara stood unnaturally straight, almost-clasped hands hovering in front of her chest. She dropped sporadic peeks toward the pills in their mother's fist. The familiar scene had London silently thanking her sister. Age and experience had left London perfectly capable of disposing of unwanted drugs, but Clara still took it upon herself to make the pills—still usually Ritalin and sometimes Adderall, except when her parents grew creative in their diagnoses—disappear.

Though he'd gone with the dawn, Trevor again gripped the bed rail at her right. Golden scruff and weary eyes hinted at their late night. In the same worn jeans and faded T-shirt, the man was a walking fantasy, one she'd watched stroll away after providing a stunning revelation about sex, and about how he planned to deal with her when they weren't having it.

Mercilessly.

Fine. For the first time in her life, London wanted to take a man down, to enslave him with physical rewards and never let him come up for air again.

The greed felt good. Trevor could deal a harsh hand when they had their pants on, and she'd gladly accept the trade.

Though her tasting experiment had technically ended in disaster, what with the hospital bed and all, she now knew Level London could take calculated risks, both professional and—she focused on Trevor's capable hands—*personal.* The horror of Dillon and his grieving father had been unplanned, but unavoidable. Last night she'd set out to learn about her wine. The people surrounding her bed could disagree, but by God she'd learned exactly what needed knowing.

The wine was fake, but some of the bottles had been mixed better than others. Many passed for cheap plonk she wouldn't deign to sell, but that on sight, scent, and sip, she also wouldn't peg as dangerous, maybe not even fake since plenty of real wines performed worse. Those better bottles had nearly killed her. The remaining samples, the ones she'd immediately spit out, were even more dangerous. Last year the complaints had been about inferior quality, not temporary blindness. This year her mysterious counterfeiter had upped the ante.

And the unpredictability.

Perhaps her risk had been too great, but if knowledge was truly power, she'd done the right thing. Plus, seeking answers had awakened a sleeping part of her with the guts to reach high, maybe as high as Trevor Rathlen.

Who currently observed her with an unnerving, ticking regard.

"Sleeping Beauty wakes."

The statement might have expressed a welcome, morning-after kind of sentiment had it come from Trevor in his soothing, affectionate rumble. Instead, it had come from a stranger and sounded like an observation, devoid of relief or approval. The newcomer stood across from Trevor, next to a man she recognized as Trevor's workout partner. The two unknowns had to be brothers, both tall and imposing with striking coloring. Suspicious blue eyes clashed against auburn hair, one head trimmed and tidy, the other boasting the type of mess a woman couldn't help but try to finger comb.

"Meet my *colleagues.*" Letting the subtle emphasis speak for itself, Trevor peeled a palm off the rail and motioned toward the neater of the two. The man wore an impeccable three-piece suit, probably custom-made, and a paisley tie in shades of lime. "This is Brian Wentworth and his brother, Kevin. Brian is a lawyer. Tereth is his client. Kevin is—"

"Kevin from the gym." London dipped her head in acknowledgement. Besides an aversion to brushing his hair, Kevin wore a gray hoodie the exact shade of his brother's beautiful suit.

He didn't look her way in greeting. "Kevin from the last time you endangered yourself and the last time Trevor saved your ass."

Her mother stiffened. "Endangered yourself?"

"It's nothing," London said quietly. "Low blood sugar, fast treadmill."

Kevin scoffed, "Not that fast, sugar."

Of course it hadn't been. London considered three miles per hour a good clip. "Brian has hired Trevor to"—what to say when her parents hung on every word?—"*assist* WW." She made the declaration to the room at large, unsure as to who would ante up a proper explanation.

"Not quite." Kevin finally condescended to look her in the eye. "Brian hired Trevor to assist his client, Tereth of Hungary, on *my* introduction. He owed us—"

"I already know that part."

Brian thumped Kevin in the chest. "Water under a bridge. I've just arrived in town. London has just been released"—he sent her a sly wink—"on her own recognizance if she promises to stay off the sauce, and I already know we've been barking up the wrong tree. Tell me, Brother, do you think seasoned purveyors of questionable counterfeits—and by questionable, I mean *full of wiper fluid*—regularly partake of their own goods?"

"She's sneaky—"

Bull. "I am not."

"She is *not*," her father interrupted.

At least London and her dad agreed on *one* thing, except London meant she wasn't devious, while her father meant she was dim. She looked at her parents. "I'm fine. I'm leaving here today. No harm, no foul. None of this concerns you."

Her mother managed to look both concerned and contemptuous. "From what I understand, you're selling counterfeit wines *and* drinking them. How long can that kind of behavior go on?"

"It's not 'going on.'" *Per se.*

"Oh, but it is, London." Brian scanned her from head to toe. The examination emphasized the stark contrast between his impeccable tailoring and her tie-in-the-back sheet. "But Trevor's right. You aren't capable of the kind of deceit that would put this on your head."

So many votes of confidence. She could *totally* be a devious trickster, if she wanted. "And you're the expert on my capabilities?"

"I work with, and *for*, liars for a living. I'm a damn good one myself. You have lies in you, but the wine isn't one of them. What is, I wonder?"

"Who was the man with the crowbar?"

London whipped around. Trevor stood, implacable as ever, cutting her a look to burn cities. Apparently he'd grown tired of listening to useless prattle and of waiting on the question that would ruin her. With the Drs. and Clara in the room, the odds stacked against continued discretion. Her nighttime light and daytime nightmare had obviously decided to capitalize on the extra mouths in the room.

He *had* warned her.

"Who broke into your warehouse?" Trevor asked again, all imperious commander of the realm. After failing to get a rise from London, he addressed her parents and Clara as though London had disappeared from between them. "Who attacked her with a deadly weapon? Who smashed her wine and went after her body? What does he want?"

The questions let the air out of the room. Where the pace and tenor of the interrogation had been cruising along, Trevor's demands left smoking silence in their wake.

Clara jerked against the bed, surprised eyes round and almost disbelieving. Mouth open, one word escaped. "Dillon?"

Victoria shot her youngest daughter a reproachful look, part surprise and part fear. "What are you talking about? Dillon is—"

"Dead," Clara finished.

"No longer with WW Imports," London said at the same time, sounding hasty and artificial in her clumsy effort to cover Clara's mistake.

Instead of hearing London, Trevor contemplated her sister. "Dead as in *deceased*?" The question dripped with speculation. He reached out and trailed his knuckles along London's cast.

Clara seemed to come back to herself. She flashed a placating smile, no doubt intended to say, "M*ove along. Nothing of Interest here.*"

"An accident," said baby sis. Except Clara didn't excel at quick deceit. Her outgoing nature tended to draw people in. Every move invited more interaction, not less.

Brian picked up where Trevor had left off, scrutinizing Clara as he talked. "So, last night, then? Since we've ruled out the accidentally dead ex-employee, who's our warehouse villain?"

London let her eyes slide shut. The conversation had become an oil pan to Clara's natural flame. Her sister meant well, but she had no way of knowing the number of snippets already in Trevor's arsenal or the skills he might employ to mine more.

London sighed and opened her eyes, looking at everyone, seeing no one. "Last night we *experienced*"—for lack of a better word—"Turner Farro."

A gasp from her mother. "Dillon's father? You stay *away* from that."

"Yes," London, for once, agreed.

"From *that*?" Kevin wondered aloud. "What exactly is 'that'?"

London refused to continue with her parents hanging by to ignorantly interject fun facts for Trevor to piece together. She could also do without them picking up more of their own. "Go," she implored them. "I won't take another sip of bad wine." Or wine period if it would make them leave. "I'll visit tomorrow. We can talk then."

Both Whitleys appeared on the verge of stepping away from the bed. The short fuse between London and her parents had always been mutual, and even *they* could detect that complications like the ones being batted across the bed couldn't be fixed with a prescription pad and a lecture. But when her father turned and strode toward the exit, her mother held out the inevitable orange bottle.

"You haven't been diligent." *You don't say?* "Bad things happen when you aren't."

Right. In her mother's mind, one after another since London had been prepubescent. In reality, London was more like Eeyore stuck in a tar pit than a person with ADHD.

Clara slipped the pills from Victoria's hand and gave their mother's shoulder a comforting squeeze. "She'll take them."

The promise won Clara one of their mother's staunch, but approving, smiles. "You always watch out for your sister."

With a stiff nod, Clara stepped aside and looked meaningfully at the door. Victoria followed along, and, mission accomplished, Victoria and Warren Whitley took their leave.

As the door closed behind them, Clara mercifully slipped the bottle into her purse. "Back to business."

******

Trevor looked down at a much rejuvenated London and took stock of what he knew. On the day they'd met, London had mentioned attending her lover's funeral. All that shock and worry had been hazardous to her health.

That day he'd tallied up one dead boyfriend. Since, he'd added one dead employee. One broken wrist. One pallet of deadly wine, origin unknown. A crowbar swinging, disenfranchised father. And a finger-squeezing, sell-your-soul orgasm he couldn't wait to watch her repeat.

London sat at the nucleus of all six knowns, which left Trevor mired in offshoots. Who was the boyfriend? Who was Dillon the ex-employee? How did they die? Why would Dillon's father feel the need to burn aggression on London's wine stores? How did the wrist get broken? Did any of the answers mean jack in terms of the origin of the fake wine? And had

London asked for that orgasm to throw him off the scent?

She'd have to learn that when a man coaxed that kind of reaction from a woman—the kind that had him getting hard in front of her parents twelve hours later—he might do a lot of things, but leave her alone wasn't one of them.

Her cast chaffed against his knuckles, so different from her smooth skin. The plaster broke London's elegant perfection, an anomaly that reminded him of the divisions simmering inside her. Without those complexities, the nurses might have found him in her bed that morning.

Maybe he'd still be in it.

Across from him, Brian was in the process of breaking character. The man treated London with his usual full-bore irreverence, half flirting and half sniping, but he watched Clara with a calculated care that Trever hadn't seen before. Clara and Brian had met when London's "friends" and family had converged around her still-sleeping form. A quick round of introductions meant the two were officially acquaintances.

Pushing away from London's side, Brian sauntered over to Clara at the foot of the bed. She didn't pull away when he bent to her ear. Whatever he said was short, but judging from Clara's expression, it was anything but sweet.

To the room, Brian said, "Yes, let's *do* get back to business. I'd love to know—"

Brian could wait. Trevor had more information and better questions. "A dead boyfriend *and* a dead employee?" Hell of a coincidence.

The color London had regained abandoned her. Resignation schooled her features into a blank mask, and he watched her un-casted fist curl. "One and the same."

Clara leaned in. "*London.*"

London flicked a hand at her little sister in a gesture that said, "*I give up.*" Out loud she said, "I need them. The wine is officially a problem, and we don't have the resources to ferret out the source and stem the flow. What if WW is infected with fakes beyond the Olaszrizling?"

"Then *we* sort it out."

"Yeah?" Brian cut in. "How? You gonna volunteer for the next taste test? You'll need us to haul your ass to the emergency room before you go blind."

By Trevor decree, further testing would occur in a lab, and Clara ignored Brian's taunt. "I'm on board. So are Grey and Trent. These men"—she gestured at Trevor, Brian, and Kevin—"want you to be at fault. We should stay far away from them."

For a heartbeat, London tensed. She looked up at Trevor, and he watched as she digested her sister's accusation. The *last* thing he wanted was for London to be responsible. If the London who'd opened to him last night was the kind to lead him on a merry chase, then he hadn't learned a Goddamn thing about how or who to trust.

She'd been vulnerable, aroused but also afraid, and she'd put herself in his hands. Unless she proved him wrong, that gift deserved to be honored beyond the sunrise. He jerked his head one way, then the other. It was all the reassurance the Whitley girls could expect to get.

"Not *all* of them have condemned me," London said.

"Of *course*." Kevin plunged both hands into his mop of hair, laughing at Trevor as though he'd finally learned a secret. "Here I didn't think you had it in you. You're in hip deep, my friend. Except you went about her all wrong." He flicked at London's shoulder with a thumb and forefinger. "Fucking this babe is a *tool*, not a treat."

London's gasp punctuated Kevin's cruelty, and Trevor's chest wrenched. Whatever man had happened to London, he'd left her sensitive, distrustful. She wasn't a woman to shrug off being used. When Trevor responded, his voice was deceptively soft.

"Get out."

A crash interrupted the threat, and Trevor instinctively reached to guard London. He swiped empty air. Across from him, her arm flew back from the rolling table she'd jostled in her haste. Kevin had backed away. A broken vase littered the floor amongst clumps of mangled pink roses.

She'd worn pink at the gym and currently flashed a pink pedicure. Red roses said too much, too soon, and the gift-shop lady had insisted that yellow said friendship. So, pink, because Trevor would never be merely her friend.

Right now his silly gift camouflaged jutting shards of glass beneath the spot where London sat poised to launch herself from the other side of the bed.

******

Pink roses. London hadn't noticed the flowers until they'd flown from her water tray. Trevor must have brought them while she slept. Petals had fluttered into a loose heap on the floor. Stems lay twisted and broken.

Trevor's voice invaded her preoccupation from a distance. "London, stay where you are."

No, London had to get to the flowers. She wouldn't be the destructive one in the room. As she scrambled from the bed, a sharp pain flared in her foot. Blood welled, seeping into the water and running in crimson fault lines across its surface. Funny, she didn't feel pain. Everything would be fine if she could salvage the blooms.

Muffled commands swirled about the room. Harsh jabs, sharp but indistinct, signaled Trevor getting rid of the crowd. He'd want privacy to fix

Kevin's slip. He'd want to assure her their almost-sex had been genuine.

That it hadn't been a tool.

London crouched among the blooms. Another pinch flared in her knee. Looking down, she saw the glass at the same time she heard the quiet click of a closing door. They'd left her alone with *him*.

The one who'd promised to be merciless outside her bed. The bastard who'd been merciless inside it, too.

Nothing but a tool.

"London," he coaxed, "get up. You've cut yourself."

A towel dropped into her peripheral vision, swinging from his fingers. London stopped reaching for snapped stems. As soon as she could pull words from her twisted gut, she'd rail at him. So far, her voice wouldn't come.

Her throat closed around her pathetic admissions from the night before. She'd worked up the courage to insinuate the truth—that she'd practically let Dillon abuse her—and now she found out Trevor had been the wrong man to tell. The fact that knew something so personal and so demeaning when he'd been seducing her as part of a role was humiliating.

Disgusting.

He didn't wait for her to stand. London felt herself lifted and set gently on the opposite edge of the bed, facing the windows, far from the broken beauty strewn about the floor. Trevor wrapped the towel around her leg from the knee to the foot and dabbed at the cuts.

"I can explain," he began.

Yes. Everyone had their explanations, their reasons. Her parents had their reasons for attempting to medicate the crazy out of her at every turn. Dillon had had his reasons for seeking to control and to punish, most likely in ways that ultimately involved sabotaging her business with planted counterfeits. Dillon's father had his reasons for seeking retribution in the aftermath of his son's death.

Even London had a stack of justifications to keep her warm at night. She had her reasons for evading her parents' efforts, for defending herself against Dillon's escalating violence, and for blowing off Turner Farro. In the end, her parents lived life gravely disappointed, Dillon was dead, and Dillon's dad would likely make her downfall his personal mission.

Yet London clung to her demons. After all, seeing oneself in a good light was basic human nature. No doubt Trevor had easily talked himself into her bed because pliable, well-pleasured targets made better business.

More effective tools.

His hands roamed over the towel, and she jerked from the grip. "Try to explain," she taunted. "Go ahead and try."

He backed away, hands up. "Kevin has his own way of getting things done."

"You're not Kevin."

"Exactly. And you're bleeding. Let me help you."

At the continued evasion, London's muddled confusion coalesced into rage. Once again she slid from the bed, only this time she hobbled to a neat stack of clothing by the couch. She snapped her jeans to attention and stabbed a bleeding foot into a pant leg.

"London, I said you're—"

"I have Band-Aids at home!" First the gym, then the warehouse, now the hospital. The man hovered like an insurance policy on a pair of million-dollar legs. Still dressing, she started his countdown. "When these clothes are on, I'm walking out that door and down the hall to check out. That doesn't leave a lot of time for you to tell me you never considered manipulating me with those big hands." She trembled at the memory. *Screw that.* "Be extra nice to the wine girl? Make her feel real special?"

Trevor barely reacted, but she didn't miss the slight flare of his nostrils and the sudden stillness that too often accompanied an unwelcome realization. His carefully masked denial told her he *had* thought of plying her with well-placed pleasure.

And she'd given him ammunition to spare. "I told you I don't like it rough, so you knew I'd be amenable to a slow, good time. You figured I'd be so grateful it didn't hurt that I'd open up. Well, congratulations. It worked. Today I admitted more than I *ever* intended." She'd told him Dillon was dead and that he'd doubled as her employee and her ex. It wouldn't be long... "I did so because I thought you were helping me. I guess we've come full circle because I thought you were helping *only* after the way my body trusted you, opened to you, on the most basic level possible."

She thrust her arms into her shirt. "*Christ.* I'm as rash and reckless as my parents say."

Foolish. *Crazy.*

Trevor grabbed her hands. "Kevin did mention getting close to you for info. I categorically refused." The admission flew out of his mouth with conviction. "The closest I came to taking his advice was to recognize the truth in it. I knew I could have gone that route. I didn't."

"You *did.*"

"I put my hands on you, yes, but not for the reasons you think." He sucked in a long breath. "Chasing the Tereth fakes is a *job*. I take on a contract. I get a payoff. The jobs and the payoffs vary. Some are nobler than others, but I'm pretty sure I already told you I don't fuck for money."

London shuddered at the harshness in his tone, at the profanity he'd never before directed her way. If he thought he could shock her...

She surged up and met his mouth with hers, suckling his bottom lip hard, relishing the heat she brought to the surface. When he released her hands to cradle her face on a low, desperate moan, she wrenched free to tread through the bloody roses on her way to the door.

With a brief look back, she said, "Only because we didn't fuck."

CHAPTER 12

Brian trailed Clara Whitley down the hospital corridor at a pseudo-safe distance. If she spared a look back, she'd notice his interest. So far, she beelined for the exit without a care for her older sister's cohorts.

He'd built a tidy empire for himself, mostly the result of employing keen observation skills among idiots. Generally, ignoring Brian Wentworth brought unsavory consequences. When London had landed herself in the hospital trying to test wine he already knew was fake, he'd hopped a plane from New York City—a perfect place he tried not to leave if he could help it—to Denver.

Where idiocy apparently ran rampant.

London had hurt herself with the counterfeit wine, and she'd turned out to be the least of his problems. Trevor had come highly recommended by one of Brian's few true friends. Lissa Blanc would soon marry Trevor's younger brother, Cole. In true Lissa style, she'd called Trevor's will "iron" and his balls something even harder. Plus, she'd assured him, Trevor was stone cold, though genial enough on the surface—maybe even *nice*, which would be key in dealing with London—but a truly hard man with a difficult, shadowed past staining his core.

Perfect.

The list of Trevor's pros had been long: smarter than everyone in the room, stronger than everyone in the state, personable, disciplined, disinclined toward strong emotion, and, most importantly, *distrustful.*

Plus, Trevor *owed* Brian—or owed Kevin, but whatever—a favor. The man had needed a top-shelf pad in a scarce real-estate market. Brian had urged Kevin to make it happen. At the time, Brian hadn't known whether or when Trevor might come in handy. But Brian liked to hedge his bets and routinely stacked the favor ledger in advance.

After all that careful planning in choosing the right man to out London

Whitley and her shoddy operation, Brian had arrived to find his man half in love with his problem.

And his own brother going hotheaded on a pile of preconceived notions.

And a set of parents who'd obviously only complicate an already complicated situation.

And a fucking little sister who liked her scripts too much to be counted anyone's ally, least of all London's.

Admittedly, from his vantage point about twenty feet back, no one could fault the view. Where London's golden skin and plush curves turned a hospital gown into an event that could sell tickets, Clara was built along slender lines—the sprite to her sister's goddess.

The two had matching black hair, but Clara's didn't coil around her face like London's. Instead, it fell in layered sheets past her shoulders, straight and glossy and sleek. That shiny hair swayed when she walked, just like her pert little ass. Brian bet if he threw coins at it, they'd bounce right off.

Big sister exuded a fragility that made a man want to gather her up and take on her world. Brian sensed London had to buck up to be strong. Little sister smiled while she sniped. Brian *knew* Clara had to buck up to be weak.

This one with the perfect body and the practiced smile had the world fooled.

"You like your pills, don't you, sweetness?"

Yes, she certainly did. But she hadn't liked his question. Whispering the accusation in her ear had been a test.

Clara had failed.

Oh, she'd taken on the Whitleys' proffered prescription, all right. Though the pills had disappeared into her bag with an air of self-sacrifice, the move had been too automated, tinged with a hint of relief that would only stand out to a consummate watcher like Brian.

Ahead, Clara pushed through a set of double doors and into the afternoon heat. She donned a pair of dead-sexy sunglasses, at least from the side view he got when she turned onto the walkway. Tiny and feisty, and no doubt jaded and chock full of deceit, Clara was a poisoned carrot dangling before a demonic stallion. The carrot might give the horse a bellyache, but in the end, the carrot would be no more.

And it would be delicious.

Clara climbed into an old diesel pickup. Why wasn't he surprised to see this one didn't own a Prius? Before she cranked the engine, she dug into the bag she'd tossed in ahead of her. The brown bottle reappeared. She cranked the top, poured out a *pile*, and threw the pills back with a toss of that hair he wouldn't mind wrapping around his fist.

Bad girl.

At least this trip wouldn't be boring.

******

Not three hours after returning home from the hospital, London opened her front door to a Trevor look-alike and panting dog. The man shared Trevor's height and coloring, but he was a leaner—and possibly, from the looks of him, also meaner—version of the real thing.

"I'm the brother." He looked down at Sasha, who must have become a pro at elevator riding while staying at Trevor's. "You can probably guess the rest."

Actually, no.

The man eyed her with bored objectivity. Trever had surely sent him, but he didn't appear to care whether his mission met with success. Then, "I come bearing gifts. You'll let us in to receive them."

She would, would she?

Intrigued, and knowing she'd never face danger from an obvious member of the Rathlen family, she stepped aside. Her apartment didn't have a proper entryway, only a rectangle of tile that flanked the door. Sasha blasted past the tile to fall into a heap on her cream-colored carpet. When she thought about coaxing the dog into the kitchen, he opened his mouth, yawned, and then rolled half over, one foreleg in the air in an invitation for a chest rub.

She fell for it. On her knees in a heartbeat, she went at Sasha with both hands until his yard-long tongue lolled out to soak her rug.

"I'm Cole," the man said behind her. "Trevor tells me you have a stalker or four. Since the two of you are, he says, 'Temporarily engaged in your first non-lovers spat,' he wants you to borrow my pup."

London looked over her shoulder, letting her efforts on Sasha's exposed belly dwindle. "You're kidding."

A dry chuckle. "I return from parts unknown to be informed my dog can be retrieved from the offices of a local wine importer. My brother wants me to let a strange woman he admits to, 'Not trusting but also not risking,' keep my sidekick. I know Sasha gets around, but usually only in the family. What did you do to him?"

"To Sasha, or to Trevor?"

Cole looked slightly baffled. "Frankly, both."

More questions from more Rathlens. This one, thankfully, didn't look like he'd offer up an orgasm in exchange for answers. "Very little," she hedged. "You mentioned gifts."

He pointed at the dog nuzzling her knees. "Obviously."

"You can't just up and leave me with the care and feeding of a mini water buffalo. I don't…"

Cole disappeared around the corner of her still-open door and into the hall. He reappeared carrying a huge rubber container and a mangled-looking grocery sack. Before she made it off the floor, a crisp printout dangled in her face. Typed and tidy, eight points fairly jumped off the page.

- Morning and night: 3.5 cups of food (total of 7 cups). Don't feed within one hour of exercise. Only use the food provided because he's allergic to the corn used as filler in cheap foods.

- With each feeding: Include 1 Glucosamine tablet (for his joints), 2 blue thyroid tablets (labeled thyroid on the bottle), 6 Benadryl pills (he has hay fever), and 1 fish oil pill (for his skin and fur).

- On Wednesday and Saturday: Use a fresh syringe (provided) to give him 1 cc of the liquid in the glass bottle (it's his immunotherapy drug, for the hay fever) in the scruff on the neck. The liquid must be refrigerated. He gets a treat after his shot.

- Every Sunday: Clean his ears with the cleaner provided.

- Every evening (he's tired in the mornings): Walk.

- All the time: Water (he drinks a lot). Make sure to keep towels handy for the slobber.

- Never: Table Scraps (you don't want a 200 lb. dog with explosive diarrhea).

- On August 22nd: 1 beer (he likes pilsners).

She cracked up after three bullets. "Immunotherapy?"

Cole didn't bother to misunderstand. "He's a sensitive animal."

"Who typed the list?"

A smirk. "I'll give you a hint—*not* me."

She'd pegged Trevor for detail-oriented, had figured he didn't like surprises and went to lengths to minimize them, but this?

This was more like love.

Cole propped a hip on her table, examining her reaction. "You think with your eyes. You know that?" Then, "My brother doesn't love, or even like, in half measures. My brother loves my dog."

She considered Trevor's meticulous list. *He's tired in the mornings. He has hay fever. He likes pilsners.*

With a final pat to the obvious king of the concrete jungle, London rose to her feet. Rummaging through the sack, she found cotton balls, pill bottles, treats, and disposable syringes. Cole had even brought a sharps container.

She set everything out in a row. "I'll take him." Because Sasha was Trevor's olive branch, a big, hairy, slobbering, lover of an apology.

Cole accepted with a shrug, ever distant and watchful. He held up a finger. "One week." A thoughtful pause. "You realize he's not a guard dog. He provides the *perception* of having a guard dog. In reality, he'd most likely welcome an intruder by snoring loud enough to help the bad guy go undetected."

Fair enough. "Why are you doing this?"

Cole helped himself to one of her dining chairs. He looked out of place in her small apartment, like he'd rather be anything but confined and had to force himself to stillness. Yet he did stillness so well, a pot of barely boiling water with only the tiniest bubbles escaping to the surface. He didn't hurry when he spoke, like each word was mentally vetted for its appropriateness for an outsider. "After my wife died, I went through... challenges. Trevor delivered food to my house on a rotating schedule that he devised with my uncle. I didn't run out of milk for *years* because they were too stubborn to let me."

London took a chair of her own.

"For much of that time, when he was dropping off eggs and bread and beef stroganoff, I blamed him for my wife's death. I thought my brother and my wife had had an affair, and that she'd killed herself after I confronted her. I was wrong, but he let me go through the process, never blaming me, forgiving me before I knew I needed forgiveness."

The story sounded like one of family devotion—an inspiring tale—but the bottom still dropped out of London's stomach. Cole wasn't building to a happy climax. An ominous weight settled over his presence.

"Do you want to know why?" he asked.

"*Should* I know why?"

He smiled darkly. "A smart one. I like that. Trevor let me lash out because he accepts that real life is a fucking mess, and he has the patience to wait it out, so long as it's reality he's waiting on. You can chop down his cherry tree, but you better cop to the deed. My anger was misplaced, but real. My blame was wrong, but honest."

London swallowed. "And?"

"My wife never had an affair with Trevor. She had one with Trevor's wife, Rhea. The two were lovers, and Rhea imploded when Kate decided to remain in her marriage to me. When we discovered Rhea's deed, Trevor snapped. All along the scarlet A had belonged to Rhea, not Trevor, and no one had known that more than the woman herself. Yet while I was busy blaming my brother, Trevor's wife had been jumping on the bandwagon, also blaming him. She played the scorned woman card, spewing vitriol all over this family until the moment she confessed to the affair and the killing. Her actions had been bad enough. But trying to get away with it? Trying to keep her husband? To *blame* Trevor and make a mockery of his trust? Well, that's not who my brother is. Trevor isn't just some whiz with brawny biceps and a big brain. There's a reason he's so dedicated to both."

London held her breath. Cole led her along with such methodical purpose that she knew this wasn't a spontaneous fact-letting. He wanted her to know things. Once she knew them, his mouth would stop moving, and that would be all she'd get. She hoped they weren't yet at that end.

"Trevor joined the Army in college," Cole went on. "There was boot camp right after graduation, and then more specialized training. By the time he got out several years later, he was a warrant officer for a special ops team stationed in Germany. He wore several hats—a combat leader on one hand, a tech advisor responsible for integrating emerging technologies on another, a strategic advisor to commanders at all levels on yet another. He was determined to play those roles—and, *oh*, how he loved that techie shit—but the Army was always a dollar short, inundated with special needs but lean on support and funding."

"Radical groups had begun attacking civilian targets across Europe— newspaper offices, museums, synagogues, a Catholic hospital. The attacks seemed to have a particular signature, but no terrorist group claimed responsibility. The international intelligence community watched chatter for months. Hell, I think even Russia listened in. Attacks kept coming. A couple resulted in massive manhunts, and random individuals were apprehended. Between the surveillance and whatever it is we civilized countries do to get information out of uncivilized people, word trickled down regarding the group responsible—a Al Qaeda offshoot working from within Europe to target Europeans. Since America polices the world these days, Trevor's team was tasked with capturing or killing the brains of the operation, a few men working out of a flat in Amsterdam."

At least London knew how the story ended, with Trevor hearty and hale enough to turn her life upside down. But she also knew about the power of the mind and about how a person with perfect eyesight might forever see the sightless eyes they had wrought. Already Dillon's fall had changed her, an accident with unimaginable power. What if she'd killed on purpose, like she feared Trevor might have been forced to do?

Cole didn't seem to notice her distress. "Trevor drew up a plan. He has a knack for that. He requested several new devices, at the time, called flybots—tiny robotic flies that can be sent on reconnaissance missions in places too dangerous for soldiers to tread. They're smaller than a pin, remotely controlled, and, at least then, extremely expensive. Trevor was promised three."

The story glided along safely, blunt in the middle, but with razor-sharp edges she knew they'd yet to reach.

Promised three.

"Trevor planned accordingly, acting as detachment commander. Amsterdam came, along with the designated date. The flybots did not. When Trevor sent word up the food chain that the team would have to wait, that his life, and the lives of his subordinates, could hinge on their ability to remotely understand the dangers awaiting them in that flat, he was commanded to execute the plan immediately. He was told the team had to take advantage of the element of surprise and that, because murmurings were beginning to surface, surprise wouldn't be possible for much longer. Trevor argued that murmurings meant the time for surprise had passed, making the flybots even more important."

Cole scrubbed a hand over his hair, growing impatient with his own story. "Trevor went in first. That fact likely saved him. Almost impossibly, the initial blast sent him through a second-story window. He broke a few bones. Only one other member of his team survived. They found him wedged in a still-standing closet without even a scratch on the door. The men they sought died alongside Trevor's, martyrs in the end. By all accounts, Uncle Sam deemed the day's loss a worthy sacrifice. Trevor doesn't know for sure, but he suspects those flybots failed to arrive by design, for they would have quickly revealed the danger and caused him to abort a mission that needed to happen and that needed to happen a certain way. His team could never smoke out men waiting to die. The Army either incinerated a Dutch apartment building from afar—very bad press—or lost a few heroic men in their valiant efforts to diffuse a threat—much better press. Either way, the bad guys were scratched off a list."

London's head was a mess of unwilling understanding. "So he left the Army."

A viscous note dropped into Cole's voice. "And dove headlong into marriage with a lying, murdering bitch. And a profession of protecting secrets and ferreting out lies, if he *and he alone* finds the task worth the effort. Trevor shed the bitch, and these days, he doesn't take anyone's word at face value. He lives by the motto 'trust but verify,' minus the trust. The whole thing makes him bad with blind faith. Worse with orders. Hell on lies."

"Yet he sent you here with protection for me." Correction. "Or at least the *perception* of it."

Cole stood. He walked to London's chair, where he looked straight down into her face. "Interesting word choice—*yet*. Almost like you know Trevor's concern for you is an anomaly in his war on deceivers. You admit you are one and can't figure out why you're still standing."

Actually, yes.

"I thought as much." He stroked Sasha's flopping ear with a foot. "I came to meet the woman my brother lets lie. In that, you're unique, but I predict also temporary."

At the door, he pointed at Sasha and reminded London, "One week."

CHAPTER 13

The warehouse didn't have a hose. After picking through the broken glass leftover from London's close call and throwing it into the recycling bin outside, Clara found herself washing away drying puddles of pooled wine with buckets of soapy water. Each toss cleansed her conscious as well as the concrete floor.

Dillon had disappeared from her sister's life.

Good.

Dillon's father and other more notable naysayers had replaced him.

Bad.

While London had been forced to grow quieter over the years, Clara had been free to grow louder. London had avoided risk. Clara had courted it.

The price for London's good behavior had been high.

Clara used the office push broom to scrub at the dried remnants of wine and push the dirtied muck out the bay door and into the encroaching evening. When the floor gleamed under the fluorescent lights, she began to systematically open every remaining bottle of Olaszrizling and dump it into the industrial sink.

There were hundreds of bottles, but Clara remained undeterred. Energy vibrated her insides, feeding on the clarity that came to her courtesy of the pill bottle waiting inside her purse. All those risks London hadn't taken rose up inside Clara like a storm. With each bottle she dumped, a faint whiff of conscious whispered that the chemicals lacing the castoff liquid probably called for a less compromising disposal method.

But there wasn't time. Clara had taken the risks her sister had refused, and she wouldn't let London be called upon to pay for them.

At last, the warehouse no longer smelled of rotting fruit and moonshine. Every smoking gun had been dumped. Clara approached an aging forklift parked in a dark corner. The lift sputtered and rumbled to life with only a little coaxing. Soon the pallet of empties sat on the loading dock, flush with the dumpsters, ready to disappear in the morning like so much trash.

Ridding the warehouse of the fake wine had been a crucial step, but only a first one. Clara washed her hands, applied a fresh coat of lipstick, and brushed her hair. Youth and beauty often told a story of innocence.

Tonight she would spin the ultimate tale.

For her sister. For herself.

She stepped from the warehouse to the office, breathing a sigh of relief to find the space unoccupied. Lipstick or no, she didn't want an audience to witness her building her case or composing her threats.

She took a seat at her desk, knowing exactly where to look for proof of Dillon's perfidy. An hour later, she closed her laptop and left the building carrying a manila envelope with several printouts, each one a breadcrumb leading straight to Dillon Farro.

Dillon's father would swallow his petty need for revenge once he saw the credible threat to his son's legacy and Clara's willingness—*eagerness*, really—to deploy it, which was why Clara had made sure the trail to Dillon's shadowed door didn't make any pit stops in front of hers.

******

Trevor let his fingers skim Brutus's keyboard. Like braille to the blind, computer keys lifted the curtain and revealed the hand working life's levers, a magic wand he used to make sense of the world.

The time at the hospital, with its discoveries and its accusations, worked like gears in his head, grinding away with curiosity and denial. London had fled. So had he, in a way, back to his loft and the ones and zeros that could reach out into the city and snatch up the answers she refused to give.

Fuck waiting.

Cole had reported a successful passing of the dog. London had taken the bait, which meant she'd be back.

Trevor would be ready.

Outside, the night waited quietly, the music of summer drifting through open windows—crickets, faint strains of pop music, only the occasional car several floors below. Even the pace of the city had slowed so he could concentrate.

One and the same, she'd admitted. Dillon the ex-employee doubled for Dillon the ex-boyfriend and tripled for Dillon the mourned, beloved son.

A dead man.

London hadn't wanted Trevor to know how Dillon fit into her life. *Or* the identity of the guy with the crowbar. *Or* why Turner Farro felt she should be punished for his son's demise. Did her concern lie in Dillon's triple identity, or in the fact that he didn't have an identity anymore?

Trevor had thought to respect her privacy. But she kept bobbing and weaving, and now she painted him the bad guy. *A familiar pattern I don't plan to repeat.*

London had become personal before she'd become a job. The time to dance around the truth had run dry last night, first when he'd seen her barely elude an imminent attack, and again when it had become apparent that holding everything in led to experimental poison consumption. The death knell in his patience had sounded along with her gasp against his chest as she'd convulsed around his fingers.

And now he knew where to start the search: Dillon Farro. For her own damn good.

Google coughed up a generalized online obituary—*wonderful son, gone too soon, to be missed by all who knew him.* An outdated bio from some long lost sales job pre-dating WW Imports revealed more nothing. After weeding through links to every Twitter account in existence attached to the name Dillon, Trevor landed on a three-paragraph article from *The Denver Post* that gave Trevor his first burst of useful info.

Dillon Farro had died in an accident at the famous and sometimes infamous Red Rocks Amphitheater located about ten miles west of Denver. Situated between huge, vertical outcroppings of red rock, the open-air concert arena had seen its share of death over the years, but usually those accidents were attributed to people going rogue on the rocks—climbing where they shouldn't, drinking too many beers before climbing where they shouldn't, smoking too many joints before climbing where they shouldn't. On and on.

Dillon, on the other hand, had died on the steep steps leading away from the stage. According to metro police, he'd fallen during a domestic dispute, no mention of drugs or alcohol. The death was described as an accident. Case closed.

Bummer for Dillon.

Because Red Rocks was owned and operated by the city and county of Denver, case closed meant Trevor could order a copy of the police report online from the Denver Police Department. He debated the above-board route, but even expedited orders were only filled within three business days. Tonight, sooner trumped later. He had a hunch a certain beautiful wine importer had been involved in a wrist-fracturing incident at Red Rocks around the time Dillon had gone down.

With a flick of the wrist, Trevor pulled up an open-source tool configured to discern firewall filtering rules. People talked about "bypassing" or "infiltrating" system firewalls, but those were common computing misnomers. A firewall basically operated by checking incoming and outgoing data packets against a set of predefined rules, often based on metadata such as an IP address, protocol type, or even the type of data or payload being sent. Incoming packets falling within a firewall's rules were allowed to pass. Packets outside the defined parameters bounced, meaning slipping through was more of a seduction than a bludgeoning. The key to making nice with a firewall lay in understanding its rules, allowing an attacker to formulate queries, whether malicious or benign, that obeyed them.

He set the script running and left the application to ping at the department's record-keeping data bank in the background. In a number of hours, a picture of the firewall configurations would began to take shape. He'd look for useful anomalies.

Then he'd exploit them.

He'd have the report—easy, convenient, and marginally illegal—in his hands sometime the next day. In the meantime, the money trail through London's company burned brighter, more elusive, and possibly more relevant to the counterfeiting. Using the name and IP address of WW's server, which he'd lifted when accessing London's e-mail after they'd first met, Trevor accessed a suite of VPN software and connected to WW's virtual private network. In less than a minute, he was in WW's systems, masquerading as a dead man who just couldn't give up his day job.

An hour later, he'd combed through the invoices received from Tereth and saved in the system within the past year. The Olaszrizling invoices were virtually undetectable from those for the Cab Franc and Sauvignon Blanc. Each one looked to have been delivered via e-mail:

> To: Dillon Farro <dillonfarro@WWImports.com>
> cc: Clara Whitley <clarawhitley@WWImports.com>

Like many small companies, WW's virtual filing cabinet included folders with general company information. He found one that contained employee data and, low and behold, login info for all of WW's employees. Lazy recordkeeping happened a lot. If a systems guy like him needed access for maintenance or to find and fix a problem, he often entered the system through individual user machines. So while each employee's login and password weren't commonly known, they typically weren't confidential.

Small fish like WW never gave much thought to their lax system security, leaving them ripe for exploitation.

Dillon Farro was third on the list. A classic password, too: $oneyonmy$ind!

Fitting.

Dillon's outgoing e-mails had stopped on the day of the Red Rocks incident. Trevor picked a Tereth invoice from a year ago and methodically began to connect the invoices used for WW's official accounting, and saved in the electronic filing system, with those Dillon had actually received via e-mail, previously deleted but all-to-easily recovered. Forty minutes later, he'd turned up a handful of saved invoices for the Olaszrizling. Not one of them had actually been received in Dillon's e-mail. Tereth was telling the truth. It hadn't sold Olaszrizling to WW.

The invoices saved in the system hadn't come from the vineyard. They'd merely been made to *look* like it.

A wave of something unforgiving and equally unpredictable danced around the edges of Trevor's awareness. This discovery dumped a few more titles into Dillon's cold lap—corporate defrauder, counterfeiter, endangerer of the public. Perhaps Dillon's array of interests had led him to wrist-breaker, too. Perhaps karma had demanded the ultimate price. And, perhaps, Dillon hadn't been the only traitor in London's midst. After all, another had been copied on each of the legitimate receipts for the Cab Franc and Sauvignon Blanc and even listed on the fake ones for good measure. That person ought to have noticed that the supposed Olaszrizling receipts had not materialized in the same way as the others.

For my sister, I'd take a bullet, London had said. Later, at the hospital, Clara Whitley had showed a fervent devotion to her sister. She'd looked scandalized at the mere mention of Dillon Farro and his vengeful father.

For my sister... Trevor's whole body clenched. London looked back at a dead employee and ex-lover and forward to a devious employee and sister. *I'd take a bullet...*

He'd crack heaven and face hell to ensure London never had to.

A soft ping pulled him from violent musings of re-killing the dead. Time and effort had softened his instinct to bring violence to the doorsteps of enemies. One *would think* slogging through the muck with Rhea would have blunted his instinct to protect.

Not tonight. He glanced at the instant messaging app that had popped up in the corner of the VPN client screen. London had just logged on.

His smile was lazy, even expectant. He waited, first a minute, then three. Better give her plenty of time to notice him, too.

******

A life without nights behind her scarred metal desk would hardly constitute life at all. The overhead lights in London's office flickered, taking turns hiding and then highlighting the stains in the industrial carpet. At her feet, London's new pet lounged beneath her old one. Both Sasha and Harriet were proving to be the useless guard animals they were, and Harriet had taken about three minutes to climb on top of the St. Bernard's snoozing form and settle in for her own nap.

Granted, the two had met while pent up together during her stint in the hospital, but they could at least pretend interest in their caretaker.

After Cole's departure from her apartment, London had diligently performed Sasha's evening routine, all the way down to the walk, the pills, the food, and even a shot with a real, live hypodermic needle. Then she'd come straight to the office. Ignorance only stayed blissful for so long. That bliss had run out about the time she'd peeled her lips off Trevor's and vomited in her warehouse trash can.

The bulleted list in front of her set out items to track with respect to the fake Olaszrizling: purchase contracts, invoices, copies of the bills of lading, and bank records. She pulled up her import/export contract with Tereth and began reading the deal she'd negotiated, back before business had gone sour. Rote terms swam across the screen, everything from quantities and pricing, to shipping carriers and the point at which title to the wine transferred from Tereth to WW. She hadn't agreed to minimum quantities, and they'd left the varietals on offer open-ended, meaning the contract terms applied to any type of wine WW decided to order—red, white, rosé, even sparkling.

The contract looked like at least fifty others WW maintained with suppliers around the world, but it put her in the right frame of mind. Turning to individual records, she called up files detailing each purchase from Tereth.

A text box popped up at the bottom of her screen. She hadn't been paying attention, but now she noted that she wasn't alone in the system.

Dillon Farro appeared to be working late.

Dillon. Farro. In her system, reaching out as if from the grave.

Her hands flew to her chest. Instead of a folder on the screen, she saw blood spill across concrete, wet and accusatory. The image flashed before she could button her defenses and call upon reason.

Guilt and sorrow—some for the man, more for the mistake that had taken him—forced her attention inward. She pinched her eyes closed. "Not real. Not even *kind* of real."

Chancing another look, she saw words waiting in the text box. An *impossible* message: *You'll never win the game if you keep handing out the passwords.*

Breath leaked from her lungs, first a trickle, then a flood. An image of Trevor seated behind a bank of blinking computer screens flashed to mind. His eyes would be lowered in concentration. The glare from the screens would yield to the harshness of his profile. Those big hands would glide surely across the keys, as though each press of a button would, without fail, conjure up the desired response. The devil thought he could work her strings from afar, that she would eventually waltz to his tune.

The message practically dared her to defy him. Interesting, since she had a history of doing exactly that.

Or maybe not.

This afternoon she'd accused Trevor of using her desire against her. In reality, he'd done the opposite. Their interlude had been focused on her—whatever she wanted, however she'd wanted it, all hers for the asking. After he'd brought her shattering pleasure, when she'd been soft and amenable, he'd gone, leaving only a warning: In bed, he'd give her everything, out of it, nothing. Those weren't the actions of a man using sex to manipulate or to achieve another goal. They were the actions of a man who couldn't resist her bed even though getting into it might *undermine* his goal.

The realization kicked up a heady sense of power. She wanted Trevor Rathlen enough to hide herself for a chance at a temporary taste of him.

He wanted her enough to let her do it. If they indeed played a game, it seemed she was one up.

Hands clammy but light, she set them on the keys and typed: *You'll never win* me *if you keep stealing them.*

Not ten seconds passed before "Dillon" disappeared.

CHAPTER 14

Trevor poured a splash of orange juice into a chilled glass and topped it with a generous helping of club soda. The loft looked like it always did—clean lines and shiny surfaces, the early morning sun shining through the window. No invoices littered the desk. No news articles clung to the corkboard on the wall. His firewall script crunched away discretely behind a screensaver showing a picture of his mountain bike. The clandestine discoveries of the previous night *almost* remained hidden beyond the murky pathways of the web. Only his blatant, purposeful hint had tipped London off to his midnight date with Brutus.

The risk had paid off, seeing how London had nearly beat the sun to his place. Spurring her had been the point, though he'd hoped to retrieve the police report from the night of Dillon's death prior to her arrival.

He handed her the drink. "My gut tells me you're avoiding alcohol." That and that fact that it was seven in the morning.

She accepted the glass and took a sip, letting her attention flow to a series of abstract prints coloring the opposite wall. "Is your gut ever wrong?"

"*Yes.*" Army. Rhea. And his impressions of London made three.

His stark answer bounced right off her red sundress. Wide shoulder straps and a high bodice framed a tempting square of golden skin beneath her throat. Lower, the skirt flared to a hem that fell a few inches above the knee. Lower still, yellow ballet flats made the siren look sweet.

He stood above her, Sasha between their almost-mingling legs, wanting to trace the line of material darting across the tops of her breasts, blocking them out, making her look demure and almost innocent. She likely expected a show of humility after last night's stunt.

She wouldn't get one.

London looked up, lips pursed and eyes narrowed. "Your brother paid me a visit."

Obviously. She'd trotted in with Sasha at her side, looking like the perfect city lady with a well-manicured behemoth on a short leash. "You kept your new pet a whole night."

"I'm keeping him the whole week."

Ah ha. "So you're here solely to compliment me on being a master strategist?" She *had* insinuated she could be won. If that didn't cement his status as a master, nothing did.

"More like a master manipulator," she countered. "First Sasha, and then a dead man running through my computer as though he occupied the next desk."

Trevor slapped a hand over his heart and did his best scandalized impression. "*No way.* Guess we should talk." Strategist, indeed.

"About your compunction toward *corporate espionage?*" Her voice dripped enough sugar to poison an elephant.

He stepped over Sasha and pressed his hands to the back of the couch, caging her in. "Whatever the lady likes." London claimed to resent being used—never mind that he hadn't and wouldn't use her—but the dress and the hour said she looked forward to his process, regardless of his point.

"There are so many conversation choices." He stroked across her shoulders, along her arms. "We could talk about my brother and whatever he told you. That one doesn't get out much, but when he does... We could talk about your computer systems, their weaknesses and their... other weaknesses. Or we could talk about how those weaknesses have led me halfway to answers. I no longer desire your cooperation, London. That makes *you*"—he stroked a finger into the valley between her breasts— "entirely extracurricular."

Her heart thudded against his light touch. "What did you learn?"

"Nervous?"

The shake of her head was too emphatic to be real. Maybe Dillon had been the fall guy, with London playing mastermind to her little sister's foot soldier. That would explain why she remained mum about the whole scenario. She knew exactly what he'd found in her systems and was more than willing to let him draw erroneous conclusions that painted her in an innocent light.

That or she *was* an innocent whose trust had been betrayed by those closest to her.

A kindred spirit.

No, a deceptively dangerous obsession. Trevor swallowed his rising doubt, not to wash it away, but to wash it down. He'd save the distrust for another day when what London had become *to him* didn't obliterate the probable reality. Today London was a golden girl between his knees, the kind of woman who thought like him and didn't waste a second without taking action. When he'd shown up to investigate her warehouse the other night, she'd already been halfway through the wine. Even after that painful, degrading setback, she'd immediately pressed on, digging into her electronic records and mirroring his next step.

She shivered, and a curl grazed his exploring hand. A whiff of vanilla floated upward, and he recalled the appreciation she'd shown his pie.

"I said"—she caught his wrist with her good hand—"what did you learn?"

"That I'm fascinated by you." London the bold or the soft spoken? The victim or the curse?

"You shouldn't be—"

"I *know*." *I simply no longer care.* Lazily, he rolled his grip to find hers. Sticking to the theme that she'd go first or not at all, he pressed her fingers beneath her bodice, then lower, until she cupped her breast. He kept his grip light. She could pull back with less effort than it would take to flick a feather.

"Trevor," she warned. Her gaze dipped. Then a flickering glance incinerated whatever willpower he'd thought to harness.

"Yes," he grated, "say my name. That's what I want. Then I want you to pull this pretty dress aside and let me lick between your legs until you scream it."

Those fluttering eyes practically smoldered. "You're a hedonist."

"Occasionally." Her hesitant but curious accusation decided him. He could separate work from play, the London of WW from the London that made him wish he was ten years younger and twenty less jaded. He pressed her fingers against a nipple, knowing the tips of her breasts had puckered and needed some love. "When it comes to sex, you need to be. How about I give you a few hours of soft sheets and knowing hands, an eager tongue and all the sex you can handle in between—slow, easy, irresistible morning sex. I bet you've never had it like that. I also bet you've wanted to." Fuck his ideals. If he couldn't cop to needing her for himself, he could always call his suggestion a favor. Before noon, she'd forget all about the man who'd hurt her. She'd be clawing the sheets and begging Trevor to rock her into next week.

He looked down, loving the way she relaxed into the feel of their combined touch. Strength and vulnerability looked back, her smarts warring with an innate shyness, maybe even naiveté. She convinced him that his uncompromising take on life—black or white, right or wrong, good or bad—oversimplified the complexities hidden behind a pair of arresting green eyes.

He released her hand and skimmed downward, finally ready to get complicated.

"Part your legs."

******

Fingers cupped between her thighs, pressing in a gentle pulse, compressing the dress crushed against her. London whimpered, sinking into the couch.

He tempted her with risks she couldn't take.

"You know how I want you," he said. "I want you more than I've ever wanted anything. And I've wanted much. Tell me you'll take me on. Come with me into the bedroom."

"I can't." Not until she told him she embodied his worst nightmare, one he had already survived and made no bones about refusing to revisit. The cinch of her past tightened around her chest like a corset, threatening the pleasure.

He didn't see. He mistook her refusal for a *nod* and a *wink*. He thought she wanted to be asked again, asked so nicely she couldn't refuse. A kiss, open-mouthed and drugging, burned across the bared skin at her collarbone. He nipped and then soothed, all the while gathering the fabric hiding her legs as his clever fingers continued her seduction.

"Part them," he said again. "Or come with me to the bedroom."

Urgency, almost panic, lit up her system. Blood roared in her ears, thrummed at her pulse, raced in her veins. Like before, London found herself reaching for one more stolen moment. What was the harm? She could come clean when his touch didn't skate along the smooth skin at the juncture of a thigh. She *would* tell him then. He deserved the truth as much as she deserved the rejection that would follow it.

London looked down at his hand helplessly. *But not yet. Please, please, not yet.* She let her legs go loose.

Those teasing fingers slid beneath her panties—*finally*—and into her warmth. "Come with me, London."

A coherent response had become impossible. London arched up into the perfect friction, again and again. "Trevor!"

"All right," he said, sliding and then dipping in a maddening rhythm. "Come *for* me."

The command rocked her control. She whimpered, biting down on her tongue as her sex spasmed with wave after wave of decadent pleasure. The apartment whirled around them, offering up only Trevor for stability. His steady heat warmed. His sturdy presence calmed. Yet with a few blunt words and soft touches, he'd stolen her wits.

He withdrew leisurely, as though he meant to emphasize just how much she wanted him to stay. Above, his eyes had slid shut, and the push and pull of his breath reminded her of a bull set to charge.

At length, he spoke, his voice deep, mesmerizing. "Come to the bedroom, London. If you do, I promise the best sex of your life." He straightened, looking like every inch away from her caused pain. "No, I promise the best sex of what I hope is your wildest imagination."

Of my life. Of my imagination. The man already understood the maze of her mind. Her life hadn't contained much in the way of sex to write home about. Her imagination, on the other hand…

She let a secret smile rule her lips. What woman couldn't claim an ocean of fantasies? So, brain fried from the deliciousness he'd already wrung from her, London let an earlier logic prevail.

Joy now. Pain later.

She slid her hand into his, and leveraged up off the couch.

A short while later, she lay stripped on the plush sheets he'd promised. Trevor had eased her clothing from her body, lips trailing behind the zipper of her dress, beneath the clasp of her bra, behind the wisp of her lace panties on her thighs. Then he'd left her with a veiled promise. "Three minutes. Relax. *Think.*"

Fantasize.

Dishes… a cupboard… then the fridge clinked and chimed from the kitchen. A minute passed, a minute in which she struggled against the urge to reach for the parts of her he so liked to watch her touch.

Long before three minutes ticked by, he returned with a covered tray and set it on the bedside. "Do you trust me?"

Trust. The operative word that wove through the very fiber of their relationship. Sometimes the seam sewed straight. Other times it zigged and zagged in an unpredictable pattern.

With that one question, he traced a satin sleeping mask upward along her body until he reached the crown of her head, which he lifted gently to cradle in his palm. The mask slipped over her eyes.

Unease settled in her stomach. A blindfold called for *blind* trust. "Wait—"

The satin slid upward and light flooded her vision. Sight restored, she saw the concern banked in his eyes. "Are you afraid? Don't consider this an *implement.*"

Nothing but pleasure lay behind that mask. Intellectually, she knew it well. "Not fear—"

"Caution?" The question fell lightly against her temple.

At her nod, his voice dropped. "Remember what I promised. Not just tonight, but before as well. It'll be slow, angel. Nice and easy. And you'll *like* it."

The determination in his tone swayed her. She opened her mouth, looked at him—and froze, eyes locked on his. He didn't appear impatient, like he was saying all the right things in order to get on with it. Instead, his wary expression offered choice. He wanted her, badly, but he wanted her trust more.

If she could fight her demons and believe in him, maybe he'd be able to do the same when the time came.

A hand—hers, she realized—floated upward to the mask that rested on her forehead, slipping it into place. "I know." She patted around until she blindly rubbed over his lips. "Show me. Please."

A nip pricked her index finger. Then he whispered, "Lie back," and pressed her into the pillow top.

Lying before him nude, sightless, and totally open, she shivered when his fingers skimmed over her collarbone. She heard a murmured, "How do you like to be touched, London?"

Surprise and anticipation stole the breath she'd been about to take. *I like how* you *touch me*. "I'm not sure I know how to answer that."

He emitted a low sound from deep in his throat. "Let's find out."

Instead of the clanking dishes she'd anticipated, she heard the rip of foil and knew he'd rolled a condom over his impressive erection, which meant...

"Oh *God*." She whimpered when she felt him slowly pressing inside, without preface or warning. Gasping, her body greeted him with a great rush of warmth. "I didn't know."

"You love being filled like this," he growled through obviously clenched teeth. Then, without altering the rhythm of his dragging, torturous strokes, his low whisper sounded in her ear. "Today"—his hips bucked forward and she gulped the warm air engulfing them, relaxing to take him deep—"we start here. Your body accepts every inch so beautifully."

She couldn't have imagined the erotic feel of him sliding inside her without the ability to see or to guess what would come next. In offering blind trust, she'd gained a freedom to physically feel him differently. Trevor, undiluted by her past or their present.

And so far, extremely *gentle* Trevor.

He entered her again and pulled free in a long, agonizing slide—once, twice, then a third time—exactly what she needed. But when she extended her legs to encircle his hips, encouraging the drugging strokes, he pulled away. Completely. She keened at the loss, panting and sawing her legs together.

"I think we've learned you like *that*." Trevor's punctuated words barely registered as he kissed his way down her throat and licked between breasts, stopping to blow hot puffs over her abdomen.

"I like it." She *loved* it. Desperation clawed at her. Empty, yet ready, her swollen tissues clenched on air, demanding the return of that decadent glide as she extended her arms to drag him close.

"Not yet," he said just before his warm, wet tongue found her center. He lapped at her softly, thoroughly. When she knew she'd go mad, he slid one thick finger inside, timing the tender thrusts to the beat of his tongue.

She gasped out her pleasure, body tightening as she scratched at the comforter below her, imagining what he looked like settled between her thighs, indulging in her arousal. "Trevor, please, let me—"

He rubbed his chin against her, literally bathing in her core. "Come again. Right now. Let me taste more of you," he demanded, before flattening his tongue and letting her drag her clit over its softness as she lurched in climax.

Before the shudders dissipated, she sensed a hint of movement. Then his engorged erection nudged her entrance.

"Harder." The plea escaped without thought for what she wanted, only for what she *needed*. Soft might be nice in her old world, but she craved Trevor's strength, knowing he'd only use it to make her happy. "Harder, Trevor, I—"

He slammed inside, kicking off another round of pulses that massaged them both.

"You're so responsive. I need more of you." His voice sounded strained as he rooted out mutual pleasure. "The feel of you is killing me."

When he plunged in at an angled thrust, she felt a hot, melting sensation that was somehow different than the times he'd made her come before. Stilling, he growled and licked into her mouth. "There?" He moved again, rubbing over that same searing spot inside.

A prickling sensation rippled from the inside out, and she thrashed beneath him in an effort to get more, feeling her body pulsing around him in wet welcome.

"Definitely, there." Keeping the slant perfect, he repeatedly dragged his cock over the throbbing internal nerves. With each pass, she heated further, offering rushes of desire until she feared she'd drown in her own response. In the past, she'd tensed before orgasm, but now her limbs relaxed until she lay limp and boneless, writhing beneath him as she cried, "Don't stop. Please, not this time."

"I'll do this as long as you want me to."

She moaned, lost to a series of internal contractions that made the rest of her twitch. "Keep going."

"Forever, angel." And he did. All strength and coiled muscle, he worked her though the most compelling moments of recent memory. Only when she resurfaced and reared up against him did he shift. With an arm beneath her shoulders, he lifted her up and into his lap, never breaking contact. Then he drove into her in sharp, almost fierce, thrusts. "Going to come. *Fuck*, without the condom, you'd feel it like a thrust."

The words flooded her with new heat. Trevor stiffened, jerked his head to the spot where her shoulder met her neck and, *Jesus*, bit softly. She shuddered, tensing around him in an orgasm that should have been physically impossible after all they'd shared.

Slowing, but maintaining a lazy glide, he murmured, "You like that, too." She confirmed the languid smile in his voice when he lifted the satin mask and cast a glance at the tray next to their bed. "And we haven't even availed ourselves of my carefully laid plans."

Her body threw an involuntary clench. "Couldn't we still?"

He groaned and bent to her nipple. Licking around the hardened peak, he said, "You're sore—"

"No, I'm—" *Perfect. Ecstatic.*

Rocking forward, he pulled away ever so slowly, repositioning her on the bed before disposing of the condom. His eyes devoured every inch of her tousled form, limbs askew. "Not too hard?"

She shook her head, still dreamy. He hadn't ramped up until she'd asked, but when he had... *divine.*

"Look at your neck, those pretty nipples, your soft center. All swollen. *Lovely.*"

She stayed still, tracking his movements as he leaned over and removed the cover from the first dish. He dangled a few cucumber slices before her eyes, gently placing one over her lips, then the mark at her neck, followed by two more over her reddened nipples. "Did you know these have anti-inflammatory *and* cooling properties? I've used them as compresses for years after training." At first, the small pads shocked, but then, as he'd said they would, they calmed her tender skin.

The lid vanished from the second dish—this time a basin of ice water—and Trevor plunged a cloth napkin into the cold bath and wrung it out. He trailed the cloth over her arms and stomach before dragging it below. When the icy chill met her heated flesh, she bucked, dislodging the now-warmed cucumbers, which he gently replaced with fresh rounds. Then, pressing the cloth against her body in small circles, he began talking. "You're so beautiful here. All rosy and soft. I want to nuzzle in. Open a bit more... perfect."

To her amazement, the ministrations weren't embarrassing. His obvious enjoyment lent the task a searing sensuality, leaving no doubt a lover saw to her comfort. She allowed her lids to grow heavy, enjoying the moment, when she heard him reach for the third, insulated dish.

Snapping to awareness, she saw him extract a fresh ice cube, not one that had partially melted in the water. He eased the ice inside her.

On a low moan, she surged downward toward him. "Trevor, what are you doing to me?"

"Caring for you. Learning you," he answered simply. Bending his head, he began to lick over and around and finally, into, her melting channel. The juxtaposition of the soft, warm tongue brushing over cold tingling skin and into ice sent her flying all over again. He looked up with a wink. "And hopefully creating a monster."

As she floated back to Earth, she realized that for the first time, she'd dared to be free, utterly sexual and uninhibited and without fear or self-consciousness. He'd shown her how.

"And you *really* like that," he said, his voice smug and self-satisfied.

She smiled to herself, half appreciation, *all* gratification.

A sex(y) monster. She liked the sound of that.

******

Rustling sheets woke Trevor from a dream about having London from behind, mewling with pleasure as he stretched her over a stack of wine boxes in her warehouse. The scent of freshly cut wooden crates floated around them, and she bit down on his wrist to keep quiet with each surge.

His eyes winked open. Instantly, all he saw was London, nude and as curvy as a frescoed goddess kneeling overhead. Her breasts swayed heavily above that tiny, tapered waist. Her hips flared to a perfect cradle that begged to cushion him as he sank deep.

A light touch swirled around his navel, painting circles and then figure-eight patterns that drifted lower and lower. Trevor realized she wasn't currently concerned with his face. London focused on the erection that had showed up courtesy of his dream.

"You're awake." His voice sounded hoarse from the orgasm-induced nap that had followed their earlier play and the fact that her soft hand had *arrived*.

Green eyes, dark with arousal, lifted to his. A subtle blush followed, pinkening her honeyed skin to a rich, burnished taupe. "Part of *you* has been awake for a while." She turned back to his dick, like she couldn't stand to look away.

His hips rolled of their own accord, and her grip tightened. Looking almost mesmerized, London began to drift lower, closer and closer, inch by inch.

Fucking hell. His grip weaved into her hair. "Christ. Suck my cock, London."

She jerked, and he immediately relaxed his fist. He didn't—couldn't—let go, but he kept his hand light, petting her hair instead of pulling it.

"You'd want that?" she asked.

Did he honestly hear surprise in her question? Surprise that he'd want her plush lips stretched around him? "Seeing you like this, *every* man in the world would want that."

"Even if I'm not very good at it?"

He would kill Dillon all over again. He would desecrate the man's grave. "Honey, I don't care if you suck hard or soft. I don't care if you lick or rub or give the head a chaste kiss." *Just touch me.* "I don't care if you bite me, for God's sake. Believe me when I say *you can do no wrong.*"

London started moving again, sinking until her lips pressed against the wide head. She licked. "You're gorgeous here. The veins almost look like they hurt."

Right now, they *did.*

She licked again, then slid her mouth over the slit. A light suction enveloped the whole head, while she let her small hand slide back and forth near the base. "London, *this.*" A sigh escaped his tight control. "I knew you'd suck me like this."

Tentatively, but with growing enthusiasm for each lick, each pull.

The heat of the late morning combined with their movements released hints of her vanilla scent. They hit him in the face with every indulgent surge. His fantasy was playing out. London had her mouth on him, and she was so warm and giving and *fucking good at sucking his dick.*

After endless moments of torture, London began to glide lower over his shaft, eventually kissing her pumping fist on each upstroke. His eyes shot wide. The words he tried to say shifted on his tongue, coming out garbled and primal. Below, his hips bounced, and he slid his hand to her shoulder to keep himself from forcing her rhythm.

She didn't need the help. With each stroke, she murmured and cooed soft, pleased sounds to his cock. He could almost *feel* her smile.

Lush pleasure built until he knew he couldn't hold back. Suddenly, she pulled the head free with a loud pop. "Now *you're* going to come."

He bucked up. "*Yes.*" *Undoubtedly.* But not inside her sweet mouth. Not today. He would do nothing to detract from her gift.

"Fist me hard, London. Don't stop." At the same time, he moved his hand to her neck and eased her upward so he could kiss that talented mouth rather than flood it.

"Let me—"

"My mouth," he said in a rush. "Kiss me here." The demand was guttural, nearly incoherent.

But she understood. Her lips met his as he growled and pumped an endless stream of heat between them.

CHAPTER 15

"I didn't think you'd show." Brian stretched his legs long in front of him. He couldn't help but examine Clara as she sank primly onto the park bench at his side, her black hair glinting bright enough to be blinding in the sun. She wore cobalt skinny jeans and a gray tank. Her little feet rested on a pair of gold gladiator sandals. The look, Brian could appreciate, came off as effortless, but cool.

Suggestive as hell.

Her sunny smile didn't waver. "Free lunch. Handsome man. Why wouldn't I be right here?"

He shrugged, knowing his return smile had more in common with a smirk. On a shark. "Because a smart girl like you knows what they say about free lunches."

"Ah. Have you come to scare me, then, Brian Wentworth the *Third*?"

So they'd both done their research. Brian plunked a paper bag down between them. He hadn't reneged on his offer of sandwiches. She'd better like turkey. "I'm not aiming to be particularly scary"—*yet*—"Clara Elaine Whitley the *First*."

He'd spoken with Trevor late the night before. They'd swapped stories—Brian's eyewitness account of Clara's discrete indiscretion with the pills in her truck and Trevor's feeling that WW's trail of invoices pointed at Dillon the dead guy but proved that Clara had to at least *know* some of the Olaszrizling hadn't come through approved channels.

If to divide was to conquer, then Clara had become Brian's half of the war.

She dug into the bag and pulled out a sandwich, holding it up in question. He nodded. *Be my guest.*

"So, super sleuth," she began, "you sent your hounds after my sister, and now you're dogging me. How can I help you with the burning questions plaguing our time?"

This wasn't the bubblegum Clara he'd seen at the hospital or the Clara Trevor had described from conversations with London. According to London, this sister was the friendly, outgoing salesperson that could charm a bedpost. She loved wine, which London believed was an offshoot of a healthy thirst for life. London had told Trevor she would "take a bullet" for Clara.

Today's Clara brandished a sarcastic streak. Brian's ire almost transformed into something more like interest. He could appreciate a dark side. He could respect it. He could even get behind the skill it would have taken to convince her family she was all rainbows and ponies and everything nice.

The tough act might even be real. Guess they'd see.

"I have a secret." He had many, actually.

Clara stopped on her way to a first bite. "And you felt the need to share it with a stranger over sandwiches in the park?"

"Since it's *your* secret, yes."

The hoagie didn't so much as fall from her grip as it did bust in half and break from her clenched fist. "I don't have any secrets, especially not secrets that would concern you."

"Maybe, maybe not."

She stood and brushed crumbs from those tight, colorful jeans that made him wish he was here to get on her good side instead of to annihilate any chance of that ever happening.

"I won't tell you anything, *anything*," she emphasized, "about my sister."

She was a good guesser, and so eager to protect. Brian could have clapped with giddiness. Instead, he handed her his sandwich. He wouldn't call Clara too thin, but she appeared delicate. Breakable. She needed a few sandwiches to withstand what she had coming. "You, your parents, London herself… you try to prove your sister is the staid little angel she appears. By painting her such a bore, you might as well hang a blinking sign around her neck. Your denials only heighten my interest."

Even though—maybe *because*—Clara denied so prettily.

"There's nothing to deny."

True, for London, though Brian wouldn't admit that he'd pretty much cleared WW's owner. Not so for Clara. The fresh calories he'd donated hung from her trembling fingers. Brian knew plenty about drugs, though he'd barely dabbled, letting off steam with booze and sex and the occasional recreational mind fuck when life got him down. He knew, however, that decreased appetite, heightened emotions, physical fragility, an inconstant personality, and now jittering limbs all pointed to one thing.

Clara had a problem.

"Nice purse, sweet thing." He didn't bother to look at the bag. "Is that dyed lamb? Rather small. A bag like that only holds the essentials. What do you consider essential, I wonder?"

She rolled her eyes, right back in her head as though she'd been practicing since turning sixteen. Too bad no matter how hard she tried, his question couldn't be taken for a joke. The heat beating down on his dark suit had grown uncomfortable, and every second he spent sparring with this damaged beauty was another one lost for his impatient client back in the motherland. The Whitley women had proven to be wily adversaries, but this investigation was about to jump to the fast track.

Clara reached for her green satchel with one hand and pelted the bench with his sandwich—no respect, this girl—with the other. He stopped her with an easy grip. "Now, now, no need to get hasty."

Despite the sun and a disgusting lack of breeze, her wrist scalded his palm. Touching Clara felt like dunking his hand in boiling water—all kinds of hot and bad for him.

"I'm not rushing," she clarified, and he heard the jitter from her hands enter her voice. "I'm simply done with your food, your questions, and you."

Brian thumped his chest with a mocking gasp. "Not me! You can't be done with me!" He sobered. "Because I won't let you be done with my questions."

Ready to be right, he tugged the bag free and jangled it over her head. Then, done with the game, he gripped the purse high against his chest and unzipped.

The bottle bobbed straight to the top. *Well, fuck.* "I wanted you to surprise me."

He pilfered the bottle and let the bag drop into her grasping hands. One look at the label confirmed a Ritalin prescription for London Whitley, straight from the hand of Dr. Victoria Whitley and filled the day before. Three pills rattled around the bottom of a damn long tube. "You know they call this stuff 'kiddy coke?'"

Clara recoiled. He swore he saw a flash of pain in her eyes before her bravado returned in the form of a hard stare and narrowed lips. "Sounds like *you're* the one in the know."

A diversion might have worked earlier—perhaps wild gushing over his sandwich? Even a hello kiss?—but not now. "'Coke,'" he drawled, "because if you take it in massive quantities—like I saw you do yesterday in the hospital parking lot—or if you crush it and snort it, you get high. Addicts add 'kiddy' because the high is short, and the crash is long. It's not quite up to par, I'm told, with the real thing. But it'll do, and it's hella habit forming."

Clara made a half-hearted swipe for the bottle. "I don't owe you an explanation." Her voice had gone hoarse, each word a struggle.

"But you do." That's why he'd asked for the meeting. Gathering leverage took foresight and planning, after all. "I suppose when I explain your drug abuse to your sister—the sneaking around, the sheer quantity of pills missing from this almost-empty bottle—you'll have good reasons for her to understand."

Clara stared over his shoulder, only acknowledging his taunt with a faint nod.

"Then why not tell me before I tell her? Otherwise she'll be getting the short of what *I* know." He let his tone insinuate that his version wouldn't do her any favors.

"It's not a regular thing," Clara whispered. "You wouldn't."

"Oh, sweet thing"—he tipped her chin to face him—"I *would*. I *will*." Clara might nick the occasional bottle of pills from her sister under the guise of a helping hand, but that wouldn't keep her supplied if the empty bottle was, as he suspected despite her protests, evidence of a childhood habit that had vastly overshot childhood. If that was the case, Clara likely used London as *one* source of many. There were others who, unlike her sister and parents, demanded payment. In the quantities Clara appeared to use, she required money to pay, lots of cash that might cause her to sell her sister's business down the river for a quick buck.

Which made Clara's problem and London's reaction to it his number one target in the game of Pin the Poisoned Wine Bottle on the Whitley Sister. "I'll sing like a canary, all about drugs and the dangerous booze you've planted to pay for them."

Clara shrank from his touch, folding herself back onto the seat. She crossed her arms over her chest, letting the little purse dangle, open and nearly empty, from a wrist. Her gaze straddled the thin line between vacant and desperate.

Contrary to popular belief, Brian didn't enjoy breaking people. Most of the time. Mainly he understood that buildings required bricks, and puzzles required pieces. Without all the bricks or all the pieces, a job couldn't be done. Fortunately—or unfortunately, depending on one's perspective—the missing pieces generally fell in his lap in the form of others' harnessed desperation. He had only to recognize the potential and manipulate accordingly. If he could do that, people tended to land in their preordained positions.

Enter Clara. As he took in her pretty, upturned face, he saw a deep sadness chase across her features. Her kind of haunted didn't come from being wronged. It came from the regret of wronging others. He understood the feeling all too well. So while her hidden Achilles heel left her squarely in his pocket, he stayed quiet, hesitant to tighten the proverbial thumbscrews.

"The wine isn't what you think," she began haltingly.

He sat, keeping to his end of the bench, unsure if another touch would come off as a kind of condescension, a veiled threat. "The most intriguing things never are."

Awkwardness grew between them, the brightness of midday failing to relieve the palpable tension.

"Dillon Farro," Clara blurted. "He wasn't good for my sister."

Okaaaay. An unexpected turn.

Clara looked him in the eye, the blankness gone as though it had never been. Here was a woman to be reckoned with, pills or not. "He hurt her, and she let him. Can't you see that man had to go?"

CHAPTER 16

The Denver Broncos jersey London had foraged from Trevor's closet exposed an entire shoulder but covered her knees. She noted her sundress stretched neatly at the end of the bed. Trevor had even dug her bra and panties from the mess of sheets and folded them neatly next to the bodice.

She couldn't put the clothes on yet.

The warm, sensual haze of their stolen hours had fled the moment she'd come to alone in his king size. If she re-dressed, the final lingering flickers of closeness would disappear behind the formality of sliding zippers and clicking heels. His kiss on her neck would become his mouth saying good-bye, and the most tantalizing hours of her life would end in a late day walk of shame.

The two of them had agreed to one hell of a truce. They'd dropped his job and her secrets outside the bedroom door. Yet, from her silent stance near his nightstand, she heard the creak of Trevor's industrial office chair in the common room, its leather and metal gliding across concrete. The printer hummed over crinkling sheets with noisy abandon. Even Trevor's nonsensical murmurings to Sasha pounded in her ears.

Like Trevor had done after round one, she'd dozed after round two. Staying awake had been a pipe dream after all the exertion, not to mention his huge, fluffy bed and the sun lulling her through the oversized windows. Only instead of waking her with his mouth, Trevor had left the bed, arranged her clothes in a manner that screamed *get dressed*, and snuck off to his desk.

She stepped out of the bedroom and padded his direction on soft, bare feet. Halfway there, Sasha gave her away with a groaning lift of his head and a lazy flick of the tail. Trevor stilled his typing hands. A Google search popped up to replace a black screen with ungodly tiny script. To her, his methods were smoke and mirrors, but disappearing command prompts spoke of his earlier warning.

We could talk about your computer systems, their weaknesses... Or we could talk about how those weaknesses have led me halfway to answers. I no longer desire your cooperation, London. That makes you... entirely extracurricular.

So far the man had proved exceedingly good at gentle when *she* needed it and ruthless when *he* did. She affected a shallow cough and waited.

After a pause, he typed something in the search bar, saying, "Good nap?"

She could only nod, worried that "answers" meant her life story—Trevor had proven himself a detail guy—and wondering how much time she had to come clean. Before she realized the back of his head couldn't hear her body language, he spun in his chair.

Their eyes met, and a complicated sensation knotted in her chest. They spoke over each other.

"If I'd have known you were a football fan—"

"I'm sorry about your shirt—"

He kept talking over the apology she didn't really mean. "I'd have thrown your dress from the balcony."

Then *quiet*. The next look between them passed more raw emotion than the previous several hours spent touching, kissing, licking. *Fucking.*

London knew Trevor wouldn't call it that. He'd rarely said the word in her presence. She also knew they'd both shelved a part of themselves—he his ulterior motives and she the very answers he meant to find—in order to have each other. With that much of them hidden, how could sex be anything *but* fucking?

And, still, this look said they might be more than the sum of their lies. He was saying she meant something beyond the bunk wine, while she plead with him to understand that her withholding was done only for a chance at this moment.

Except neither of them actually spoke, and like all fleeting miracles, it passed.

She gulped down a breath. If the axe was to fall, she might as well get it over with. "Just now? What were you working on?"

Careful deliberation flickered behind eyes that could be equally giving and shrewd. "A bank. A bank chain, actually. A security breach compromised member information across the country—names, addresses, passwords, *pin numbers*. Lots of people will be getting those letters they hate, the ones enclosing a new debit card along with a recommendation for a fraud alert with Equifax and Trans Union."

"So you?" she prompted.

"I work out how the little deviants got in."

She forced a smile. "So tell me, *how?*"

The dark contemplation she'd watched cross his face a minute before resurfaced. He didn't want to explain. "The same way I would."

London winced at the bite in his tone, at the warning it carried. Trevor meant for her to know that any time he wanted her secrets he'd reach out and grab them. The aggression shouldn't surprise her. After all, they'd abandoned the safe haven of the bedroom. He was back to being ruthless.

Which she preferred. Those moments at the hospital, when she'd thought he'd used her body for easy answers, had been some of the worst of her life.

She sidled to the couch and sat, tucking her legs against her chest inside the oversized jersey. "This morning you mentioned finding answers when you helped yourself to my files."

"Yes." His eyes asked what his mouth didn't. *What more should I know?*

"Dillon was behind the fakes, wasn't he?"

Dillon had liked money and lacked respect. He'd had the knowledge, the access, and the motive to use her company as a front to make a few bucks at her expense. Their final night together had proven his true feelings for her had run less Dr. Jekyll and more Mr. Hyde.

That last conversation on the steps of Red Rocks would never be forgotten.

She'd tried.

When forgetting had proven futile, she'd *ignored*. Because every time she let that night in, she feared the term "accident" didn't quite cover Dillon's death. Curling into the warmth, the safety, of Trevor's shirt, London let herself delve into memories she'd been desperate to destroy.

A new shipment of Olaszrizling had arrived in the warehouse that day, a towering pallet that far surpassed WW's order numbers for the previous vintage. London hadn't been babysitting Dillon, but the sheer volume had been hard to miss, especially in light of the complaints they'd received on older bottles.

Later in the afternoon she and Dillon had arranged takeout on a blanket, ready to watch the sunset amongst other picnickers and after-work warriors who ran Red Rock's steep stairs for exercise. Much of her relationship with Dillon had been spent doing normal things in abnormal ways. They had cooked meals in silence, watched movies from separate couches, and escorted resentment on dates like a trusty third wheel.

Making conversation more than anything, London had asked Dillon about the order. Why that wine? Why that much? The risk had struck her has unnecessary.

The idea that the wine might be counterfeit hadn't occurred to London until long after Dillon had died, when Trevor had burst into her life with his strange balance of easy acceptance and unwavering distrust. That night at the amphitheater, she'd simply worried about where her company would land if Dillon had exercised poor judgment. What if Tereth repeated its problems with this year's Olaszrizling, leaving her with thousands of dollars of wine she couldn't sell?

The conversation had started with a few simple questions. She hadn't necessary pegged Dillon with a wrong call, but as the owner, she'd been curious as to his thoughts and motivations. Separated by a pile of Chinese takeout buckets, Dillon's usual antipathy had turned to seething agitation. Her intervention had been an overstep, but, accustomed to Dillon's more passive-aggressive attacks, London had powered through his visible anger. This was her business, her livelihood, her *everything*.

London would always marvel at how she'd gradually allowed her workplace subordinate to become the unquestionable king of her castle. Bit by bit, she'd let her power erode, until Dillon had felt justified, even at ease, in questioning her intellect, her physical value, her very worth. Near the end, he'd been willing to cross the most shocking boundaries without fear of reprisal.

But his fall *had* been an accident. London hugged her knees tighter to her chest, searching Trevor's glinting gaze for any hint that he'd let this go for one more day—a day of facing the truth and coming to terms with her story, a day of contemplation about how to let Trevor in.

Because if *she* saw blurred lines between her innocence and guilt, then Trevor would never see beyond them.

Cutting into her reverie, Trevor answered her question about Dillon's involvement in the counterfeiting. "Yes," he said, searching her face. "My guess is Dillon forged receipts from Tereth, then got the wine from who knows where. We need to search bank records. I bet we find split payments that aren't reflected in WW's well-cooked books."

Sickened, London's fingers curled into her shins until she felt the bite of her nails. That sick bastard had stolen more than her confidence. He'd taken her *money*.

Trevor cocked his head. His eyes roamed her folded body, down over the bright orange material that shielded her clenched form like a tent. "It's amazing you manage to keep anything hidden. Right now I can *see* your confliction. Do you feel bad that he's dead?"

There was no stopping the gasp that whistled through London's teeth. Trevor's simple question kicked off a series of snapshots. One after another, she relived the horror of that night.

Flash. Dillon reacting to her questions about the wine with unexpected vitriol. "*I have it fucking handled.*"

Flash. Her uncharacteristic doubts. "*Maybe, maybe not.*"

Flash. His demand—his *warning*?—to let it go.

Flash. Her demand that he respect her oversight—no orders over five thousand without her approval.

Voices rising. Both of them standing. The concrete amphitheater echoing Dillon's wrath and her resistance.

Joggers slowing. Picnickers staring.

Her claim that she could only be his boss, not his girlfriend. Being both didn't work.

A curse. A shove. Then... *pain.* The sound of her wrist snapping between the crush of her falling hip and the unforgiving concrete.

Dillon looming overhead, outwardly extending a hand to help her up, eyes secretly blazing with the promise of retribution.

The knowledge that if she dared to let him too close, he'd make her pay in private, when she least expected a fight.

Fear. Of blood on her thighs. Of tears on her cheeks.

A mad scramble away from danger.

A defensive kick to his shin. Another, even more panicked.

Stumbling. Flailing. A surprised bellow.

Silence.

Then so much blood and too many questions before the world cried "accident" and buried its dead.

"Do you?" Trevor pressed. "Do you regret his death?"

"Regret?" she croaked, now shaking beneath his shirt. What did he know?

"From what I've seen, the man was an ass." An understatement. Trevor's expression said if Dillon had lived, he'd soon wish otherwise. "Do you miss the guy? Wish he was here? Are you stalling this investigation for someone who wouldn't have done the same for you?"

Relief unwound the tension in her balled limbs. These were normal questions, not suspicious ones. A deep breath lent her the strength to sit straight. "I don't miss him." She only *wished* she did. Plus, in a way, she *had* been stalling the investigation by giving in to her fear that Trevor would learn the details of Dillon's death and disappear from her life forever.

The stalling had to stop.

Trevor flashed a cool smile. If he saw her despair, he didn't let on. "Good." He spun in the chair to face the monitor. Soon a map popped up. Red dots peppered the streets of downtown, mere steps from his building. "For now, what do you say to a roving dinner, a la food truck?"

London shelved the memories of Dillon's fall behind the mental wall she'd built to cage them. *Dillon* had died. She had not. And every breath in Trevor's unrelenting presence jolted like an electrified prod. He was teaching her. If she owned the ugliness, life could be beautiful. If she denied it, life could fall apart.

"I'd love that," she said. More than anything.

Knowing she shouldn't, helpless to resist, London promised herself *one* more day. After a last night with Trevor, she'd use the time to dig through her records and trace the paper through Dillon's foray into disorganized crime. Then she'd tell Trevor everything.

Everything.

******

"You *have* to try these." Trevor started her on fish tacos. The truck's bright pink sheen belied the serious food coming out the side window. Cilantro and grilled meat spiced the air a half a block away, and when he passed over their shared plate and she took a first mouthful, he watched the tension slip from her composed features.

Bliss. London had called him a hedonist. Yet she'd lowered her guard for pie and tacos and the steady tide that swept her to orgasm. He rubbed a thumb over her lips, which were closed and undulating with each hinge of her jaw.

She tried to pass the plate back after the one bite, but he held up his hand. "Have as much as you want. I'll polish off the rest. Remember, though, this is the first truck in a long route."

"That's what the map was?"

He nodded. "I'm surprised you haven't noticed the food truck extravaganza that's taken over the city. I swear Denver's best food rolls with these trucks. You just have to know where they are."

After a third bite, she pushed the plate his way and refused any more. "I'm saving myself." Her gaze roamed over his shoulders and then… down. A whistle sounded from the back of her throat. "I have a feeling I'll be outmatched at an eat-a-thon."

He patted his stomach. "I'm a growing boy." When she let go like this, he could feel the life roaring inside her. He loved relaxing her to the point that she let herself be carefree. If left to him, London would do as she liked, not as she'd been taught. No more moderating her voice, stifling her laughter, or counting every calorie. The London that simmered below the surface liked to roll on the floor with dogs. She craved new foods in exotic places. She longed for more boundaries with her family and fewer with him.

For God's sake, her mouth had smiled around his dick in the light of day.

They walked the streets as late afternoon faded to dusk, using his mobile map as a guide. As far as finding the trucks went, well, there was an app for that. The taco truck paled in comparison to the traveling wood-fired pizza, and by the time they reached his personal favorite, N'awlins Cajun and Creole, he had to down the lion's share of their muffuletta sandwich.

He licked at the olive tapenade oozing from the side of the bread that had been piled high with salami, ham, and mortadella. "I'm glad you like meat. I don't think I could be with a woman who doesn't eat meat."

Her mouth quirked, and he realized what he'd implied. "I mean that *literally*, as in salami and meatballs."

A fake wince told him he'd only made things worse for himself. "Must like 'meat,'" she confirmed. "What else do you want?" Her light tone didn't mask the seriousness of the question. At the same time, he hadn't hid the answer.

"I've been telling you all along."

"True."

A brief acknowledgement, but one that slammed her barriers back into place. Trevor could sense tension building within her like a cold rubber band, ready to snap if stretched one more inch.

Without another prompt, she filled in the blanks. "You value honesty above all things." A pause. "Your brother told me about your military background."

During the double-edged dog drop. "Of course he did." Cole in love had taken on many of his talkative fiancée's traits. There weren't many boundaries that Lissa, and now apparently Cole, refused to cross.

"Cole said you'd requested—and been promised—certain technology. When the equipment didn't show, you were ordered to move on a dangerous mission without it. People died because your team went in ill-equipped."

"My brother was thorough."

She shrugged. "He loves you. Bringing Sasha to me was a scouting mission. Turns out our younger siblings want to take care of us."

Given Brian's report on Clara Whitley, Trevor had a feeling his brother and London's sister had very different goals.

London's gaze flicked to her wringing hands. "Clara couldn't stand Dillon. She never warmed to him. In fact, time only made things worse."

"Smart girl." Maybe Brian had misjudged.

London ignored the dis, saying, "So you left the military and entered a field where your job is to find the truth using whatever means, shady or not, are necessary."

"I try to wear the white hat, but that about sums it up."

"Except in all your planning for a simple existence where *you* pull the strings, you didn't count on Rhea. She came along and surprised you with her double life."

Which had made things so much worse. In the service he'd relied on people capable of deadly deceit in the pursuit of whatever "higher" purpose they served, so he'd been on the lookout with Rhea. "I knew she had secrets"—*like you*—"for years." He threw their empty paper plate in the trash before he ended up mangling it in a fist. "I didn't guess the extent of them. You asked what I look for in a woman, and you're right about honesty, but let's add 'non-murderous bitch' for good measure."

London might be holding back, but he knew she wasn't a killer. If he could get her to open up, she'd check all the boxes on his short list, a list that didn't apply to her because he didn't particularly care about her qualities or her faults. He cared about *her*. Flawed, complicated, secretive London, who loved her family too much and herself too little, who was beginning to see Dillon had betrayed her in big ways and small, but who didn't speak out against him.

Beautiful London.

Giving London.

London who'd instantly sobered at his talk of murder, her ocean of questions run dry. A sheen of unfallen tears made her eyes shine in the evening light. "I'm sorry for what happened to you."

She cried for him, when he'd promised to find her out. This very second his software program pinged away at the police firewall. Later tonight he'd deploy a remote administration tool and then print the file covering Dillon's accident like he was Officer of the Month. Trevor didn't know exactly what the report would say, and he didn't expect exciting reading, but he knew accessing the info without her knowledge was an invasion of her privacy. She'd guarded the fact of Dillon's death too closely to be comfortable with him gorging on the details.

That hesitance was exactly why he had to do it.

He leaned in and pressed a kiss to her brow. "Don't cry." Not for him. Not as he went behind her back. "Those days are over. They shaped me." Into a distrustful bastard who couldn't let time work things out. "Special forces left me strong"—*and suspicious*—"and gave me skills I use every day." To make a living. To make a difference. "When inclined, I can be the watchdog I couldn't be back then. And Rhea was a lesson, one I'm glad I learned." Even though it was one London might not appreciate.

She blinked at the appearing stars, visibly wrestling for control. Not one tear fell, but her mouth opened hesitantly. Then closed. Then opened again. "Trevor…?"

"Yes."

He could see the yearning in her expression, that of a woman who wanted to unburden herself so they could move forward. Just as quickly her face went blank, smooth and carefree as though the longing had never been. "I remember you promised dessert. The night's not over until you fulfill your promises."

He managed a nod, stifling the urge to roar at her to talk. Taking her hand, he started down the street. "Never say I don't keep my promises."

Unfortunately, not all his promises to London had been kind.

******

London let him pull her along, over concrete sidewalks with grates playing classical music, across three one-way streets, and through clumps of college kids checking their smart phones. Her head was thick with the heavy dinner conversation and what she'd almost revealed.

Tomorrow. Tomorrow. Tomorrow.

He slowed at another truck, this one simply called *PB&J*. After a few quick words to a jovial guy in the window, the man disappeared wearing a huge smile, promising to "impress the lady."

Trevor spoke conspiratorially. "This one's my creation. Allow me to blow your mind."

He already had.

But when she took her first bite of a fried peanut butter-Nutella-banana-honey sandwich, London almost—not quite, but *so* close—understood the phrase "better than sex."

Thank God she'd met Trevor, or else she might try to marry a sandwich.

When he leaned in for a bite, she snatched it away. "Mine."

A low chuckle. "Possessive, are we?"

"Exceedingly."

"Good thing a peanut butter truck never runs out of the P&B." Keeping his tone lighter than their dessert, Trevor asked, "You float away sometimes. A few blocks back, I'd swear you were ready to get serious, to get *real.* Now you're clutching that sandwich and staring dreamily into space."

"Have you *tried* this sandwich?" she muttered, swallowing too much. "I take that back since I have no intention of letting you do such a thing."

"So?"

"Uh?"

"What," he drawled, long and low, "have you been thinking?"

At first she'd been thinking of the amount of sleuthing she'd have to do early in the morning if she was to hit Trevor with a treatise on WW's counterfeiting problem by the afternoon—banks and boats should tell the tale. Then she'd panicked, hoping her forthrightness with respect to the wine would soften the blow of learning she'd killed her boyfriend and, all too purposefully, kept that fact to herself. That comforting dilemma had caused her to wonder whether Trevor would be able to see a difference between her and Rhea.

London *knew* she hadn't done wrong.

She shivered despite the melting peanut butter and honey. Except she also *knew* she'd killed her lover and experienced crushing relief instead of remorse. She'd kicked out at Dillon to keep him away, never intending more than a stern message about what she would and wouldn't tolerate. When he'd gone down, she had finally—and metaphorically—begun to stand up.

She popped the last bite. "I was thinking about what wine to pair with this kind of perfection."

His voice dripped skepticism. "And?"

"Something deep purple with notes of mocha and licorice. I'd pair this"—*and you*—"with a robust wine. The kind of wine that goes down like hard liquor, lingering in the throat. The kind of wine you have to remember forever because it's hard to replicate. It tastes so good because of the moment, and moments are easily lost."

Hell.

She eyed Trevor a little madly, knowing they were doomed. Even a frivolous truth about booze sounded like a bad omen.

CHAPTER 17

The weather turned in the night. By the time London arrived at the office the following morning, the previous day's light had fled, leaving the sky heavy and threatening. Even Sasha appeared disinterested in exiting the car for the soggy parking space outside WW's warehouse.

"Harriet awaits," London coaxed. "You can steal cat food." She probably shouldn't allow that, given the dog's allergies.

Sasha cocked his huge head, dark eyes unconvinced. Still, when she opened the back door, he unfurled his long body and dumped himself from her backseat. He reminded her of a sloth trying to run a marathon.

She laughed in the gloom. "Such a perfect puppy. Yes, you are." When Sasha returned home too soon, she might have to get him a playdate all her own—maybe a teacup poodle that could ride around on Sasha's head like a trainer on an elephant.

Grabbing the leash, she strode for the door, ready to dig—hard, fast, and, this time, smart—for the origin of the bad Olaszrizling and the paper trail connecting it to Dillon. Once she proved to Trevor and Brian that Dillon had gone rogue, they should get off her back. After all, Dillon was beyond causing further trouble.

With that problem solved, she would confront the other head on—explaining exactly how the gangrenous limb had been severed—and let Trevor make his choice about what she'd done.

She stared up at the menacing sky. *Please let him choose a second chance.*

Forcing positive thoughts, she yanked open the chipped metal door that led to her equally appealing office.

And stopped cold.

Grey, Trent, and Clara huddled around her desk, each face appearing more stricken than the last. Several open bottles of wine stood between them.

For tense seconds, her employees stared at everything but her, hesitant, yet obviously full of news. Their silence said too much.

"I'm sorry, London," Grey finally began. "If we weren't sure about the counterfeiting before, we are now."

"Don't say it." London wasn't sure she could bear hearing the obvious. Letting go of Sasha's leash, she shuffled forward. The first bottle she picked up had crooked label. The second claimed to be a Pinot Gris, only it was missing the "s." The third label had been printed on an inferior machine, or maybe one running out of ink. While the image at the top had bled and smeared, the bottom grew fainter and more pixilated until the print disappeared altogether.

Trent pulled the third bottle from her clenched grip. "We've tried to carry on as usual over the past few days, but these new shipments are *impossible*."

When she reached for another reject, her hand shook with the effort, and she snatched it back. She didn't need to hold the offender anyway. The amateurs had poured red wine into a Champagne bottle and called it Bordeaux.

All the bottles had been opened. *No way.* "Tell me you didn't try the wines, that you didn't take that risk."

"A thimble full," Clara rushed to say, shifting from foot to foot. "No harm done."

London sighed in resignation. Leave it to Clara to jump in mouth first, no matter the risk. If the three were physically fine, she had bigger problems to address, ones worthy of the ulcer brewing in her stomach. "And?"

The trio erupted.

"Hideous—"

"Dangerous—"

"Unconscionable. Not fit to pair with a bean-and-Velveeta burrito."

London couldn't help but smile at the last. Leave it to Grey to match his snooty wine sensibilities with a decidedly low-class stomach.

Seven different wines sat before her. She knew without asking that each of the bottles translated to useless cases stacked beyond the cinderblock wall at her front, destined for destruction rather than delivery. None of the wines claimed to be from Tereth, or even from Hungary. These new fakes dotted the globe, at least in name, from Italy, to France, to California.

Clara handed London a stack of papers. Flipping through, London realized they were invoices retrieved from the crates, paper copies without an electronic footprint. Half the selling price had been paid up front, no doubt from WW's account. The remainder was due now, upon delivery, but the invoices didn't say to whom payment should or could be made.

Shadows began to emerge from her previous confusion and disbelief, merging into a picture she could finally see. Suddenly, the "how" of Dillon's treachery became clear. He had to have made independent contacts in Eastern Europe, most likely during scouting trips on WW's dime. Last year's Olaszrizling had been a test run. He'd planted legitimate bottles to be used for tasting and sales purposes, but ultimately delivered fakes to the purchasers. The previous "vintage" hadn't passed muster, and Tereth and WW had been inundated with complaints and returns. This year, Dillon's source must have promised a better product. Maybe they'd pointed to a more established process or better grapes. Or maybe Dillon had found a new supplier. Regardless, Dillon had ordered the motherlode, thinking his problems were solved. The "Olaszrizling" had arrived first. Instead of masquerading as the real thing, the wine was the lowest level of fake, a dangerous concoction of chemical additives and flavoring agents that wouldn't fool, but could possibly kill, a horse.

Now Dillon had died, and London was staring at the rest—she hoped—of Dillon's spree.

"Well, well, well." Brian's drawl interrupted her macabre discovery. "Looks like *my* client isn't the only one with problems."

London and Clara spun to face him, while Grey and Trent moved to shield the offending bottles. For his size and intimidation factor, Brian indulged a flair for color. He'd lost the three-piece suit and wore a pair of gray jeans with a pink-and-green pinstriped shirt rolled above thick wrists. A battered leather satchel—some might call it a man purse—hung across his chest.

The mean messenger-boy thing worked for him.

Immediately London noticed that Brian didn't focus on her. He looked her sister up and down, and Clara squirmed under the scrutiny.

Brian clucked his tongue "You really *are* a busy girl."

Clara? WW had enough problems without Brian snooping around and adding imaginary suspects to their short list of one.

Next to her, Clara cringed. "I didn't do *this*."

Of course not. "Brian." London spat the name with as much scathing authority as possible for a person standing in front of clear evidence of wrongdoing. "Don't you—"

Wait? Why the emphasis on *this*? Clara had done something, which Brian had apparently ferreted out, but not *this*. London turned to her sister. "What *did* you do?"

Brian yawned and sat on the edge of an empty desk.

Clara's eyes darted between London and Brian. That defining charm and confidence withered a little. The woman who had an answer for everything opened and closed her mouth, a choir girl robbed of sound.

Without warning Brian lunged for Clara's purse, situated on a chair not five feet from the lot of them. Leather in hand, he returned to the desk and calmly retook his seat, not attempting to open the bag. Instead he seemed to hold it hostage, as though his possession constituted some kind of leverage.

"Yes," he said loftily. "Do regale us with the tale. What *did* you do?"

London's little sister took a huge breath, staring Brian down.

He popped the snap on the outside flap of her purse.

"*Dillon*," Cara whispered, for once showing fear, looking at the bad wine as though it might attack. "I did *Dillon*."

The news was a battering ram that splintered London to bits, leaving pits of pain dripping blood and bone.

On the sidelines, Brian's lips curved in a predatory grin. He'd come to light a fire. Now he set in watch it burn.

*****

London hardly remembered the drive to Trevor's building, only that she needed to reach him. He could help make sense of the senselessness. She hadn't found the answers she'd promised herself she would find before returning. Grand plans of presenting him with a clear picture of the counterfeiting debacle and why it wouldn't continue and couldn't happen again had been obliterated, first by the news of the new shipments of fakes and then by her sister's admission.

Much of WW's inventory could never be sold. Even though London had discovered the problem before delivering any bad wine, her customers wouldn't take kindly to broken contracts that left them without supplies. WW lost either way.

And Clara… London hunched over the wheel, shaking and rubbing her face along her forearms. She jerked into a parking space, lucky not to swipe the surrounding cars.

Five, four, three… She sucked in a slower breath. *Two, one…*

London had been forced to listen to her sister's rationalizations as she'd done her best to stuff Sasha into the backseat. The dog had been fascinated by Clara's gesticulating hands and loud excuses, leaving London raw and exposed to pleading she hadn't wanted to hear.

Clara claimed to have approached Dillon on London's behalf, to have *slept* with him on London's behalf. In all her wild prattle, Clara seemed to indistinctly implicate herself in the counterfeiting, again for London's own good. About that time, London had gotten tough with the dog and left her sister yelling at the street.

London's heart beat in strong denial, telling her Clara couldn't possibly mean the things she'd said or the admissions she'd made. Her head countered with the facts. London had *turned* her sister into a wild card. She'd retreated into Level London, safe and staid, and left Clara to miss what London had once been. Clara had morphed into the person she thought she'd lost. That kind of inauthentic transition could backfire, and if it had, London had herself to blame.

She glanced at the clock and saw that it was only eight in the morning. They hadn't been apart twelve hours, and already she was back at Trevor's empty-handed. *Worse* than empty-handed.

"Go home," she said aloud. "Get some sleep. Let him work." Let him devote more time to his pressing bank project, though her tingling senses said the project had been fabricated to cover up the fact that he'd been researching an inept wine merchant with too many holes in her story.

Her reasonable side wasn't listening. She wouldn't demand much. A kiss. A cup of coffee that somehow tasted better when he poured it. Maybe a quick cuddle. And then she'd swallow her pride and admit to being in over her head. One shipment and one kind of wine was a very different problem than multiple shipments of several varietals, with monies still owed to a group of total unknowns. She needed Trevor's special skills to resolve the source of the counterfeits. Where had the wine actually come from? How did she make the shipments stop? What would happen when she didn't pay?

Or maybe she only needed Trevor to hold on to her and tell her things would be all right.

Exiting the car, she led Sasha up the stairs all the way to Trevor's floor, hoping the burst of energy would drain her nerves and lend her a sense of normalcy.

She raised a hand, ready to knock, then paused before her fist fell. Though the answers she'd promised had merged into more questions, London did have *one* thing to offer.

The truth. The ugliness of Dillon's death and her role in it, without reservation or rose-colored glasses.

She took a moment to conjure up the speech she'd prepared over and over in her head. Mostly she sought to appeal to Trevor's logical side, to make him understand that meaning well and making mistakes were not mutually exclusive. Barely satisfied, she rapped on his door.

Nothing.

She knocked again. Not anything untoward. Certainly not desperate.

Silence.

After coming this far, after mentally prepping for the look on his face when she described her kick and Dillon's fall, London wasn't inclined to give up.

She rang the bell.

The door opened.

London hadn't seen this Trevor before. He towered over her in worn gym shorts—of course he'd already been to work out—his chest and feet bare. Dark smears below his eyes spoke of a restless night. Behind him shades had been drawn over the huge windows of his common room, leaving the usually airy loft dim and shadowed. Rain pounded the glass beyond the shades, and a clap of sudden thunder made her jump.

Menace rolled off him, shrouding her in an emotion he typically dispelled rather than engendered: Fear. She considered turning away, but he grabbed her right arm, barely clearing the cast that would soon be removed, and pulled her into the apartment. In a blink, she and Sasha were shut in, their companion looking huge and disheveled and *cruel*.

She took solace in Sasha's demeanor. Ever relaxed, the St. Bernard plodded a few steps and dropped to the floor in a knee-crunching flop. Whatever Trevor was feeling hadn't fazed the dog, which confirmed what she already knew. No matter what, Trevor wasn't capable of real evil.

"Hi," London managed to say. "I guess it's kind of early."

Hey eyed her blankly.

"I've been to the office already." More *nothing* crossed that dark face, so she added. "I got some news."

Normally he'd want to know what she'd learned. He'd ask whether they were making progress. His stare shifted. Now it bored into her, invading in a way that almost cut. "I don't care about your news, London."

The warning Trevor delivered in those few words was unmistakable.

"All right," she said. Wanting to regain the closeness of a few hours before, London reached for him. Before her hand could connect with his arm, he reared backward, the movement too pronounced to be casual.

She threaded her hands behind her back, letting him know she'd respect his space. "I won't stay long. I promise." Forget the new fakes. She would keep to the salient points. She'd share what she owed him and leave. "But first I need to tell you something."

"Really."

Definitely not a question. And no interest in the answer.

Level-headed, pragmatic Trevor had fled. In his place, malevolent Trevor reigned, and that version didn't much care about unburdening her of secrets. Feeling anxious, she almost wondered if he already—

"What could you tell me that I don't already know?"

A growing uneasiness joined her anxiety. "It's about Dillon's death," she said softly. "I owe you an explanation."

"Stop." He spun on a heel and went to his desk. Instead of churning through numbers, Brutus sat as quiet and as dark as the rest of the loft. Trevor plucked a stack of papers from the printer and, keeping most of him as far from her as possible, slid them into her waiting hand. "If you stay I'll go fucking crazy. I'll... Get the hell out."

One look told her she'd arrived too late. Trevor had handed her a copy of the police report on Dillon's accident. She knew what the papers revealed—her interview, witness statements, a description of the gory scene. Trevor must have hacked into the police database the night before, on the heels of their perfect day. She'd gone home, preparing for hard work and hard truths. He'd done the same.

"*No.*" Not when she'd finally come to reveal the truth. Her body lit with grim anguish. After all her efforts, she wouldn't let the last bit of traction she'd built burn away in a single morning. WW might not recover. Even though she'd feared this moment was inevitable, she couldn't let Trevor be the second casualty of her choices. "It was an accident."

Trevor's eyeballs spasmed in their sockets. She approached in the slowest degrees. Had he always been so daunting? *Yes.* Chest thick with muscle, arms roped with steel, all an effective carriage for the confidence, and now the judgment, he carried like a hammer.

With each small step, she added a little more to the story. "I *did* lash out, Trev. I kicked him, at his knees, but I didn't intend for him to fall. I only meant to keep him away. He'd gotten so angry, both about the breakup and about my taking a firm hand with WW's orders. His anger could be so…"

Very, very different than Trevor's.

"The police"—her tone sounded increasingly desperate—"ruled the fall an accident, not even rising to self-defense. There were several witnesses. All of them confirmed my story when interviewed. There was even video feed from the security cameras at Red Rocks. You saw all that in the report?"

"I *watched* all that from the file."

"I came here to tell you." As she neared his huge, straining frame, she realized dimly that this was all happening too soon. She wasn't ready to be alone with his size and this shaking rage directed her way. She wasn't ready to lose him either. "I'm so sorry," she whispered brokenly.

"*London.*" He shrank back, but didn't actually move as she shuffled closer and closer. "Don't."

"You deserved my honesty from the beginning. I didn't give it to you because I feared you'd shut me out, *like this*. I was a coward."

This time when she touched him, he exploded, the frenzied movement pushing her backward. The papers in her hand fluttered to the floor in a wash of white. Her shoulders hit the closed metal door behind her, and he drew her hands above her head before he pressed into her from the front. "I warned you."

Trevor was *aroused*. The grip on her wrists didn't hurt, even over the cast. With his vibrating tension at her front and the door at her back, she surprised herself. *Bring it*, she thought with frustration and impotent, inexpressible love. *Do your worst.*

His lips crashed against hers in a brutal kiss that London answered with total surrender, telling him with her body that he could have anything, silently pleading for forgiveness. She opened her mouth and welcomed the dominant slide of his tongue. They tussled in a clash of scraping teeth and desperate breaths, him no doubt holding back, her egging him on. In time, his mouth softened against hers, and she thought dazedly that she'd won. But then she felt the press of her hands into the metal of the door. "Keep them there," he grated, before gripping her sides and spinning her around.

Against her back, he pressed close, bringing her cheek flush against the door's cool surface. "Do you think I'm stupid?"

She gasped out a "No" against her shoulder as he yanked her skirt above her waist. Had he forgotten her history? She deserved his anger, but she couldn't take it if he used sex as a weapon. "Trevor—"

"Then why did you think I couldn't or wouldn't handle your *incident* with Dillon?" He yanked her panties down to her ankles and lifted one foot free.

She gritted her teeth, ignoring her rising panic. "Because of Rhea. You told me—"

As Trevor knelt behind her, still clutching her lifted ankle, she heard the whoosh of his shorts as he pulled her hips outward. He stood, but instead of a heavy, painful invasion, she heard a sharp intake of breath above her curved spine.

He murmured a viscous curse. Then she felt a baby-soft stroke, starting at the tips of the fingers she still pressed to the door, down her arms, over her shoulders, and along her torso until he skimmed the bunched skirt.

London would do *almost* anything for him, but he wanted too much. "I won't apologize by letting you hurt me."

His answer came like smoke, dark and elusive but once again calm. "I'd never ask you to." His lips moved to her ear at the same time his palm glided between her legs from the rear. Gently, he opened her, coaxing a response. "You know it, too, or you wouldn't be here. I am angrier than I've ever been. I want you more than I ever thought possible."

She could only whimper as her body softened and yielded. "Then take what you want."

He ignored the invitation. "You lied to me."

They'd lied to each other. "I said nothing."

"You said nothing *strategically*. After all I know of you and all the chances I gave you, you didn't trust me to see the difference between killing an innocent and protecting yourself from a monster."

She gasped as the meaning of his words penetrated her lust-clouded mind. *He understood.* His fingers swirled and stroked until she thought she'd go mad. "You said so many times—"

He fondled her without rhyme or rhythm, now punishing her with the knowledge that she wanted an elusive thing only he could give. "I said my wife was a *murderer.* Are you a murderer, London?"

She swayed her hips, sliding into his magical touch. "No." She hoped not.

With a tortured groan, he flung himself away. When she turned to look, she saw him sprawled on the floor, elbows to knees, palms to forehead. "I knew you held back, but I gave you the benefit of the doubt. You didn't do the same."

Pushing off the door, London went to him. She swatted at his hands and lowered herself into the vee between his torso and thighs. "I—We're different."

"*Too* different."

His heavy shaft brushed against her softness, and he simply leaned back, leveraging his weight on his hands. How could she have feared him?

"You had righteousness on your side," she said, "and I thought I'd done the one thing you wouldn't tolerate. I'd have given *anything* to not be the most perfectly imperfect person for Trevor Rathlen. And you reminded me, as did your friends and even your brother, that you knew I hid myself. I knew when you found out, we'd be over."

"Yet here we are."

"Yes." She couldn't help rocking against the pulse of his erection. Soon the whisper of her name replaced the curses she'd heard before. It was enough. London rose to her knees until she could grip his sex. "I'm on birth control." That was all she gave him before she sank down, the invasion slow and stunning. The feel of him plundering through throbbing tissues stole her breath, blitzed her sanity.

Trevor stayed perfectly still, jaw and eyes clenched, making her work above him. She rose and fell, griping his hardness inside, using his shoulders and chest to push and pull in slow, savage pumps.

They didn't kiss, and he didn't touch her anywhere but where they joined. Finally, he eased his back to the concrete floor. In utter surrender, he pleaded with her not to stop.

Her eyes stung. Her breath caught. She'd never known sex could be about so much more than two people trying to feel good. The plunge and retreat of his body inside hers was so basic, so elemental, that it reshaped her ideas of intimacy.

She didn't *want* Trevor. She *required* him.

This man hadn't broken when faced with her past, but by the fact that she'd felt compelled to hide it. Not once had he found the real her—the one others had tried to change and to drug and to protect—anything other than perfect. He hadn't been fazed by her relationship hang-ups, her refusals to cooperate, or her secrecy. Only her refusal to believe in his goodness had finally pushed him over the edge.

Stock still and straining beneath her, Trevor's lips moved in silent fervor. Watching him fight the pleasure served to build hers, up and up, until the dam broke, and heat flooded and spread to every extremity.

Trevor let her collapse to his chest, winded and ecstatic. His hands rose to her hips, squeezing and then soothing, even as his shaft throbbed within, and she knew he held back. The moment she'd first uttered, "*I don't like it rough*," had changed everything about how he touched her.

Her inability to let go of what had happened before—always so much emphasis on *before*—had tainted her dealings with a man who deserved more. Trevor should have a woman who could start fresh and welcome him for him.

Him. Big and wicked and fundamentally male, a veritable jungle gym of sex.

Smiling to herself, London wiggled forward, pulling off him until her lips barely brushed his. "Trevor," she said, injecting every ounce of her inner seductress into her voice. "I want you to *fuck* me."

CHAPTER 18

Trevor threw a full-body twitch that cracked his head against the concrete. He felt like a yo-yo in the hands of a child with short legs and long arms. Every unfurl sent him bouncing off the ground. He could only hit so many times before his brain shorted out completely.

I want you to fuck me.

He could have said, "I just did," but he knew exactly what she meant.

What she wanted.

And, God, help him. *I'm going to give it to her.*

Trevor snarled. He rolled her to her back, careful of her injured wrist, but otherwise freeing the dominance he'd kept under wraps. He shoved the concern he'd felt out of the way. She knew her mind, and if she wanted to get acquainted with his darker side, who was he to refuse?

Flipping her on the concrete, he unzipped her scrunched skirt and dragged it down her toned legs, along with a pair of red panties that really deserved closer inspection. Then he made short work of her white top and lacey bra, until the lowered shorts hanging from his thighs were the only clothing left between them.

Trevor rolled her again, and, holding her wrists hostage above her head, he took a second to admire the gorgeous curves splayed out on his shining floor, her melting warmth against the unforgiving cold. He gave her hands a firm squeeze that clearly said, "*Stay*," and climbed over her, nosing the vanilla scent at her knees, her thighs, the indention at her waist. Even her nipples smelled like an invitation to feast.

He did.

Had a woman ever been so soft? Had he ever needed one to yield so much?

London's legs sawed beneath his exploration. He muscled them apart and held. "You need this don't you? You need me suck your nipples and lick your clit and take the choice away."

Words fell from her lips, all incoherent.

"Don't you?"

She nodded, and her open thighs pushed against his forearms as she rocked her pelvis into the air, reaching but not finding. All her tight control—from her careful decisions about what to share and what to suppress, to her fear of letting go during sex—went up in flames before his eyes.

She rocked and thrashed and thrust beneath the pressure he applied to her legs. When he walked a pair of fingers across her abdomen, finally pressing rhythmically above her pubic bone, she bucked upward, gasping and crying out for the direct stimulation he denied her. London became any other animal frenzied to get what she wanted.

"I *will* fuck you," he promised, dark and a little menacing. "When *I'm* ready. First, I want my tongue inside you."

He licked the tender skin on the inside of either leg before letting himself taste her slick folds. Her scent, her flavor, the quickly indrawn breaths floating down from above, combined to drive him wild. With every stroke of the tongue, he drove his cock forward, slipping his length along the shellacked cement.

The smooth coldness against his skin, her hot wetness on his tongue… A groan escaped between tastes. Beneath his open mouth, she got even wetter. She began to tighten. He slid up her body and entered her.

Hard.

Her whole body shuddered, and his attention darted to her face, searching for signs he'd gone too far. What he saw filled him with awe. Lips parted, lids heavy, London had arched up at the neck, thrusting her breasts forward, offering herself up. She let out the sweetest sound he'd ever heard, and her tight little sheath grabbed hold of him and squeezed from all sides.

Head reeling, he tussled with the buzz that lit at the base of his spine. *Don't come. Not yet. She asked. You'll give.*

Rising up on rigid arms, Trevor pistoned in and out of her warmth. He didn't hold back, riding her rough, pushing her across the floor with every surge. When her release finally subsided, he pulled free.

London mewled at the loss. When he didn't thrust back inside, she turned her head and nipped his wrist. All he could do was laugh, but even that turned to a groan when she looked up and said, "You're so *good* at this."

Jesus Christ. If he was good, she could teach lessons.

"Roll over." The command sounded more like a growl, but London didn't hesitate. She flipped onto her stomach and looked back at him, her eyes asking, "*Whatcha gonna do now?*"

He laid a hand on her rear and pressed, pressed until her entire front met the floor, arms and legs spread wide with him kneeling between her thighs. "Feels good doesn't it? The cold against your skin?" Finally gentle, he slid two fingers into her slit from behind, opening her, positioning her so that with every move, her slick clit would slide along the cool smoothness below.

"Mmm," she whispered. "Wow."

"Not yet," he countered, scrambling to rid himself of the tangled shorts.

She gasped as he lowered himself over the length of her, covering her like a blanket. Palming his heavy shaft, he brushed against burning skin, back and forth along her backside, teasing the flushed softness waiting below. His growl was possessive, almost foreign to his ears, his whole being riveted on the feel of her.

Centering himself, he listened to the rain pummeling the windows. The continuous pounding isolated them, making it seem like he and London were the only people in the world.

Maybe they were. He wanted them to be.

He thrust into her waiting heat, rocking them both, knowing each rooting surge pinned her between him and the floor. "You're wetting my concrete, aren't you? I want you to come all over it. Come all over me." The pace started slow and rose, a race they'd both win. Building to a violent rhythm, Trevor wrapped his arms around London and rolled them to the side. He had to be able to touch her, to squeeze her breasts and lick her neck and slide his thumb low to the place where she took him so desperately.

He petted and circled until she let out a keening cry that matched the fierceness he felt. Only then did he let go, rough but careful as ecstasy took over. "London, my London." He flattened a palm over her heart. "You make me crazed."

She nodded, catching her breath. "You make me new."

New. As in remade. A fresh start.

His hand clenched, turning from the steady beat he valued above all else. London had taken the sex—relished it, even—but would that level of honesty and trust still be denied to him elsewhere?

"New," he suspected, could be a relative term.

******

Morning had nearly passed by the time London disentangled herself from Trevor's arms and staggered to her feet. The movement set off a chain of miniscule aches and pains, each one attesting to the fact that, yes, she *had* gone full acrobat with Trevor on his bare floor.

Reliving the things they'd done left her feeling giddy and light. Trevor had eased her in, first showing her the joys of gentle, careful lovemaking before getting wild and raw.

Oh, how she liked both. Needed both.

Dillon had viewed sex as a way to make himself feel good, whether physically or emotionally. Sex had been about proving his power and getting off, pure and simple. London's needs and desires hadn't entered into the equation.

Trevor seemed to burn her pleasure as fuel. He touched her body to reach her mind, and he only enjoyed the ride when she did, too. His approach had led him past all her carefully constructed defenses, and she realized she was ready for a true partnership.

Still lazing on the floor, Trevor watched her progress with a careful expression. Once she'd slipped into her skirt and managed to sort her bra from her blouse, he pushed up and reached for his shorts. They dressed in silence, both lost in the magnitude of what had happened.

Finally clothed, Trevor sauntered toward the door. He knelt down and gathered up the mess of papers littering the floor. *The police report.* Stack in hand, he went to the kitchen island and began the obvious process of reordering the sheets.

"You don't have to do that," she said. Neither of them needed to read those words ever again.

"I want to." Trevor almost sounded bored, purposefully so.

Why?

"Do you remember"—she licked her lips, suddenly dry—"my mention of learning more about the counterfeiting scheme this morning?"

"I do." Again he answered in a slow drawl that didn't quite mask a building tension.

"The problem is bigger than we thought. Crate after crate has been delivered to the warehouse. The new wines—all fake—are half paid for, at least according to the invoices that shipped with the bottles. Dillon apparently arranged for a great deal before his death. I'm expecting the shipping paperwork to lead to a dead end of dummy entities, and the invoices"—she went to her bag and pulled the roll free—"don't tell me anything. I don't even know who shipped the wine or who's missing their money."

"Would you pay them if you did?"

She slapped the roll of invoices against her leg. "That depends."

"On?" He rescued the papers from her fidgeting and began to flip through them.

"How dangerous it is not to."

He blinked. "So you'll find a way to end the relationship."

True. But if significant quantities of wine were making it to the United States, then she was dealing with a sophisticated organization that could be supplying dangerous product to countless other merchants. Simply turning the fakes over to the U.S. authorities and washing her hands of the problem wouldn't suffice. A WW employee had colluded with the counterfeiters, submitting multiple orders and even paying for them from WW's accounts, all under her supervision. Maintaining any semblance of innocence would be next to impossible, especially since the employee at fault had conveniently turned up dead at *her* feet. If London went to the police, she might as well hand them a manifesto detailing a conspiracy to sell counterfeit wine. Even Dillon's accidental death might begin to look less like an accident and more like a cover-up.

"I have to stop this," she agreed. "I also have to stop whoever is *doing* this." By *stop*, she meant locate the source of the counterfeits and call the authorities from a safe distance. With a productive raid on their hands, who had time to look her way?

Emotion flickered in Trevor's eyes, an initial speculation that dissolved into cold calculation. London had never considered herself particularly intuitive—case in point being her current predicament—but in that moment, she knew in her bones that Trevor gauged her potential. And her gut said he considered her tendency toward harm, not good.

He tilted his head. "Have you talked to your sister?"

Not *that* question. *Not yet.* "Of course I have." Though not in the way he meant. "Why would you ask that?" Acknowledging Dillon's treachery had been a long road after a hard battle. London couldn't sacrifice Clara without first talking to her about what her admission had meant. Clara would *never* betray London. Despite her wild ways, Clara had proven herself trustworthy since her childhood days of drug muling from the kitchen table to the toilet.

The drive to vouch for her baby sister rose automatically, an instinct rather than a decision.

Trevor's knuckles went white against the counter. A muscle beat at his temple.

Dazed, London went to him. The closeness she'd felt a few minutes ago dissolved as his tension morphed into rage before her eyes. He wouldn't look at her, and the bristling in his big frame screamed: *Stay away.*

"Trevor? Look at me. What's going on?"

"You've talked with her?" he prodded, suddenly spearing her with those icy blues. "You look at *me*. Stare me in the face. Tell me we shouldn't be focusing on Clara."

Panic shorted all the synapses firing in her brain. "I—please, listen. I know Clara's clean." Except for the fact that Clara admitted to sleeping with Dillon, who'd masterminded WW's counterfeiting.

"You're lying again." A speck of surprise crept into Trevor's voice. He stepped forward and ran a thumb over her cast. The gentleness in the gesture, especially in light of his seething anger, made her eyeballs prickle. "*Again*," he said. "To *me*." He moved quickly, snatching up papers and ushering her back. London didn't understand his plan. Not until the door opened. Not until she stood in the hall without Sasha. Not until he thrust the police report and the invoices into her hand, and a lance of pain drew imaginary blood that dripped from her ravaged heart to the floor.

Before closing the door, he stood strangely still and coldly informed her of their status. "I gave you one chance too many. It's funny. I'm supposed to be the one with trust issues, and yet I tamped them down, forcing myself to see you in the best light. In reality, you're unwilling, maybe incapable, of trust. You'll never be *made new*, no matter how many times you say it, and I'm through with your kind of broken."

Staring at the closed door, clinging to the bliss she'd known on its other side, London pictured Brian that morning, watching Clara with knowledge in his eyes and her purse in his hands. Brian must have reported to Trevor before London's arrival at the loft, probably as she'd driven over. Trevor had known about her sister's sick admission all along. He probably knew more than London did about Clara's involvement in the newly arrived fakes.

His question about Clara had been a test.

London stared blankly the door barring her from giving him an explanation, at the cast that bracketed her wrist. The jumbled invoices in her grasp said she hadn't stewarded WW like the businesswoman she strove to be, and the police report reminded her she'd done so much worse than that.

A realization sliced through her, an invisible chokehold tightening around her neck. In response to Trevor's test? She'd done what she did best.

She had failed.

CHAPTER 19

Hours after fleeing Trevor's hallway, London cornered her sister at the office. Grey and Trent had gone home. Even Brian had abandoned his post as her sister's keeper. She could only imagine that Brian and Trevor would soon compare notes on the disastrous deeds of the Whitley sisters.

Her head spun. Her heart hurt. But anger and Advil were fighting for supremacy. Either way, she'd end up better off than dwelling on the unseen chokehold she'd battled since Trevor's dismissal. London had allowed her bond with her sister to jeopardize—to *destroy*—Trevor's belief in her. She hated the result but couldn't regret believing in Clara.

Maybe their bond could reap dividends in another quarter.

Dragging a chair toward her prey, London sat down across from her sister. Just the two of them now, alone with the cheap desks and flickering lights. Someone had removed the open wine bottles from earlier. While she couldn't see the evidence, she also couldn't forget the fact that all those wines sat less than twenty feet away in her warehouse, looking pretty with nowhere to go.

Before London could begin to interrogate, her sister started with a classic. "It's not what you think."

To believe or not to believe? London examined, really looked, at the woman facing her. Beautiful and petite, with glossy strands of straight midnight hair falling around her shoulders, Clara presented a picture that fit Dillon's type more than London ever could have. Clara didn't have unruly curls that resented the brush. Clara could eat pizza for dinner and dessert and still be a size four. Clara laughed and joked and appeared not to take life, or herself, too seriously.

Clara also sported blue smudges beneath both eyes, and the longer London looked her over, the more her sister began to thrum her fingers on the desk and dart her gaze about the room. Clara's shirt hung off her shoulders—*had it always?*—and a smudge of makeup stained the collar.

The silent, brooding routine soon had Clara squirming in her seat. "Things got out of hand," Clara said, rubbing at her temples. The admission lacked her usual confidence, that teasing note that drew people to her side.

London couldn't imagine any "thing" so extraordinary that her sister would lay hands on Dillon. "Tell me."

The stalling went on.

"Clara," London snapped. "This morning you admitted to sleeping with my boyfriend. We both know that's not your style. Even if it were, *Dillon* was not your style either. You did this right about the time WW couldn't ignore the fraud problems I know Dillon had a hand in. You said you weren't involved with the latest bunk shipments, but you never mentioned *before*. What about last year? What about this year's first shipment of Olaszrizling, the one that nearly blinded me?"

Tears glistened in Clara's eyes, and London knew she flirted with the truth. "God, Clara." London's throat hurt, and a creeping sense of unease twisted in her chest. "What did you do?"

Clara didn't answer. Instead she reached down and lifted her purse to the desk, the same purse Brian had seized that morning with obvious intention. When Brian had grabbed the bag, Clara had rushed to admit her involvement with Dillon, almost as though Clara longed to keep the contents private. Did the purse somehow hold answers?

Confused, London waited. Clara unsnapped the outer flap and reached inside. One by one, she pulled free three orange prescription bottles, then a baggie of unmarked pills.

The first two bottles had been prescribed for London—Ritalin and Adderall, compliments of their mother. Clara had taken them under the guise of disposal. Ever helpful. Always making it easier for London to pretend their parents didn't find her lacking. Both bottles were nearly empty. The third bore Clara's name. If that bottle had been the only one, it could have been called normal, maybe necessary—if one didn't know Clara.

London swallowed. "What's in the bag?"

"More of the same," Clara answered quietly. "Ill-gotten gains, you could say. Not from a pharmacy."

"How long?" A shaking stared deep in London's belly, working its way higher and higher.

"Since high school. Before, I didn't know the pills could be... fun. Then all the sudden I couldn't understand why you'd ever want to toss them away."

Years. Her sister had been hiding her addiction for years. All the while, London had unknowingly been feeding the problem. London had *kick started* the problem. "And Dillon? Why him?"

"You needed... I meant to..." Clara's halting speech sputtered to a stop. She appeared to think better of her approach before continuing. "In moderation, the plan seemed like a good one. We both got a little extra money since it cost a lot less to purchase the fakes than it did the actual wine." Another pause. "London, we planned to start and stop with the Olaszrizling. I never knew he would or did go any bigger."

London physically bit her tongue. Her mind whirled with thoughts of rehab and twelve-step programs. In a few totally overwhelming seconds, she considered moving Clara into her apartment, how they'd explain Clara's problem to the Whitley's, whether she could give her sister another chance in recovery, how she could have missed it, how she could have *fed* it, how either one of them could ever forgive the other.

Eventually embers of resolve began to crystalize from the ashes of the last weeks. Dillon's fall, her broken wrist, the poisoned wine, Turner Farro's foiled attack, her heady affair and crushing set down, the unresolved invoices calling from her purse, the deadly wine calling from her warehouse, the look on Clara's face as she'd laid out the pills, the look on Trevor's as he'd called her *broken*—all of them demanded that instead of reacting to the forces that batted her around like a ball on a pool table, London *become* the force dishing out the hits.

If WW went under, London couldn't help anyone else, least of all herself. With a single swipe, she brushed Clara's stash into her own purse. Clara winced but didn't protest.

London took a deep breath, wishing something so simple could actually help. "We'll handle this. I promise. Can you try, just *try*, to stay straight until I deal with a few other issues?" London knew she sought the impossible, but their choices were limited.

Tears tracked down Clara's face. She nodded. "Of course I can try."

"For now, I have to know where the fakes are coming from. I need a name, Clara, and an address."

Clara rummaged in her desk and produced a file-sized envelope. "I gave a copy of these to Turner Farro. Technically, they only relate to the Olaszrizling because Dillon went rogue after that, but Turner won't be tormenting you again."

The envelope had *heft*. "Why?"

An innocent shrug from her sister. "He doesn't want the world to know his son was an abusive, embezzling scumbag?"

Whoa. The time would come to piece Clara's addiction and betrayal together with the parts of her hesitant explanation that didn't quite fit, as well as the unexpected forward thinking that would save London at least one battle.

No more visits from Dillon's unhinged father.

At London's stunned look, Clara smiled smugly through her tears.

"They're pills, London. Do I rely on them more than I should? Yes. Have I let them cloud my judgement? Yes. Do I have a collection of rubber tubes hanging in my closet next to the scorched spoons? No."

There was her Clara—a joke in the storm, a smile in a fight.

One day they'd be okay. For now, London split the envelope and confirmed what she already knew.

She was headed to Hungary.

CHAPTER 20

August—Budapest, Hungary

The beauty of Budapest—both natural and manmade—promised the city couldn't have an ugly side. *Almost.* Centuries upon centuries of wanderers and invaders alike had left their mark. A stroll around the Buda Hills flanking the gentle curve in the River Danube or onto the Great Plain spreading to the east of Pest bombarded a visitor with an architectural buffet, everything from Gothic and Baroque, to Renaissance, to Ottoman, to Art Nouveau. In one spot, London might be visiting Berlin. In another, Buenos Aires. In yet another, the beating heart of Istanbul.

She hadn't visited often, only enough to know she needed more time. On this trip, she had none.

Clara's packet had her blowing through the city, straight from the airport to the main coach station on the Pest side of town. While only a two hour drive, she planned to endure a couple busses and a final train ride into prime wine country on the shores of Lake Balaton. Hungarians drove on the right side of the road, but London had never gotten comfortable navigating cars in foreign countries. She'd use the trip to further map her battle plan.

A few crawling, but comfortable, hours later, she alighted in Badacsony, a town she affectionately called "Badassy," but that really sounded liked "Bad-a-chon" rolling off the tongue. Lake Balaton glimmered along two-hundred square miles of Hungary's most lush terrain. While the southern side offered a smattering of resorts—Europe's party pond, they called it—where beautiful people on holiday went to club by night and beach bum by day, the northern side couldn't have been more different.

While London had previously come to Badacsony to appreciate its rich history in robust white wines, until recently she hadn't been in charge of

153

Hungarian imports. The first stop on her first "official" visit would be Tereth. A tiny operation, she would most likely be able to speak with the owner. With any luck, he would add insight to the story he'd told Brian about the Olaszrizling complaints from last year.

Straight from the train, London strolled up a road no wider than an American bike path. Every few minutes, a bicycle or even a puttering compact car edged past, all moving at the same pace.

At the top of the hill, she turned to see the lake sparkling in the sun like a sea of blue jewels. Before her, the village spread out in a leisurely smattering of well-kept homes, complete with shutters and thatched rooftops and painted picket fences. Most of all, there were *vines*. Behind her, the larger producers blanketed forested hills, a blur of lush kelly green. The competing puttering of tractors and sprinklers drifted down from above. Three young children galloped by, a pretty little girl leading her budding suitors on a merry, giggling chase.

A preloaded map and her phone's GPS guided her along the narrow pavement, wet and steaming from a recent rain shower. She'd forgotten the roadside plonk sellers. Every few hundred yards, she came upon an obscure, nameless cart selling wine by the pint and the liter. It seemed every hobbyist in viticulture along Balaton's shore had set up shop to lure unsuspecting enthusiasts.

Fifteen minutes later, she stood in front of a swinging wooden sign with her meager backpack, sipping from a bottle of seltzer water, or szoda, an invention the Hungarian's proudly called their own. The sign read "Tereth" in curving letters, and a pebbled path took her past it and through a pruned rose garden, a row for each color—red, yellow, even pink. She thought of the roses Trevor had brought her in the hospital, how she had knocked them down and cut herself on the glass.

Crazy, some might say.

Broken, another had.

At the end of the path sat a two-story house with a gabled roof—pure gingerbread. Steep stairs climbed to an upper veranda with an ornate railing. She'd known Tereth was small and that WW had been lucky to get its hands on any of the Tereth Olaszrizling, but this?

This was a home—lived in, cared for, only big enough for half of the seven dwarves.

An elderly lady bustled out of a sliding door and onto the deck. At the sight of London, her face lit and she let loose with a burst of bright Hungarian, with its long, loud vowels and aggressive consonants. At London's uncertain smile, she came down the stairs and approached, now talking slower as if the reduced speed might help.

London peered at the vines peeking from behind the house. She tried the most obvious approach. "Wine?"

The woman spun for a look, appearing nonplussed. Then, without another word, she scrambled back up the stairs and disappeared.

All right, then.

Just as London thought she might need to move to plan B, or come up with plan B, her host reappeared carrying an outdated flip phone with actual push buttons. She talked rapidly into the speaker before holding the phone to London's ear.

A new voice. "Yes? I am Attila. I can help you?"

Attila. The very man she needed. And he spoke English, a rarity in these parts.

For now she would play tourist. She asked about wine tasting—the wooden sign had said "open" after all—and Attila promised to stop by in ten minutes. He instructed her to "Stay with Mother" for the short time until his arrival.

"Mother" turned out to be quite the host. By the time Attila arrived, London sat at a long planked table in an extensive wine cellar beneath the house. A plate of cheese, olives, and nuts tempted her to enjoy of the hospitality of people who might call her Enemy when she told the truth. The exhausting trip from Denver to Lake Balaton showed its toll in the form of one bite of cheese, then a nut, then a cup of szoda from the glass dispenser Mother had plunked down on the table. After realizing they didn't share a word in common—not London's English or her French, and certainly not Mother's Hungarian or German—the woman simply mimed with sweeping hands.

"Eat." "Drink." "Be welcome."

London giggled at the thought of what Victoria Whitley might do to the poor soul that darkened her door, asking about wine and looking tired and hungry.

A diet pill, perhaps?

"You seek to taste?"

London looked up to see a man in the shadows. He stood about six feet tall and could only be a few years her senior. Dark-haired and golden-skinned, he reminded her a bit of *her*, only taller and more direct.

She ventured, "Yes."

"You visit the Balaton alone?" He sounded depressed at the thought. A cliché, she knew, but the man could absolutely impersonate Sad Dracula in Hollywood movies.

"American," she explained, hoping it would be enough.

"Ah!" He smiled. "Independent and..." An obvious search for words. "Tough! Like cowgirl. You are welcome to my home."

For now.

Attila obviously wanted his independent American visitor to get a taste for the best. Over a period of two hours, he plied her with samplings of no less than fourteen different wines. With each one, he explained the grape, the grape's history, and how Tereth did it best. The outside world got Hungarian wines that fell in line with traditional international standards. In country, one could try indigenous varietals like "blue stalk" and "sheep's tail." They washed the full-bodied whites down with liters of seltzer water—"Hungarian's invented!"—and piles of cheeses and olives— "Homemade, American. A family recipe!"

Throughout the presentation, London worked to build a rapport with Attila. She asked a million questions, mostly because she *had* a million questions, and didn't dump a single drop of wine into the spit bucket. At the close, only after she'd purchased several bottles of his finest, she had to break the moment.

"Attila," she began, wringing her hands below the table. "I told you my name is London, but my last name is Whitley. I… own WW Imports in Denver, Colorado."

He nodded, suddenly shrewd, cutting her off with the slash of a hand through the air. "You think I don't research the American woman who sells swill and calls it Tereth? You are her. And you are sad and in my cellar to— how do you say?—put my hatch in the dirt."

"Bury the hatchet?"

"To say you are sorry."

"I *am* sorry."

He stood. "Sorry is not enough, London Whitley."

So said Disappointed Dracula.

"I know. I came to apologize, but I also have questions. I'm trying to track who sold my company your wine—"

"Not *my* wine." *Increasingly Angry Dracula.*

"No, not yours, but they labeled it Tereth. I can't stop the counterfeits until I find their source."

Stubborn elbows landed on the table. "You sound Hungarian. No trust in police." *Exasperated Dracula.*

She winced, then shrugged. What could she do? Certainly not share the long, sordid tale that had brought her to the wilds of Hungary over her local police station. "Attila, what do you know?"

"Nothing." The answer carried a dissatisfied ring of finality. "Why you think I pay American lawyer to find out? Why he pay for computer investigator mumbo jumbo? I make wine. Real wine. You've tasted! Is delicious. I don't hunt a thief."

London tapped her temple, set back but not defeated. "Think," she demanded. "You *know* something."

"You stay where?"

At the closest guesthouse down the lane with an extra room. She hoped. "In town."

"In *upstairs*, more like. Look at you. Tired and beaten like a cat pulled on you."

Yep, the cat had dragged her in all right. If this was a Hungarian example of making a pass, she might get violent. "No, not upstairs."

His smile was angelic for one so scrappy and determined. "My mother is beating me if I send you off, American. This is her house. She is *beating* me." He fluttered a lofty hand toward the cellar exit. "You stay."

Obviously considering the matter closed, he picked up her pack and headed for the cellar door. As she rushed after him with her new wine purchases—under no circumstance did one leave good wine behind—she heard his deep voice floating down the stone steps.

"Tomorrow you walk the town. Interview the plonk sellers on the street."

The men selling cheap local wines?

"Some of them neighbors." Then, a bit too fiercely, he added, "Some of them *not*."

Not neighbors, and apparently not welcome. London had, albeit inadvertently, damaged Attila's livelihood. Yet he invited her into his home for an epic tasting and a free bed. The interlopers had garnered the vintner's dark attention. To get a rise out of the jovial Attila, they had to be a sinister bunch, indeed.

An unwilling groan escaped through London's compressed lips, but she followed him up.

Seemed London liked Helpful Dracula most of all.

******

Mother greeted London bright and early with a breakfast spread on an ornate brass tray—a soft boiled egg, thick slices of buttered toast, a wedge of white cheese, and peeled orange slices. Sun and the scent of freshly cut grass poured through her open window.

A bed and breakfast had *nothing* on Tereth.

The fresh air, delicious wines, and the unexpected kindnesses of the night had helped London find rest, even though her dreams had proven anything but restful. Trevor had come to her in sleep, dipping his head to hers. The detachment he'd shown in their final moments had bled into wonder, and he'd told her so, calling himself ten times an ass for pushing her away. An instant and powerful desire had taken root. London had wanted to draw him close, breathe in his clean, masculine scent, and lick his lips. She'd wanted to pretend that less than an ocean stood between them, and that her mistakes—both of the past and most certainly the future—could be forgiven.

Instead, London had shaken herself, appalled by the impulse. The moment she'd broken free, fury had paled his skin and tightened his features. The control he wielded over himself, and over her, had unraveled, and he'd laughed.

He had laughed at her ridiculous compulsion to have him.

London had roared awake to Mother's soft tapping at the door. Smoothing her hair and adjusting the T-shirt she'd slept in, she told herself the gracious smile she presented in greeting was real.

The house really was inhabited solely by Attila's mother. After their tasting the night before, Attila had trundled off in his Mercedes to his own home and family. Mid-breakfast, a cheering horn blasted from the drive. When she leaned out the window, he stood blithely in front of his hood, offering to, "Walk the American."

What a lucky family this man had, though she couldn't accept the offer. Anonymity didn't come in the form of the town's most prominent citizen.

Soon London again traversed the sloping roads of Badacsony, playing the flirtatious tourist on a wine-tasting holiday. Larger vineyards didn't make the cut. Her interest centered on the carts dotting the roads, a phenomenon she likened to lemonade stands, only for wine. Brilliant, really.

The first three salesmen passed out tastes of cheap whites and needled for the sale of a jug. Each man talked in practiced English of his beautiful home—"Just there!" "Across the lake!"—and how he kept vines for one innocuous reason or another—"Wife so expensive!" "In the blood!"

From the information Clara had provided, London knew Badacsony had been ground zero for Dillon's escalating purchases. Had he stuck to Olaszrizling of poor quality, as he'd done the previous year, she might have suspected one of her friendly roadside sellers of cutting him a deal. But Dillon had progressed to the type of counterfeits that could only make their way to her warehouse if built upon a pyramid of sophistication and financial backing.

A sleepy lakeside village couldn't possibly be the endgame. A professional operation sending bottles to Denver would be too conspicuous and require access to cheaper shipping and delivery routes, manipulable banking options, a sizeable manufacturing site, and plentiful cheap, and chillingly quiet, labor.

Still, it had all started here…

The fourth man she encountered behaved differently than the other three. This one didn't have a practiced byline or a big smile. He was younger and moved with restrained desperation, shifting back and forth on the balls of his feet and asking her what she needed between puffs on a cigarette. Surely no Mafioso, but perhaps an underling's underling. Or a smalltime criminal who had an in on some cheap "juice" he could move.

She got the feeling she could request a pallet of wine or a hit on dear Aunt Olga. Equal work for equal pay.

The sample tasted nauseating, but not deadly. London smacked her lips and bought a glass. Appearing surprised, the man stood back and watched her drink. When his Hungarian didn't translate, he, too, tried German. At an impasse, London finally pulled out her smartphone and called up a translation app she'd downloaded in the airport. Before long, they conversed in bursts of text, passing the phone back and forth.

Her: *Wine for resale?*

Him: *How much?*

Her: *60 cases of Olaszrizling, to start.*

The bald request made him wary, and he began to inch the phone back into her hand. As it slipped into her fist, London spied a marking—a tattoo?—on the fleshy part of the man's hand, below the thumb. She wouldn't have noticed, but over the last few days, she'd scrutinized the invoices that had shipped with the fakes to Colorado. Each one featured a single distinguishing characteristic—a small calligraphy "K" at the bottom of the page.

K

Beyond the "K," the invoices were devoid of information other than a clear demand for money—no name, no address, not even a date. That info had died with Dillon.

The design matched the tattoo exactly.

Seizing on the coincidence, London held her casted wrist in the air, as if to say, "*Hold up*," while she dug the invoices from her pack. Revealing the stack, she pointed between his tattoo and the identical marking on each page. If anything, the match-up acted as evidence that she'd worked with his group before, and if it led her down an iffy path, she could always explain that Dillon had moved on, and she was simply seeking those who deserved to be paid.

Oh, the irony of goody-goody London Whitley, on the street with the papers to actually back a descent into organized crime.

The guy perked at the sight of the invoices. He probably had a stack of his own to pay. Best case scenario, she'd placed herself squarely on his team.

"A Katonák," he said.

Katonák. A name? A place? She passed over the phone. The second he returned the translation, he began packing his goods, shoving plastic jugs of wine to the lower shelf on the cart and covering the whole show with a ragged tarp.

And London knew.

An *organization.*

The seller pushed off, rolling down the slope without throwing another scrap.

"Wait!" She trotted alongside, babbling in useless English. "I need contact information. An address."

"A Katonák," he repeated. Ferocity laced each syllable, as though the words themselves imparted everything she needed to know.

She slowed and let him disappear. Hands on hips, she trudged back up the hill to her pack, lost in plans to mine the skimpy morsel he'd revealed for more. The crest of the hill exposed a hulking figure crouched over her bag. He wore dark jeans and a hooded sweatshirt that hid most of his face. He stood, lifting her pack with graceful, liquid movements that couldn't belong to one so imposing, *if* she didn't know from experience that they did.

Trevor turned to her ascent, looking down at her with restrained solemnity in every breath, enough to douse the sun.

"I see you found The Soldiers."

CHAPTER 21

London jolted, stunned to see him on a hill in rural Hungary. "I *am* a soldier." Trevor might be as cool and collected as always, but she blazed with heat—joy on one hand, wrath on the other.

"Yes," he agreed. *But a different kind*, went unsaid.

"I'm afraid to ask how you found me."

A golden brow shot upward. "This town only has so many streets."

Clara had struck again. London chose to ignore his purposeful obtuseness in light of her limited time. "*Why* did you find me?" Not that his answer mattered. Not one bit.

"I regret how I treated you." Under the hood of his sweatshirt, Trevor looked weary, worse even than when she'd found him by her side in the hospital. His cheekbones tapered to an edge. His eyes had grown hawkish. Perhaps tracking her had come at a cost?

"You look changed," he observed.

Since their initial meeting at the gym, Trevor had been exposed to Level London, massively at first and then in lesser degrees. Today she'd shed that mantel for a woman who got shit done. The cart seller had provided a key piece on the way to a major accomplishment. She would *find* The Soldiers' lair and drop an anonymous tip to INTERPOL. She would *dance* when a customs raid shut their counterfeiting operation down.

Saving herself might save a life, someone's eyesight, or a criminal case of ethanol poisoning. "I *am* different, but, as I recall, you don't find me capable of change."

He nudged closer, leaning down so that his face neared hers. "You don't need to change."

Like my dream. London backed away. Would he bait her and spurn her, laughing at her gullibility?

"There are corners in your head you don't enter," he told her. "Your sister sits in one of them. I was wrong to consider your defense of her a lie. I regret saying—*thinking*—your love could ever be flawed."

Now who was lying?

"'*Broken*', you called me." Grabbing her pack from his hands, she rushed past, aiming for the visitor center. The translation app had worked well enough, but she needed a real computer and fast Internet access for the kind of research she had in mind—*Hungarian Crime Syndicates 101*. Perhaps they could point the way. If not, Attila's hospitality might be put to another use.

She stopped short. "You don't have to do this, you know. I'm off the hook with Tereth." *I stayed the night there.* "The owner tripped over himself in his helpfulness, which means you're off the hook with lawyer Brian, too." Trevor didn't need to know about Attila's happy marriage or the fact that he'd left her with his mom.

"I didn't come here for the job or for you to help me complete it."

London hustled. How much time before Cart Man made contact with A Katonák? *The Soldiers.* She preferred to find them before they found her. "No?"

He snatched her about the waist, stilling her progress with a gentle hold. From behind, he said, "I came to help *you*."

She looked around at the eyes on the street. On all sides, keen glances slid her way, assessing their argument. Men appeared wary, probably contemplating whether to interfere and whether they stood a chance were Trevor to unleash. Women looked… appreciative.

Breath deserted her. "How?"

He turned her until she stared up into grave features. "Your sister, as well as Brian and even Kevin await us in the capital."

The claim made all the sense in the world and no sense at all. "W-what?"

"Your sister went to Brian upon your departure. They went to Kevin. They all came to me. She told us… things. I know about her pills, London, and I know how it started. She got close to Dillon for the wrong reasons."

An understatement.

"I also know what you don't, a rationale she didn't share with you." He bristled, adding sternly, "You love her unconditionally. You must also forgive. Even forget."

Forget? Never. "Sounds like you want forgiveness to be catching."

"I don't deserve it"—he bent to murmur against her temple—"though I do want it. Badly."

He stepped away. The coaxing mien disintegrated, replaced with Trevor's flat, businesslike calm. "I'll fix your feelings for me later. You'll let me because I have something you want."

Pfft. She cocked her head in an effort to look bored.

"I have an *address*."

For the fakes?

He was right, then. The man had a date.

******

Where London had taken the train, Trevor had rented a car and abused the local roads in his efforts to intercept her.

He took his time getting them back.

"Are you hungry?" He held up a chocolate cookie. The hours after sending her away had been filled with grueling, angry exercise. Plus baking. None of the diversion tactics had lessened the burden of hurting her. They'd only emphasized his place at her side.

"For an explanation," she hedged. "You claim to have an address. Clara's knowledge of Dillon's efforts only went so far, pretty much ending in Badacsony. *How* do you know where A Katonák is operating?"

"Money," he said. "Dillon hid his tracks well. From WW's account, he wired the expected amounts for each wine shipment to empty holding companies he'd set up to *look* like legitimate holding companies owned by the vineyards the fakes were quote-unquote 'coming from.' Because he paid the right amounts to what appeared to be the right recipients, his activity didn't raise any flags. Dillon then paid lesser amounts—the amounts actually owed for the fakes, leaving him with a tidy profit on each transaction—from the dummy companies to accounts abroad. With a little patience"—*and disrespect for international law*—"the money was traceable from Denver to London to Budapest. The Hungarian accounts connected to an alias, which linked to a known crime boss within The Soldiers—Laszlio Magyar. Once I found Laszlio, I found his phone and the GPS tracker inside it. U.S. teenagers know better than to leave their GPSs activated for fear their parents will spy on them. I guess that message hasn't made it to the Eastern Block. Turns out Laszlio spends concentrated amounts of time in three places—his home, an office complex, and a warehouse district on the outskirts of central Pest. My money says that where we find Laszlio, we find *killer* wine, emphasis on kill."

Silence greeted the explanation. When he chanced a sidelong peek at London, she sat motionless, staring at the cookie he still held in his right hand. "I *knew* you could do exactly as you've described. I tried to explain and to ask for your help. You turned on me."

Yes. "Know you couldn't be angrier with me than I am with myself. You are *owed*." He planned to deliver.

When Clara had shown up with Brian and Kevin in tow, he'd heard the story of how intertwined the sisters lives had been. The two had depended on each other in a stifling household with rigid rules, at least for London, about how to behave. He had judged her for first protecting herself against his preconceived notions about women committing violence and then protecting her sister, whom she viewed as her one and only lifeline.

Trevor's duplicitous wife had been unique, cruelly manipulating the world to fit her desires. London was equally unique. She had manipulated her desires to fit a cruel world. No longer would Trevor view her through the jaded eyes of a man scorned.

Horror, and then aching regret, had suffused London's face when he'd called her *broken*. Yet she'd stood firm, refusing to give in, even though her problems had recently multiplied by a factor of ten, even when he'd turned his back and shut the door in her face.

She'd burned through her grief, hopped a plane, and gotten down to the business of setting her problems right.

London accepted the cookie. She savored it slowly, in that way of hers that reminded him of how she approached all things sensuous. The woman had no idea of the power in her mouth and in her hands. When she'd had him on the floor of his loft, stroking his chest and moaning and *using* his shaft with newfound abandon, he'd known he would easily kill for her.

When she licked chocolate off her fingers in his car and refused to look at him because he didn't deserve it, he decided he'd die for her.

"So Attila Tereth no longer sees you as the enemy." Trevor hadn't missed her jab about the winemaker's eagerness to please. Who *wouldn't* wish to make London the happiest of women?

"The two of us were never enemies."

"He thought you were."

"I can be persuasive."

Trevor refused to bite. "You'll find I can be persuasive, too. And stubborn." He pulled over. Interesting how they'd strayed to the most secluded of country roads.

"Now what?" she asked.

"I'm about to persuade you to give me another chance. Then I'm taking you to Laszlio's warehouse to watch you ruin his world."

She shrank against the passenger door. "If you think you can screw your way into my good graces, you cannot, I assure you."

So prim and proper and *fierce*. "I don't intent to 'screw' you at all."

Confusion, and, to his intense satisfaction, disappointment, warred in her gaze. "Good."

"I intend to talk to you. But I'm going to plump your nipples while I do it. I'm going to plead with you. But I'm going to rub your clit while I do that."

Her lids slammed shut, scrunching as if to shut him out.

"I plan to beg you. But I'll feel you come around my knuckles before you give in." *I'll ply her with pleasure for as long as it takes.* "Do us both a favor and play hard to get."

******

Trevor smiled as he reached for her, a lazy stretch across otherwise pained features. Never what she'd call playful, he approached now as if his very life depended on her response. His palm drifted closer until the back of his fingers met her cheek. "You deserve more than a passenger seat on a lonesome road. I'll make it a throne."

She leaned into his touch. Outside the car, rain drizzled, obscuring the windows and closeting them in. "We shouldn't—"

"We *must.*" His thumb brushed back and forth, grazing her lips, her brows. "If you feel the need to rush on, all you have to do is tell me *yes.*"

Yes?

"Even better say, 'Yes, Trevor, you get another chance. We'll try again.'"

The stroking along her face slid downward, over her neck. Soon he traced the wide opening at her T-shirt.

"You're remorseful," she observed, giving in to the quiver in her voice. "Because you were wrong, and you no longer view me as unfixable? Or because you want me enough not to care?"

His fingers dipped below the thin material covering her chest, until those gentle stokes glided along the demi cups of her bra. "I look at you and see strength and determination and a capacity for love that, once, boggled my mind. *You* were never broken."

She clenched the seat, trying to hold back. *Failing.*

"That kind of love was an emotion I didn't understand, but it doesn't confuse me anymore. What seemed elusive is now within my grasp." At the last, he delved beneath the lace shielding her breast and softly, ever so lightly, dragged a fingertip across her nipple. London whimpered. Sensation tingled over her skin, at her breasts, her belly, her thighs.

His caress deepened for a moment, then pulled free of her clothing and slid lower, until he cradled her abdomen in his palm. "I like how you love, angel." He rubbed gently. "You love how I touch."

How he touched and *so much more.* She loved the man who'd scooped her off the gym floor and asked her name, who had made her pie and watched over her in the hospital, who had shown her real men made woman feel unimaginably good.

Her head fell back. "*Trevor.*" Her bold trickster, wearing a white hat he wasn't afraid to dirty.

Fingers cupped between her thighs, stretching the maxi skirt she'd donned for wine hunting between the two of them. "I'm already your lover." His touch built a magical friction. "Will you let me be your love?"

The offer presented the ultimate temptation. She lifted her head and met his gaze, saw the smoldering, scorching *prayer* in the harsh planes of his face, and felt helpless. "This isn't fair." She should have been able to breathe, to reason.

"They say life isn't fair. Love *definitely* isn't." He grabbed handfuls of her skirt, gathering the fabric in his solid fist. With each exposed inch of her legs, she tripped closer to falling.

"Tell me, London. Say *yes*."

She shook her head and grabbed his thick wrist, meaning to press him away but instead snatching him close.

"Give me some space, just a little."

The knowing glint in his eyes lured her to his cause. She relaxed against the seat, thighs barely parted. Knowing what he'd do next made her urgency worse. Her whole body lit with needy heat. She wanted to rip at her clothing, tear at his.

Entirely seduced.

He humbled himself, giving everything, asking for nothing but a part of her.

One finger slid between her ready folds. London grabbed the armrest.

"See how I keep my promises?" he said.

I'm going to plead with you. But I'm going to rub your clit while I do that.

"You can count on me, London." He circled and swirled. "I'll be there to taste wines and manage computers. I'll cook your dinners. I will paint your toenails if you wish. And I'll fuck you."

She bit her lip. A low, breathy wail erupted from her throat. When he slid two fingers inside, filling the ache pulsing within, she raked her nails down his arm, trembling and gasping out her delight.

"No," she breathed, as the car swam around her. "I'll fuck *you*."

"Touché." His smile, edgy and determined only minutes before, turned blissful. "I'll take that as a *yes*."

CHAPTER 22

They connected with Brian, Kevin, and Clara at a small Budapest hotel, not far from the majestic Elizabeth Bridge crossing the narrowest stretch of the Danube. The three struck London as unlikely conspirators, but she and Trevor found them huddled cross-legged on the room's one tiny bed with a map and several satellite photos spread between them. Heads together, they studied the layout of outer Budapest with the fervor of long-time partners.

"If the wine sits here"—Clara pointed to the map—"then we should observe from"—her finger swirled above the paper in indecision—"here."

Kevin whistled, the sound low and contemplative. "A strait shot in, and we can park inconspicuously."

Brian noticed their newcomers first. He hefted the pair of binoculars at his side and pretended to search the room, first stopping on London's face and then letting the contraption tilt to the hand Trevor held. "Troops!" he bellowed, emitting a fake bugle call without sounding the least bit like a trumpet. "I've discovered JBF hair looks the same in every country. Our two returning heroes have obviously—"

"I hate to break it to you," London interrupted, "but I don't think your precious Hungarian client will pay six hundred an hour for your brand of insight."

He cast the binoculars aside and veered his attention to Clara. "Occasionally I do good deeds for free."

Transplant them to Hungary, and the brothers stayed in character. Brian, the impeccable, irreverent lawyer in navy khakis and a striped V-neck that molded to every honed muscle of his torso. And Kevin, the real-estate king in ripped jeans and a beer T-shirt. Brian making jokes. Kevin looking on while devious plans worked behind hooded eyes.

Next to her, Trevor took in the apparent comradery with unveiled suspicion. London could see that while he called Kevin "friend," he called

Brian "colleague," and he didn't harbor much hope for either of them.

Trevor's free hand skimmed down her back, ushering her forward into the room. "We'll leave the good sisters to catch up." A meaningful look passed to Kevin and Brian, and the two brothers gathered the maps and pictures and hopped from the bed, suddenly eager to take their talks of world domination elsewhere. Without further ado, Trevor told Clara a stern, "You'll be fine," and London, "Hear her out."

Then the three men abandoned the room, leaving London to face her sister alone. Clara didn't move from her place on the bed. She looked up at London, eyes wide and imploring.

And clear.

"Are you sober?" London asked.

"Yes."

London nodded. After all the lies, she might be a fool to believe, but Clara had ditched the fidgeting. She sat quietly, steady and calm, waiting for London to take a seat. When London lowered herself to the edge of the bed, Clara smiled, and the pureness in the gesture ate at the stiffness between them.

London broke the silence. "I'm told there's more to know about your relationship with Dillon."

Clara's smile melted off her face. "Oh, *London*, it wasn't a relationship. I suppose that's the most important point."

Did it help that her sister had slept with Dillon casually? "Maybe we shouldn't—"

"I won't deny the pills and the money played a part, but I approached Dillon—came on to him, I guess you could say—with a plan to lure him away from you."

"I don't understand. You say that like you're *proud*." And pride in betrayal would never do.

Clara held up a hand. Whether the tremors London detected hinted at withdrawal symptoms or extreme emotion, London couldn't guess.

"Do you think I didn't know how he treated you?" Clara asked. "Do you think I couldn't see his pleasure in your fear?"

Oh, God.

Clara went on, pausing frequently, her voice flat. "I don't know the details. After all we've been through, you didn't share. But I knew Dillon Farro was hurting you, in big ways and small. I knew he was getting worse. And I knew that, for whatever reason, that escalation wasn't enough for you to cut him from your life. So I approached him, *yes*, and seduced him, *yes*, and baited his monstrous little mind with the idea of infusing WW's selection with a very limited amount of quality fakes. Dillon could make extra money and feel like he was getting the best of you at the same time. *He always wanted to get the best of you.* He believed me because he knew about the pills. He knew I needed money, too, enough to cheat the person I love most."

"I planned to expose the scheme after it did a certain amount of damage." Clara stopped, visibly contemplating the logic. "You'll take almost anything, London—look at what you took from Dillon on a personal level—but you protect WW like a lioness. I planned to expose both Dillon and myself once I felt confident your knowledge would lead to Dillon's total expulsion from your life—you'd dump him and fire him. You'd save yourself on WW's behalf, and I suppose I counted on your forgiving me. Your drive to build WW became a tool I planned to use against you, but also *for* you."

London's vision blurred, and she whispered, "I didn't dump him. I *killed* him."

"*Don't* say things that aren't true. At the time, you didn't even know about the fakes. This doesn't change the fact that Dillon died in an *accident* before I could complete the plan. When that happened, I put the Olaszrizling from my mind, knowing the whole scheme would die on the vine without Dillon around to keep it going."

London leaned forward, searching Clara's face. "It didn't."

"Exactly. I'm not sure why I trusted Dillon when I knew he wasn't capable of honesty. At some point, he switched gears. Instead of staying small-time, he built new and different relationships. He got organized using company dollars, and he threw WW into the deep end without swimming lessons. I swear to you—on my recovery, on my *life*—I didn't know."

The timing of the shipments corroborated Clara's story—from last year's sub-par Olaszrizling and this year's deadly cousin, to the most recent mega shipment of many WW staples. "Did you make money from your plan? Is that why you didn't explain this before?"

Clara's answer came in a halting admission. "I didn't tell you before because I felt you would feel worse about my deciding you required interference, like our parents have always done. I'm sorry, London, but in this case, you *did* require my interference. In the end, though, Dillon and I were—both of us—guilty."

Yes, London rushed to think. *And no*. Clara spoke true. London had only broken things off with Dillon after she'd begun to suspect mismanagement of his import work. The Olaszrizling had tipped her in that direction, even without Clara's big reveal. That burst of courage had led to Dillon's sudden attack and London's defense of herself. Without Clara's horrible, traitorous, thieving plan, London might still be under Dillon's thumb.

"Guilty," London agreed, "but, in a roundabout way, effective." London could dub it *helpful-addict syndrome*, the ultimate pure heart and empty head.

"Brian caught me with the pills." Clara ducked her chin and picked at a loose string on the bedspread, hedging on the details. "He stalked me out of the hospital after I relieved you of the prescription from Mom. While Trevor busied himself falling in love with you, Brian saw my weakness and exploited it for information. That man is merciless." A shallow cough brought Clara's head up. "London, there are moments when I know I'll regret my actions forever. Other times I swear I'd do it all over again. Either way, I'm here to begin making amends. Without me, there wouldn't be a threat in a Hungarian warehouse. Let me help you end this. Then we'll go home and heal."

London picked up the binoculars Brian had abandoned on the bed. She breathed on the lenses and then shined the twin pieces of glass with the edge of her shirt until they gleamed. Outside, dusk had overtaken the city, shadowing the spires and gables and turrets that made Budapest unique. If there could be a right time to find and expose the counterfeiters, or a wrong time to punish her sister, this was it on both counts.

"Deal," London said, soft and sad. She took her sister's hand like they were back on the cul-de-sac, and together they slipped from the room in search of their self-proclaimed sidekicks.

CHAPTER 23

Trevor tapped his foot in a quiet, ineffective rhythm, his grip threatening to bow the steering wheel. The five of them sat skulking within their rented sedan, tinted windows and all, in the exact spot Clara had pinpointed on the map. Three hours had passed with nothing but a few stray dogs and a skinny cat that had curled up on the hood.

The building he'd targeted sat in a secluded area of Budapest's seventh district. Once entirely derelict and neglected, many of the city's popular "ruin pubs" had sprouted into the district's abandoned buildings and their large vacant lots. Those parts of the area gave Budapest's party scene its best nightclubs, channeling Berlin's penchant for opening bars in bunkers and warehouses. Other corners of District Seven remained desolate, an aging salute to more industrial pursuits.

Despite the echoes of music and booze on the breeze, the concrete goliath within his sights appeared to be a former repair shop gutted of signs of life. If Trevor had done his job well, the building hid more than cobwebs and vagrants. Those cracked walls and broken windows shielded an illegal operation that supplied pockets of the western world with counterfeit wine.

The setting had a familiar feel, déjà vu of a life Trevor remembered well—the waiting, the innocuous veneer that most certainly shielded dire straits, the crawling sensation of being unprepared and without a remedy. In his experience, the scene hinted at unavoidable conflict and unattainable success. He thought of the flybot that had ended his faith in his military superiors and again wished for technology that could provide a glimpse behind the veil.

Kevin yawned from the backseat. "Maybe you got it wrong, hoss. I mean, sure, the trail led here, but don't you think these guys are smart enough to lay fake breadcrumbs."

"They're smart enough." In fact they *had* laid a false trail. Trever had blown through it to the real one.

"Then I'm telling you—wrong place, right time. Let's recalibrate—"

"Shut up." London whirled in her seat and added sweetly, "Please."

Trevor stifled a grin. London and Kevin might never make amends, and he rather enjoyed watching her abuse him for his early callousness. Kevin, too used to hero worship, deserved to have beautiful women smack him down at every turn.

Kevin bristled. "Maybe they don't work at night."

This time Brian chimed in. "Baby bro, my favorite-because-you're-my-only sibling, they *always* work at night."

"Yeah," Clara agreed, shifting to get comfortable in the three-inch gap between the two brothers. "You need to brush up on your stakeout skills. Patience is key."

Kevin swiveled his head on his neck and looked down at her, looking mock horrified. "'Patience' coming from a—"

"Don't," London snapped. "If I know my sister, one more word and you'll be flying home for emergency surgery of the testicle-repair variety."

"*Guys*," Trevor said. The crew must have sensed a shift in his tone because every head turned to stare out at a van that had pulled up in front of the building's chain-locked double doors.

Brian clapped with only the tips of his fingers. "Ooooh. We have a starless night, an abandoned building, and a black van with a shady driver. Could this *be* more *James Bond?*"

Trevor couldn't resist. "Yes, if you were tougher and better looking."

Two figures slithered from the van amid the groaning and laughing in the car. London seized Trevor's arm. "Is that?" She grabbed the binoculars. "That's the street seller from Badacsony. Why would he be here? This can't be business as usual."

They waited as the guy they recognized undid the padlock and unwound the chain. He disappeared into the space within, while the other man stood guard outside. A lonely light flickered to life in the high windows.

The lookout had fifteen years on his lackey, and he dressed like a professor in a tweed jacket and loafers shiny enough to see through the tint in the window. Trevor had seen that face online—*Laszlio Magyar.*

One answer made sense. "The wine seller warned them about your presence, and they called him back from the wilds of Middle Hungary. *Laszlio* reeled him in."

"I presented myself as a friendly," London countered, her voice sliding from surprise to confusion. "He believed me to be a returning customer. I even showed him The Soldiers' invoices. Nothing his beady-eyed bosses could find on me or my company would've shown otherwise. As far as they know, I'm an ally, not a threat."

"Then this warehouse hides more than bunk wine." Brian's lips compressed into a grim line, all joking set aside.

Trevor let out a contemplative grunt. "London *did* ask for an address. She made it clear she wanted a face-to-face. Whatever hides inside must be something not even a returning customer ought to see."

CHAPTER 24

London couldn't fathom what she was seeing. On the heels of Trevor's pronouncement, Cart Man exited the building and opened the back of the van. In quick, furtive jerks, he flung the double doors wide. *People* poured out.

People who'd been locked inside.

A girl staggered to the ground, heaving in the dirt. She appeared to be in her late teens, with dark skin and hair. Cart Man kicked at her heels until she rose and stumbled into the van. Others poured through the doors, desperate to move from one enclosure to another, as though circumstances might improve if they could only escape the warehouse.

Another woman limped and clutched a bandage around her forearm. Yet another carried a *baby*. All the women remained quiet. None tried to run.

The well-dressed gentleman didn't engage. He watched passively, almost appearing bored, while people were loaded into the vehicle like cattle.

"*Holy Shit*," Kevin whispered.

The antics in the car went silent, the sound of harsh breathing the sole sign of life. London knew—they *all* knew—exactly what played out in front of them.

Human trafficking. The Soldiers used smuggled workers to do the organization's backbreaking dirty work, locking living beings within a cavernous garage each night like animals in a test lab.

Only seconds passed before Cart Man relocked the doors, and the two men drove off with a vanload of workers.

As they drove past, London saw Trevor jotting the license plate on his wrist. Shell-shocked, she gaped at the now sinister façade. The interior light flickered, lending the scene an eerie glow. When she stared hard, she saw movement.

Not through the windows. They flew too high.

Of the doors. Tiny pulses gave the impression of outward momentum. She cracked her car door and stared hard across the empty lot. Yes, the doors were moving, and the only possible cause...

"There are more people inside!"

In a rush, she bailed from the car. Trevor overtook her, yelling to Brain and Kevin to grab the tire iron from the trunk. When they came to a sharp stop at the doors, they could hear banging from within. Some cries sounded like Hungarian, others clearly another language. In her panic, London couldn't place the languages.

"Hallo!" Trevor ventured in the German most locals could decipher. "Bitte halten. Wir werden kommenden." He slapped the metal doors with both hands. "I told them to hold on and that we're coming. Who knows if anyone understood."

Brian, Kevin, and Clara arrived with the tire iron and a flashlight. Trevor shoved the iron's flat end through the looped shackle and gave a mighty heave. The padlock protested, but held. He shoved the metal farther through the loop and tried again. With a loud clank, the lock gave.

When Trevor whipped the chain aside and began to inch the doors apart, a stampede of bodies thrust their small band of rescuers aside. Men and woman alike pushed the doors apart and rushed into the night. Stepping over the threshold, London entered a cavernous hall. The ceiling soared on the left, but on the right, two stories and a set of metal stairs stacked within the same space.

Rickety tables crossed the main room in end-to-end succession, forming what appeared to be a makeshift assembly line. At one end, empty wine bottles filled box upon box. At the other, full bottles stood upright, awaiting packaging. In between, the tables held tubs of dingy water, vats of unidentified liquids, and an entire section of store-bought juices. She saw a printer, a stack of blank labels, and even a blinking laptop. The place smelled like a cross between a malfunctioning fume hood and a tractor repair center.

She shot Trevor an uneasy glance. Threadbare pallets littered the floor in a corner. The people they'd freed had truly been imprisoned behind locked doors, forced into indentured servitude, likely in exchange for passage into Hungary from whatever country they'd sought to escape in search of a better life.

Trevor's deep voice rumbled. "Kevin, video every detail with your phone. Brian, call the authorities and then take photos. Nobody touches a thing unless it's a person who's... alive."

London rushed Brian a piece of paper from her pocket. She'd written down the number for the Tourist Police, who apparently spoke English on a twenty-four hour hotline. She'd envisioned a calmly delivered tip to the customs division of INTERPOL and Hungary's International Police. Now they needed emergency services and backup before Cart Man returned with his van, likely armed and conditioned for violence.

Coincidentally, London felt her own urge to inflict pain. Those bastards had done much worse than sell dangerous booze to people like her. They'd tortured innocents in order to manufacture it.

Relying on their solo flashlight and one low-burning fixture swinging from the ceiling, London and Clara ventured deep into the space. They couldn't leave a soul stranded in this hellhole. As they shuffled forward, the air thickened and heated. At the back of the high bay, they veered right, through a door, and into another large room. The heat intensified, almost intolerable.

"Trevor!"

He barreled in behind her, immediately letting loose with a string of curses worthy of a trademark. A little girl, maybe four or five years old, clung to his side like a monkey. She'd wrapped her hands about his neck, her legs about his waist. He held onto her with equal zeal.

Brian and Kevin followed, phones up. Kevin narrated as he recorded. "A small door sits at the back of the warehouse. It leads to... MOTHERFUCKER!"

A dais rose at the center of the room. On top, industrial-sized burners worked overtime to heat a number of drums of boiling fluid. Alcohol vapors saturated the air, and dozens of plastic jugs—some filled, others awaiting their turn—clustered around the base of the platform. The source material for The Soldiers' gawd-awful wine became instantly obvious. They began with subpar moonshine from a poorly ventilated, illegal still. From there, they branched out—probably with various industrial chemicals—to make an endless variety of products for cents on the dollar.

Without supervision, the burners had overheated in the aftermath of the exodus from the warehouse. Flames licked upward, hugging the drums, feeding off the fumes as they stretched toward freedom.

London didn't see a fire extinguisher. An explosion was imminent.

"In seconds," Brian muttered, "this place is going to be warehouse barbeque." He snapped a picture of the rising fire.

"Mamă!"

The tiny girl in Trevor's arms shrieked and kicked. Following her pointed finger, London saw a young woman curled on the floor. Kevin reached her first. He shoved his phone in a pocket and flipped her over, cradling her above the concrete. Even unconscious and grimy, her exotic beauty stood out against the ugly surroundings. If forced to guess, London would say she was Roma, some might say Gypsy, and probably from neighboring Romania. Black-haired and coffee-skinned, she had bold, striking features, even with her eyes closed. Sooty lashes fanned out over smooth cheeks, and the woman had been blessed with slender curves that made a mockery of her tattered, loose-fitting dress.

London's stomach clenched at the sight. This wasn't the place for one so pretty. The men who'd held her captive wouldn't have overlooked her beauty, or its worth.

The woman's chest rose and fell in shallow heaves, but she didn't respond to Kevin's gentle crooning. "Hello, love," he said. "Open your eyes. I'd do anything to see them."

The little girl howled. "Mamă!"

Kevin looked up at the rest of them, and London saw in his eyes a helpless desperation she hadn't thought possible.

"Pick her up." The instruction came from Clara, calm and collected. "Carry her, Kevin. We'll take her out of here."

The command snapped Kevin out of his stupor, and he gathered her up like precious cargo. Brian snapped one final photo of the two of them.

Then they ran.

Trevor sheltered the little girl with one arm and pulled London with the other. She scrambled to stay on her feet, knowing he'd drag her if necessary. The moment they burst from the door, an blast rocked the rear of the building. Once clear, London staggered to a halt behind Trevor and turned to see balls of fire spurting upward from a gaping hole in the roof.

Surprisingly, many of the people they'd freed still milled about the lot, watching with unconcealed relief and wonder.

They had only been inside a matter of minutes and already sirens blared in the distance, growing closer with each heartbeat. The back of London's neck prickled, and she looked over her shoulder. A black van slowed, then sped past the rental car, disappearing into the night.

Too late for that.

She had names, pictures, videos, invoices, and numerous eye-witness accounts. Even many of the victims held their ground as the police approached. The shipments would stop. A Katonák would pay. She had ample proof of her innocence in the counterfeiting scheme.

London would never know whether the still would have blown without her involvement.

"It would have."

London looked up at Trevor. His intensity bore down on her with nearly the heat of the fire. "I can *hear* what you're thinking. And it *would* have blown. Maybe not tonight, but the operation lacked the requisite components required of long-term success. Plastic jugs? Rusted drums? No ventilation?" He looked appalled. "Plus... fate. You may have rushed the explosion, but you were also on hand to free every single soul trapped in that building."

"Because of you."

177

"No, London." He nuzzled the gorgeous baby girl in his arms. Sensing that she and her mom were safe, the child had relaxed. She played with Trevor's shirt, and he twirled her curls. "*All* of this is because of you."

Tears leaked unchecked as she looked around. Fire crews battled the blaze. Kevin had sunk to the chewed-up asphalt, clinging to the woman he'd carried free, crooning into her ear. Brian and Clara stood by, perhaps a tad closer than necessary, their heads bowed above Brian's phone and his "epic" video.

"I told you you'd ruin Laszlio's world." Trevor's lips brushed hers. "I should have told you that whether or not you succeeded, you'd always be the center of mine."

EPILOGUE

"This got you to *yes* once, London," Trevor rasped as his body plunged into hers.

"Maybe it will again. Better keep trying." She'd fully blossomed into the sex(y) monster Trevor had hoped to create, pulling her man aside at his brother's nuptials for their own wedding-night rehearsal in a makeshift dressing room. The bridesmaids had moved along to pictures. They didn't need the room anymore.

She, however, did.

Or at least she needed the wall currently rubbing along her back.

Trevor angled her thigh so his shaft hit deep. In the months since their so-called "Bust in Budapest," she and Trevor had discovered every pleasure imaginable. Some days he took her slow and sweet, like their first time together. Others he let himself be wild, handling her like a doll and bending her to his will.

As promised, she periodically took *him*.

The freedom London felt in both love and lust blew her wildest imaginings. Life had taught her restraint and rules. A man had taught her fear and reservation. The idea of living and loving boldly hadn't been in her cards.

Two months ago, they'd flown to Hungary to testify against Laszlio Magyar and his Soldiers. The organization had been dismantled from the roots, and WW Imports thrived. Clara had completed an in-house rehab program and remained steadfast in staying clean and seeking support. London had moved into Trevor's loft. Every night she sat at the island while Trevor cooked.

While Trevor *proposed*.

He kept the ring with the spices, flashing the diamond every chance he got. So far London had pled for more time, wanting to settle into their new life before the next step. The last remaining vestiges of Level London demanded they get a plant, then a dog, and *then* talk marriage.

Lately the loft could double for a greenhouse, and Sasha was on permanent loan.

"I should punish you," Trevor threatened, pulling out. At her gasp, he slid back in, slow and steady. "But I won't." His hips pistoned, gaining speed to match her panting breaths. "I think I *like* you as a tease."

She rubbed her face along his stubble, purring that she *loved* to tease him because of where it got her—stranded on his glorious cock.

He had to stifle both of their cries with his mouth, crashing into hers as they shuddered and shook. Still supported and resting her forehead on his chest—careful not to get makeup on his impeccable tux—she caught her breath.

Outside their haven, she could hear so many new friends, soon to be family. Cole's bride, Lissa, had hugged London on sight, saying, "Sister, and I mean that literally, this place may not be New York City, but you and me? We'll still shop the fuck out of it."

Lissa's best friend and matron of honor, Scarlet, had flown to Puerto Rico on a private jet with her intense husband, Ethan. London knew Lissa had money, but Scarlet oozed class. When they'd met, she'd smiled and handed London a small black-and-white box tied with a red ribbon. The swirl pattern on the side read, "Saks Fifth Avenue," in curly letters.

"Wear this for Trevor," Scarlet had advised, with Lissa cackling over her shoulder. "Do it tonight."

London had the box hidden in her bag. She planned to don the gift at the right moment…

That moment came after dinner. Brian had finished his second-best-man speech, standing up on Lissa's side of the aisle. He'd toasted the couple's "good looks" and given them Lissa's most expensive abstract painting as a gift, a nod—London had been told—to the fact that Cole had initially despised Lissa's artwork. Today, he'd had the hotel ballroom outfitted with her prints for the reception, all flown in from Colorado, rather like a traveling museum exhibition for the guests at the party.

When Cole settled in front of Lissa to slip the traditional garter from her thigh, London didn't join the women wrangling to catch the scrap of satin in the toss. Trevor cast her a dirty look, surely thinking she planned to avoid the ultimate catch and the tradition that went along with it. Instead, she directed his hand to *her* thigh beneath the table, dragging his fingers upward until they met a garter all their own.

Trevor appeared confused, but he didn't waste time curling his grip around the band and sliding it down her leg, slowly, dragging his fingertips along her inner thigh with every inch. Always Trevor with the slow reveal, and he called *her* a tease.

As he lifted the garter from her leg, she waited for him to bring it into the light, knowing he would while the room remained distracted by the newlyweds. When he did, she laughed with joy and watched her man read the three words embroidered on the cloth: *Yes! I ! Will!*

BOOKS BY LIBBY RICE

Second Chances Series

Love Me Later

Art-Crossed Love

Love Drunk

Funny Bitches Series

Book one coming in the Spring of 2016

THANK YOU!

Thanks for reading *Love Drunk*. I hope you enjoyed the read as much as I enjoyed the write!

Would you like to know when my next book is available? You can sign up for my new-release e-mail list at *www.libbyrice.com*.

I post regular snippets from novels, pictures of character adventures, and other fun extras on my Facebook page. I also post tidbits about what's going on with me. Come join us at *www.facebook.com/libbyrice.author*.

Or you can follow me on Twitter at @libby_rice, Instagram at libby_rice, and/or Goodreads at *https://www.goodreads.com/LibbyRice*.

Reviews help readers find books they'll love. I welcome and appreciate *all* reviews, whether positive or negative.

You've just read the third book in the Second Chances series. There are two other novels in this series—*Love Me Later* and *Art-Crossed Love* each read as a standalone novel. For excerpts, please read on.

LOVE ME LATER: EXCERPT

Can they love right on the redo?

Scarlet Leore enjoys a glittering existence amongst society's elite. Ethan Blake is a prizefighter knocking his way through school, counting on his winnings to bankroll the dreams that won't fit in a boxing ring. When the two meet, neither can deny the instant attraction that wells between the hulking fighter and the heiress who is miles and millions out of his league. But a vicious attack leaves Scarlet physically and emotionally battered, and for Ethan, her allure crumbles along with the rest of his life after she accuses him of wielding the knife.

Years later, Scarlet has abandoned the high life for that of a hard-working lawyer, while Ethan has clawed his way to the pinnacle of a business empire. Drawn into his world of high-stakes tech mergers, they dance to a tune of revenge, desire, and finally, redemption. But their world won't tolerate an attorney falling for her client. They'll need more than lust and forgiveness. They must bridge the chasm of a tormented past to understand who they are today. Only then can they forge a future in the face of the resurging enemy who once tore them apart.

December—New York City

The tunneling entrance of the club opened to a packed arena and a blinding wall of light. Blood, sweat, and testosterone hung heavy in the stale air, shrouding two roped-off contenders in an invisible layer of menace. The fight had started.

Scarlet tracked the boxers with an untrained, but keen, eye. In the midst of sinking to her space on the scarred aluminum bleacher, she stopped, arrested by what she saw in the ring two rows down.

One man had blond hair, the other black, a color so dark it gleamed with a bluish tint under the fluorescent glare. The blond certainly deserved his heavyweight distinction, but next to the darker brute, his pale limbs appeared almost fine-boned. The striking contrasts didn't end there. Both men pummeled each other without reserve, yet the dark-haired fighter struck with less desperation, more calculation. From the other, she sensed a tendency to throw out every move in his repertoire, one after the other, until a fist connected.

"Utkatasana?" The question arrived with butchered pronunciation and a low chuckle that dragged Scarlet from her slack-jawed musings. She and Lissa had come to the fight to ogle her friend's new interest. From Lissa's description—"tall, dark, and rough"—Scarlet knew exactly who the man was, and she certainly couldn't fault Lissa's taste.

"As a matter of fact," Scarlet said, looking left to catch Lissa's smirk. "I always drop a quick chair pose before a boxing match. All the cool kids do."

Except she'd never been to a boxing match and was pretty sure that other than Lissa, none of the Harry-Winston-wearing, charity-hosting socialites she knew would be caught dead in a dingy fight club in Brooklyn, perfect yoga form or not. Tennis was more their style. Especially when played quietly and accompanied by one of those announcers who screamed in a whisper.

Their loss. Or so she told herself. In truth, she didn't think those women found the confines of wealth lonely or isolating, whereas she fit in at the top about as well as she did here, where men fanned money in the air, taking impromptu bets on the violence unfolding for their entertainment, while Scarlet tried to casually blend into her seat.

"Where'd you meet him?" Scarlet thrust her chin at the dark-haired Adonis who now danced beyond his opponent's reach. With each movement, the muscles of his arms and torso flexed and relaxed with the fluidity of an evening tide, dark eyes burning with quiet determination. At least it would be a short fight.

"Not him," Lissa replied with a dismissive clip, ducking to rummage through her purse. "I met mine in sculpture class." She glanced up. "Looks like I should ask yours to model."

Scarlet got stuck on "Not him." As in, not hers and possibly available. She wouldn't be violating the cardinal rule of girlfriend-hood if she hunted the soon-to-be winner down after the fight and proposed. The radical thought stuck in her chest, pushing her heartbeat from a semi-manageable trot to a full-scale gallop.

Lissa shot her a fascinated look. "Re-heely, stop licking your lips. He's not a snack."

"No." Scarlet coughed into a fist, letting herself smile. "I'll be his." Already gleaming with sweat, dark head bent low, the man was delicious, the perfect spice for a stifled life if she dare reach high.

"Touché," Lissa answered with a wide grin. Then, bold as she pleased,

Lissa reached out and tugged at the square bodice of Scarlet's dress. Scarlet jerked back, but the material inched downward under Lissa's tenacious attention, revealing a flash of flesh.

Squirming away, Scarlet yelped, "What are you doing?" And batted at Lissa's questing fingers, wrestling for control over the thick brocade bodice.

Lissa shrugged. "We want He-Man's focus to shift right"—light taps pegged the apex of Scarlet's cleavage—"here."

Heat crawled from Scarlet's hairline downward. "No, we really don't." With a final wrench, she righted the dress and turned back to the fight. One look told her she hadn't been the only one distracted by the skirmish. An aggressive gaze had swiveled her direction from inside the ring. She'd known his eyes would be dark, but like his hair, they were black, chips of midnight that examined her with the same single-minded calculation he used to size up his opponent in the ring. Before she could muster even a faint nod in acknowledgment, his thickly fringed lids dipped, then jerked toward his shoulder with the rest of his head, absorbing what looked to be a killer blow to the jaw.

Of course Lissa didn't miss the exchange. "You alone in that apartment tonight?" She slid Scarlet a sly look, wetting her lips.

Scarlet's stomach dropped in quick, clenching rebellion, whether from Lissa's question or the lost glance, she couldn't say. "Just me, Liss." Her words sounded overly bright to her own ears. She'd spoken to her father once since arriving from Stanford for the winter break. A hundred bucks said Tripp Leore wouldn't venture within a thousand miles of New York City for the holidays, leaving her the sole inhabitant of six-thousand square feet of Manhattan high-rise.

Alone put it mildly.

Feeling the need to justify her answer, to seem a tad less pathetic, Scarlet added, "But Dad left a present." A one-sentence note on the counter had announced the car waiting in her underground parking space. Maserati. Red. Hers. The typed narrative had conveyed the gist, everything except, maybe, "Merry Christmas."

Each year brought a gift more extravagant than the one before it. Beginning with a Russian sable jacket the December her mother had died, and continuing every holiday since, the presents had proven costly, yet impersonal, luxury items to be paid for by her father, but selected by an assistant. One Christmas without her dad had turned to two, then five, now ten. Time had morphed from longing for his presence into anger over his absence and, finally, into acceptance of the status quo. These days, Scarlet took the presents and tried to enjoy them, never confusing money for love.

The arena erupted around them, and Scarlet jumped up to see her future husband power drive a right hook into his opponent's jaw. The man wobbled on his feet before sliding slowly to his knees and face planting on the canvas.

The referee's hands hurtled skyward. "Knockout!" He grabbed Husband's wrist for a victory revolution, giving the crowd its frenzied fill.

Scarlet remained standing when her man ducked under the ropes, escaping without a backward glance. She wiggled her fingers, but plastered damp palms against her thighs, refusing to reach for his retreating form. A familiar glow settled in her chest, then spread upward. Want. Different than the trivial, acquisitive desires she'd been exposed to for most of her life—for a trip, a trinket, a haute-couture gown. The low burn spoke of what she actually needed—affection, closeness, passion. All the things she'd been taught never to demand.

An optimistic smile tugged at the edges of her lips. Scarlet had found her sport.

******

Ethan folded himself onto an indoor picnic bench in a dive Mexican place in none other than Little Italy. He sat on prize money for the rent, and across from a stunning blonde for pure pleasure. His post-fight mood had been light, and he'd been persuaded to join a couple other boxers heading into Manhattan with two beautiful, and apparently rich, coeds.

The aroma of seared onions and green chili wafted from the kitchen, and his growling stomach balked at the wait for a plate of cholesterol. Patience came easy, though, with the unbeatable scenery. He let his gaze track lazily across the table. A bit of frippery? Yes, but Scarlet Leore dazzled all the same.

"Where'd you learn to fight?" she asked.

Ethan heard the question but decided it was likely directed at someone else.

"Ethan, right?"

Nope. She definitely spoke to him.

"Chicago." He swallowed a mouthful of Corona. Eight hundred miles stretched between him and home. Not nearly enough.

Scarlet drummed her hands against the table and then pointed at him in a clear invitation to elaborate. When he didn't, she dug in. "Did you box in school?"

Tenacious little thing. Ethan habitually avoided questions about the life he was in the process of leaving behind, but he was equally uneager to see her turn that gorgeous face to the guy sitting to her left. So he improvised. "Still in school." A skinny wallet had dictated a late educational start. "And no, not at *Kingsborough*. Community colleges don't generally have boxing programs, Empress." He'd never been the Columbia type.

She grinned, momentarily sidetracked. "Empress?"

"I figure you blew past princess around the third grade." The dress, the flawless hair and makeup, the car she'd been lucky to park outside—and would be even luckier to retrieve in one piece—all of it pointed to a life as someone's queen. She made him wish he could afford the upkeep.

"*I* think you might be right," she conceded with a conspiratorial wink. "So where'd you learn?"

He surprised himself with an honest answer. "At home." Not knowing how to say more without saying too much, he bit his tongue, refusing to add, "*On the blood-stained carpet under my mom's old couch.*"

Unfazed, Scarlet waited patiently, calm and expectant, obviously ready for an uplifting tale. The story didn't go that way.

"My dad was a hitter." He dropped the bomb casually. Her expression remained passive, but her shoulders hitched a fraction closer her ears.

Gripping the table, he stretched through the length of his arms. "I learned to hit back." He owed much of that journey to an inner-city boxing club. Other aspects of his training could be called… freelance.

Sudden irritation spiked at what his Barbie of a dinner companion had coaxed him to reveal. He let his eyes roam from the top of her shining head to her well-displayed breasts and back again. She exuded old-school sex. The costly vintage dress and outrageous jewels conjured up images of the glamorous pinup girls of a bygone era. Women didn't look like her anymore. Too many dieted down to nothing before purchasing globular breasts of the man-made variety. She appeared to be a utopia of *au natural*. And he *liked* it.

Her back shot straight, and she reached behind her. In a blink, a black cardigan covered her assets.

His stomach, already grasping, clenched at the loss. "Think a woman like you would like a street fight, where the loser bleeds in the gutter until he gets up and drags himself home?"

She stiffened despite the cheerful conversations buzzing around them, and her once-coaxing voice dropped in open challenge. "A woman like me?"

Flawless. "Rich. Spoiled." He took another long pull from his beer. "Ever seen a street fight, Empress? If you do, nix the earrings."

Her flirtatious smile faded, replaced with a wary look. One hand rose to skim nervously over a huge diamond stud flashing at her ear. She looked to have an idea about where he might take the conversation, and she wasn't willing to go along. But she surprised him when she said breezily, "Quite the tough guy, huh? A fighter out of necessity and all that? Never had a thing handed to you and resent people who did?"

His eyes narrowed. Few people mocked him. And Scarlet had recently seen him beat a man unconscious for money. Her words stung, a little because of the sheen of disdain that threaded through the thinly-veiled joke, but mostly because she was right. *Well, well…*

She ignored his look and went on. "I suppose that makes you smarter, more worthy than someone like me? Because I was born wealthy, I'm stupid? Lazy? Dangerous in some way?"

No, he thought, obviously not stupid. And her brand of head-to-toe perfection couldn't be lazy. But *dangerous* put it mildly.

Already fascinated, it only got better as she decided to give him a run for the money he didn't have. She stretched languidly and pulled the cardigan off her shoulders. Then she leaned forward—far forward—over the table. Her golden eyes were a couple shades darker than her hair, and she smelled like anything but onions and green chili.

"Tell me," she whispered, heat simmering in her appraising gaze. "Other than being poor and able to hit really, *really* hard, why are you so special?"

Ethan stared back. The answer was simple. He excelled at doing *a lot* of things really hard.

Scarlet's taunt had ended just as their food arrived. Before they could be interrupted, Ethan leaned in to meet her. She didn't pull back, and his lips brushed her diamond earring when he said softly, "Wouldn't you like to know."

"Scarlet"—her friend slid a margarita between them—"Su amiga no get carded."

Scarlet. He liked hearing the name said aloud, a siren's name as tempting as the rest of her. Except for that smart mouth…

The thought died when he decided her mouth tantalized, too. She ate leisurely, with a sensual ease he supposed all rich kids were taught. Forget the burrito, he wanted to see her suck oysters straight from the shell, then lick an ice cream cone drizzled with strawberry sauce.

The way people ate said a lot about their nature. This rich man's daughter wasn't cold.

And that was pre-dessert. When she sucked the sopaipilla sugar from the tips of her fingers, he scrubbed his face, threw a twenty to the table, and extended his palm in her direction.

"Let me take you home."

ART-CROSSED LOVE: EXCERPT

Can love be more than a four-letter word?

Lissa Blanc is a painter on a mission. She filters the world through a lens of color, line, and form and hides her ambition behind a delicate smirk that lets her critics believe life comes easy. To her, art isn't what she sees. It's what she feels. Few know that behind the glitz of a prodigious upbringing, she's driven to emerge from the shadow of painful memories that insist she'll never be a renowned talent in her own right.

Cole Rathlen is a photographer on the mend. A crippling grief has stifled his once-rising career and compromised his creative instincts. Knowing he can't stagnate forever, he seeks a twisted absolution in the form of a woman whose paintings give life to the emotions he won't let himself imagine, let alone feel.

When the two partner for a prestigious project that will pull them from the mountains of Colorado to the palaces of India, Lissa quickly realizes that more than diverging ideals hinder their search for success and salvation. Was Cole's life upended by a tragic but unavoidable choice or something more sinister? While Lissa can't delve into the mystery but not the man, Cole can't resist a tenacious soul that refuses to leave him chained. As the truth closes in on a project finally sprouting wings, will Lissa sacrifice her chance at success to set Cole free? Or will Cole shrug the chains of lingering regrets to prove that those who love the most, love again.

February—Boulder, Colorado

Cole set the prostitute's money on the nightstand, wondering if his wife's angel was laughing as hard as the living woman would have. Low light from an overhanging lamp highlighted Ben Franklin's sagging jowls, and Cole flicked his gaze toward the cash. "We agreed on four hundred?"

"Yes," she said. "Thanks." Her voice held the cultured tones of the upper class. This wasn't your average streetwalking hustler, but an

190

expensive call girl living the good life. Boulder, Cole was learning, didn't offer much variety in the way of hired sex. For cheap love, a guy drove to Denver.

Ms. Jewel, or at least the woman who called herself that, reached across a foot of empty space separating their respective queen beds. The hotel might be respectable, but he hadn't splashed out for a suite. Most of her customers didn't, she'd told him, and he wanted the pictures to be representative of a normal gig.

Long, tapered nails scratched lightly over his thigh in a less-than-subtle suggestion. In her mid-thirties, Ms. Jewel looked to be a willing—more like eager—twenty-five, but her caress didn't stir anything but mild curiosity. No surprise there.

Cole hadn't come to fuck.

He halted her progress with a gentle hold on her slim wrist. "Beautiful, definitely, but you know why we're here."

"Close-ups and conversation," she acknowledged with a sly smile. "But a girl can hope." Drawing back with a languorous pull, Ms. Jewel stretched along the edge of the bed before propping her head up with one hand. With the other, she stroked along the curvaceous silhouette her pose presented to great advantage.

Facing off against a preening whore who looked ready to pounce only added weight to the digital camera in Cole's lap. God, the fall from regular contributions at Time to freelancing for Boulder's local daily had been far. In slow increments, he raised his bulky equipment and snapped a candid shot of this evening's companion, from the neck down, as agreed.

The woman's presence in his frame proved that pimping wasn't nearly as rare in Mayberry-esqe Boulder as one might think. Five minutes on Craigslist could get a man—or a woman, for that matter—a wealth of by-the-hour entertainment. Yet paid or not, the camera couldn't help but love Ms. Jewel's creamy cleavage and healthy, smooth skin. While hookers might abound in this hotbed of high-tech employment, they were the consensual kind, not drug-addicted runaways or kidnap victims without other options. No, Boulder hookers drove fast cars and lived in sleek apartments, pandering to white, well-salaried, workaholic techies who paid the bill before the sex, cringed at physical force, and felt a desperate need for affection.

All in all, Boulder made hooking look pretty good.

Cole stood and began a series of photographs in rapid succession, almost like he was shooting the cover of Vogue, only he wouldn't Photoshop or airbrush or taint the photos in any way. What he saw, readers would get. "Tell me how you started."

He didn't have to ask the question. Cole was just the photographer. A journalist would write the words, while Cole would provide the pictures.

But a talking subject relaxed, and a relaxed subject made for better shots.

So talk he would.

His model didn't hesitate. "I enjoy sex." There was that smile again. This time she rolled onto her back and cupped her breasts. They were covered—he'd managed to axe every one of her efforts to strip—but barely. A skimpy sundress skimmed the top of her areolas, and without a bra, her nipples might as well have been giving a dance recital on her chest.

"I suppose that's a good trait in your profession." Probably too glib, but she didn't notice.

"Yes. I'm also attractive." And humble. "School was never my thing, and after the fifth offer, I finally took the money and rode, so to speak."

Damn if she didn't get a smile out of him with that one. "And?"

Ms. Jewel didn't spread her legs. She also didn't clamp them together. The thin material of her dress made her lack of undergarments all the more obvious when she went limp and relaxed against the bed. "Since I liked the… physical aspects of the work, I let them make me rich. Lines of good-looking nerds at the door have secured my future." Her teasing look said, want to be next?

Cole took a picture of her long fingers. They thrummed her hardened nipples with no sign of fatigue. He really ought to put a stop to her little show, which hadn't been on the agenda, but he couldn't quell the curiosity she'd sparked with that touch to his thigh. How far would this sexpot have to go to turn him on? If she slid that hand down into her heat, would he finally get hard? If she moaned? What if she lifted the dress to her waist and went ahead with the spread she'd been threatening?

"Enough," he clipped. "Gorgeous as you are, this isn't Playboy, and I'm not interested." Because every last one of his wonderings had the same answer: nothing would turn him on. She could play and pant, even moan and masturbate for his eyes only, and he wouldn't respond. Pleasure had died along with Kate. In its place, he felt nothing good, only a burning desire to be close to the woman he'd loved, only a visceral need to visit her grave, only an unswerving willingness to sacrifice a rising career to accomplish those goals.

No matter how succulent the woman, a whore in a hotel room could never thaw the ice. Cole stuffed his camera and a few scribbled notes in his duffle. The evening couldn't be called photojournalism at its finest, but he had several decent pictures and enough information to cobble together semi-informative captions. Ms. Jewel had her cash. The local paper would buy this shit and assemble a story that wouldn't surprise anyone. Yes, the world's oldest profession made its home on street corners and casinos and the Mustang Ranch. But prostitution had also infiltrated lily-white bastions of education and accumulated wealth, granola moms with thousand-dollar strollers be damned.

When he touched the door handle, tasting escape, she posed a question with the barest hint of contempt in her voice. "And you, Mr. Rathlen? What are you doing here? You were one of Boulder's best-loved sons, traveling the world, having your photos featured in all sorts of fancy publications. I swear I saw your Tsunami shots in National Geographic."

"I was," he admitted. "You did." But they both knew what she meant. Now you're photographing a hometown hooker for the local daily.

No longer. Thirteen months and seventeen days had passed without a care for the fact that Kate wouldn't have chosen mediocre. Ms. Jewel, who sold her body for money, at least had the decency to excel at it. Perhaps she hadn't been forced into this line of work, but few made her kind of choices without glimpses of pain.

The woman mocking him from the bed hadn't jumpstarted his cock, but she'd done a number on his head. Cole would be making some calls come morning.

******

June—New York City

"You don't look like your headshots."

Cole paused his perusal of a painting that monopolized an entire wall of one of the Meatpacking District's chicest galleries. Though the disembodied voice came from behind him, he knew the smooth tones interrupting his study belonged to Lissa Blanc. He drew out his response, glancing between the canvas and the nearby placard that described it. "And this painting doesn't look like a park."

"Your pictures make you look friendlier. Smaller. Happier."

She didn't wait for his rebuttal before circling around to tap the crimson drywall next to her work with a matching fingertip. "What do you feel when you look at it? Not like you're in a park, but maybe you think of being young and carefree?" Her lips curled into a parody of a smile, like she was being forced into used-car sales at gunpoint. "Maybe you see something you want to purchase."

"You're kidding." Morning Park was more interesting for what it lacked. Chunks of the car-sized canvas had been left bare. Where she'd seen fit to add paint, serrated jags of black and green crawled out from the edges toward a thin seam of yellow that unevenly bisected the disarray. The mess had all the qualities—if you could call them that—of the prints his wife had framed.

Kate had loved her "Blancs"—not that Lissa had reached that lofty, last-name-only level of acclaim—while Cole had wanted to use them as bonfire kindling. Where his wife had touted Lissa as an up-and-coming genius, mark her words, Cole had questioned the mental faculties, let alone the artistic integrity, behind paintings that could potentially be copied by a posse of well-trained five-year-olds.

Lissa stiffened, all the welcome-to-the-big-tent theatrics draining away in an instant. "Unlike you, Mr. Rathlen, I don't consider my work a joke."

He bit his tongue. She flushed when she got mad. The pinkening of the smooth skin rising above her black corset held his interest more than the paint she'd thrown at the canvas. "I'm critical, Ms. Blanc. I have not called you a joke."

Mostly because circumstances hadn't thrown him the chance. He was a photographer, not an art critic, so other than becoming a bona fide Internet troll, he lacked a platform to rant about the "talent" his wife had so admired.

"Sorry," Lissa sneered, examining her nails. "I was having a gin and tonic in my mind just now and missed your point." Slender arms wound across her chest. "What gives you the right to criticize work you can't possibly understand?"

"A mouth," he said dryly, "and a rampant superiority complex." Might as well be honest. Certainly less had allowed fools to masquerade as fine minds.

Turning to the painting once again, he marveled at the blobs Kate would have called brilliant. "There," she'd have informed him, "where the green prowls toward the black but can't reach it for the yellow. That's the essence of disrupted nature—a park."

"What's interesting about you," Cole told Lissa casually, "is what you don't understand. Art is more than critical acclaim. If great, ordinary people connect with the work."

And pay for it. He let the undeniable thrust of his words hang between them. Lissa had wormed her way into a few of New York City's most hallowed show spaces, but a big seller she was not.

Her do-or-die smile receded. Inexplicably, Cole wanted that particular danger to return. But professional relationships, like all others, began best in honesty.

"I hear the highway business is booming these days." He paused, eyeing her famously philanthropic parents in the crowd. Together they ran one of the country's largest construction companies. "Rumor has it these swank gallery showings have more to do with your family's heavy machinery than your hand with a brush."

The red blooming on her chest darkened to an angry purple. He got his smile back, but only in the form of a tight stretch of lip set against clenched teeth. A shame because, apparently unlike him, Lissa Blanc was photogenic as hell. The pictures he'd seen had portrayed her looks with staggering accuracy. They'd highlighted the thick chestnut hair that now gleamed auburn in the light and revealed the dark eyes that assessed him with cool intensity, at odds with the delicacy of the surrounding bone structure. They'd even done justice to her skin, showcasing the exact shade of white tulips, at least when she wasn't flushed with anger or frustration.

Most of all, her pictures had hinted that Lissa Blanc would be magnificent were she to stretch those generous lips wide with the proper smile she withheld.

"So that's it. You don't like it." Lissa stated the obvious, probably still out mentally sucking gin and tonics. "You sought me out for an appointment, then traveled to Manhattan, all to share your—with all due respect—less-than-worthy disdain."

"No." Taking her in, he drifted closer and breathed deep. Notes of fruit and an unrecognizable spice hit like an apple orchard in August, one he badly wanted to explore. Kate had smelled like Chanel No 5.

He froze, rejecting the thrall of long-denied senses rushing to life. Betrayal started small. First an innocuous observation, then... a crisis. Had Cole not believed in the power of temptation so ardently, he'd still have a wife.

Shame lashed at the part of him he kept on lockdown, not for insulting Lissa's painting or for tearing a chink in her armor, but for enjoying the tease and wondering what color she'd turn next.

He cleared his throat. Yet Lissa's the one I need, the one Kate would have chosen. Choosing Lissa himself—no matter how distracting the woman or how virulently he disagreed with his wife's prematurely-silenced admiration—would pave a path to absolution.

Without uttering a single superfluous syllable, he made his point, "I want you to paint for me."

www.ingramcontent.com/pod-product-compliance
Lightning Source LLC
Chambersburg PA
CBHW030247130626
46549CB00002B/429